The Blue Hour

THE BLUE HOUR

J. P. Smith

THOMAS & MERCER

Text copyright © 1989 J. P. Smith
Printed in the United States of America.

Published by Thomas & Mercer
P.O. Box 400818
Las Vegas, NV 89140

ISBN-13: 9781612185675
ISBN-10: 1612185673

For CNS
body and soul

1

AS SHE WALKED PAST THE WINDOW OF HER BEDROOM SHE saw a man sitting at a table on the terrace of the café opposite her building. As he looked up at her he ceased stirring his coffee and smiled, nodding his head slightly. And as she was wearing only a thin cotton camisole she quickly shut the curtains and went off to have her shower.

It had been raining for most of the night and early morning, and only within the past half hour had the waiters at the Café Picard set out the white chairs and distributed ashtrays and sugar bowls to each of the tables and prepared to serve coffee and croissants and brioches to those of their customers who preferred to dine, so to speak, tête-à-tête with the morning traffic. The man who was now occupying a table and gently agitating his café au lait was unknown to them, though a few of the waiters recognized him from the last time he had been there, the day before, or perhaps the day before that. Seeing the half-nude woman was an unexpected treat for Inspector Cuvillier, since he had merely stopped in for a coffee and croissant, and it was only the sudden appearance of two pink legs that had distracted him from his *petit déjeuner*. He continued watching as the curtain passed rapidly before her, and he allowed his imagination to sketch in the remaining details. He pictured her removing her camisole, slowly and deftly slipping the garment over her head. He saw, too, her pale, compact backside, darkly cleft, as she bent over to turn on the tap for her bath; the soap as it foamed and swelled over her firm breasts and slim thighs. He imagined her spread-eagled on her bed, her limbs secured to the posts by thick leather straps. He saw himself standing over her, trembling with anticipation, and was unaware that the man who occupied the flat beneath hers, indeed the very man he had come to keep an eye on, was also dreaming, about a cottage in a small Swiss town some ten kilometers southwest of Zurich.

Adam and Honnie had lived in Oberwil for only two months, trying to scratch out an existence amidst the few pieces of furniture allotted to them and a kitchen that lacked the more sophisticated appliances that graced the glossy pages of magazines and Sunday supplements. The previous residents had left behind not only the accumulated dirt of their tenancy, half-empty boxes of *muesli* on the kitchen shelves and nail clippings between the floorboards, but also their dog, a white toy poodle who greeted Adam and Honnie at the door on their first day with an appalling whine. Its eyes were rheumy and a sore on its head ran with pus. Adam disliked dogs and so tried to ignore it. Honnie crouched down and spoke quietly to the frail beast and thought up names for it, Ludwig or Wolfie. Adam suggested that as they had little enough money to support themselves, it would be impossible to feed in addition a starving animal. Honnie begged to let the dog stay, she thought it might bring them luck. That first night they lay in bed and listened to the cries and howls of the creature as it sat outside the front door. The next morning, when Adam relented and agreed to keep the poodle, it was nowhere to be found.

A week later, when they returned from shopping in the village, they noticed a peculiar odor of decay. Until they grew accustomed to it everything seemed to be infected by the malign stink: the lentil soup, Honnie's bubble bath, their clothes, their hair. They scrubbed the pine floors, the linoleum, even the walls, and yet the odor refused to wash away; it had somehow insinuated itself into the very fabric of the little house. The dog was never seen again, and yet Adam felt that something of it remained there: the corruption of flesh, the bitter whiff of mortality haunting them with its ominous smell.

Their nearest neighbors viewed them with suspicion, this tall young man and his tall, slim girlfriend, as they drove their battered old Fiat around the lanes and to the shops, holding hands and stealing kisses as they did their marketing. Sometimes they would go to the local café or pub and drink tankards of lager, only to remain pinned to their chairs by the insolent stares of the worthy citizens of their canton, unable to share small talk, unwilling to smile. Back at their cottage they would read or listen to music or sometimes argue, mostly about the state of their finances, which was shocking though miraculously never truly critical. Often they made love at odd hours, or rather at the hours when the Swiss might be found otherwise engaged, such as working in a bank or repairing a wristwatch; midmorning, say, or three in the afternoon, or sometimes against the wall of the shower, their slippery bodies covered in soap, their moans and gasps camouflaged by the rush of water at half past ten in the morning.

Now the cottage in Oberwil is empty. It is the blue hour, the cool, momentary sliver between day and night, when his thoughts always turn to Honnie. He is walking about the house, treading the faded rugs, the creaking boards, searching through drawers, gently touching the damp walls with his fingertips, as if seeking something he had perhaps mislaid or even hidden away, when suddenly he hears Honnie's voice. "I am here," she seems to be saying; it is so quiet it is almost a sigh as it is caught in the cross-drafts of the upper floor, and he climbs the stairs and sees the shadow at the end of the hallway, and as he is about to wake the thought comes to him that Honnie is dead.

Adam Füst sat up in bed and rubbed his face and leaned forward to clutch at the curtain: daylight. Daylight and certainty.

The man on the café terrace abruptly emerged from his reverie, left a few coins on the table, and descended underground to the métro just as Adam stood under the shower and soaped his slim body and shampooed his thick hair and then let the hot water rinse away the soap as his head began to clear itself of the voice of Honnie.

Tying his dressing gown about him, he left the bathroom, switched on the electric kettle in the kitchenette, and then, noticing a record on his turntable, pressed a button and listened to Ornette Coleman's "Lonely Woman," the drummer and bassist working up a lather of agitation, lending the sax and trumpet an edgy foundation for their lamentations in this dirge without tempo, Honnie's favorite tune of all, the saddest she'd ever heard, she used to say; the anthem, these days, of Adam's grief.

Adam Füst did not know the woman who lived above him, indeed he knew few women in Paris, although he sometimes tried to imagine what figure suited the light footsteps that often padded just above his head each night and every morning. On more than one occasion he had met her in the lift, or on the stairs, and although at first glance there was no resemblance between her and Honnie, Adam discerned something about her, some indefinable quality that reminded him of his wife and that put him in two minds about having this woman as his neighbor. It wasn't her build, for Honnie was tall and slim, long legged. Neither was it the color of her hair, for Honnie's, like his, was black and not light brown. Perhaps it was the fact that his neighbor was a woman of Honnie's age, that she smiled brightly at him and greeted Adam whenever they met.

Yet what troubled him most was that Honnie was no longer a part of his life. No, that was not quite correct. She was very much a part of his life. In fact, since she had disappeared Honnie continued to exist for him, if not in the flesh then as an invisible presence, a sensation, a pressure on the brain, indeed almost as a form of malaise, like the oppression some feel before the onset of a thunderstorm. There were physical reminders everywhere: a wardrobe full of her clothes—forgotten summer dresses, a rain-coat, a black nightgown she had bought in a Zurich department store—even a few of the drawers in the bureau contained some of her things, lacy panties, Lejaby brassieres, a half-used tube of vaginal lubricating cream. Nine or ten paperback books: various novels; some *policiers* Adam had passed on to her.

And there were photographs, altogether no more than a dozen: Honnie in Oberwil, standing before the cottage, her arms crossed, a cigarette between her fingers; Honnie at a café table in Paris, her white T-shirt tight against her breasts, sun-glasses hiding her eyes, sipping orangeade through a straw; Honnie in Budapest, standing outside the Hungária Restaurant with her mother and father at the time of their last visit to their native country, her parents seeming so pleased, a wistful, rather distant look on Honnie's face. And there were more. He could not drive away the images that continually flashed up behind his eyes, these pictures of an altogether more intimate sort that came to him late at night while lying awake listening to the dying sounds of the day, the other tenants retiring, the Café Picard shutting down until morning, the hum of his blood as it coursed through his body: intimate pictures. And once he had driven away these pictures, once he had caught his breath and turned on his side and shut his eyes against the terrible, luminous face of his bedside clock radio, he would begin to hear her voice.

Undoubtedly the woman who lived above him, just as his other neighbors and his concierge, Madame Moreau, believed Honnie and he had had an argument and simply separated for a time. Undoubtedly they all expected she would return. In fact Honnie and Adam had had only a slight disagreement the morning of her disappearance—indeed, for a few weeks she had been a bit aloof, distant—but there had been no flareup, no violent release of emotions, no battle that might lead to a separation.

Adam Füst remembered the morning well.

He had risen at six, showered and dressed, then made breakfast for the two of them while Honnie had her bath. He had awakened especially early that morning because his employer, the film director Gabor, had intended to spend the day scouting out locations for his next project. They were to drive to Chantilly, then, if necessary, north to Beauvais or southwest to Rambouillet. Gabor wanted to see a man in Chantilly who owned a small manor farm on the grounds of which stood a century-old stone *pigeonnier*. Gabor had managed to get hold of a photo of it and others similar to it, and Adam had rung each of the owners in advance to set up appointments. "If it's in decent shape," Gabor had told Adam, "and if we can talk this guy into letting us use it for a day, we'll shoot the torture scenes there."

Adam remembered the photographs: the *pigeonniers* were low, round, stone structures with holes at the top of the dome for the birds to enter and exit. There was something depressing about the buildings; Adam could not understand why they had affected him in such a way.

He sat on the edge of the bath and watched Honnie lying in the water. The soap and shampoo had made the bubbles disperse. He saw her long legs, slightly parted; her thick triangle of hair as the ends of it floated outwards and toward the surface; her wide breasts, their dark nipples bobbing out of the water. "Don't," she said as he tried to touch her.

They had been lovers for five years, a married couple for three; strangers for two weeks.

He tried to sit her down and face him. "Please, Honnie, talk to me, tell me what is the matter."

"Nothing is wrong, I'm fine."

"You're not fine, I can see that."

"I'm fine."

"That's not true."

"You're right," she said finally, "I'm not fine; do you know why? It's because you keep asking me if I'm fine. You are driving me insane, Adam, leave me alone."

She sat in her terrycloth robe and ate her toast and marmalade, occasionally pushing her long, damp hair out of her face. She still had not found a job and refused to take any position that was not in some way connected with her training as a restorer of frescoes. The last time she had worked was some eight months earlier, in a chapel just outside Argenteuil. Every day she would commute by train, set up a campstool and begin the arduous job of cleaning and repairing the frescoes that had been neglected for so long: the death and resurrection of Jesus Christ; the lamentations of Mary; a dove in flight: scenes hastily executed two hundred years earlier; work of poor quality. It didn't matter: it was what she was trained to do, what she loved doing most. But she had made life difficult for herself, she had refused to work on anything but frescoes in churches, chapels, convents, and the like. One of the first frescoes she had helped restore was located in a mansion outside Budapest, and it was during the course of the restoration that the remains of a body were found.

The house was located in Alsógalla and dated from the eighteenth century. The original owner had been a nobleman with extravagant tastes, and as it now belonged to the state it had, over the years, undergone various transformations. For a while it housed a division of the tourist board; then it became an old people's home; afterward a country retreat for members of the Hungarian Central Committee. It had remained vacant since 1971, and by the time Honnie came to work on the frescoes on the ground floor it had been decided that the house was to be turned into a hotel. The frescoes were illustrations of scenes from classical mythology.

Every morning Honnie and her fellow students rode to Alsógalla in a van driven by their instructor, Janos, a young man with a moustache and goatee and pale eyes who reveled in so much female company and told vaguely off-color stories, or rather tales that began as harmless vignettes ("I must tell you about the time when I was a little boy and I was taken to lunch in the Ruszwurm...") and that inevitably concluded on a sexual note ("...and so the woman pulled up her panties, wrapped her coat about me, and smuggled me out of the ladies' room. Little did Mama know...").

When they had the occasion to climb ladders to work on the uppermost parts of the frescoes he would insinuate himself beneath them, the better to see up their skirts. Once he stopped the van and went off to urinate behind a tree. He called Honnie by her given name, Agnes.

A sizeable crack, treacherously wayward like a bolt of lightning, ran diagonally through the panel Honnie had been assigned, "Orpheus in the Underworld," at the very moment when Orpheus, having descended to Hades to fetch his beloved, with doubt and longing turns to look at her and, by thus breaking his agreement with the region's divinities, loses Eurydice forever. The crack was some fifty centimeters long and, toward the middle of it, nearly as wide as Honnie's index finger. She would have to remove the loose debris, add fresh mortar and intonaco, match paints and colors, and touch up the repair with her goat's-hair brushes. As she began the work more pieces of plaster came away. She realized at once that the wall was thinner than it should be, that there was a large space behind it. She borrowed a flashlight from Janos and peered into the cavity.

By half past four the wall had been pulled completely down and the remains of a young woman taken away to Budapest. Little remained of her but bones and clothes and jewels and some leathery patches of skin, some hair. One of the police inspectors who examined them believed that she had been dead for nearly two hundred years. The newspapers were full of the story for the next three weeks. Experts from two museums examined the remains in the company of a team of pathologists. It was concluded that the woman had been no older than eighteen at the time of her death. Honnie remembered the pearls around the neck, the hard shiny leather of her skin, the bones of her fingers. Although she never spoke of the experience, Adam tried to imagine what had gone through her mind at the time. He pictured her following the beam of light into the space behind the wall and the shock of seeing the skull of the victim. Sometimes he wondered if the woman had been alive at the time of her internment. He speculated on how she had faced the agony of her death.

On the morning of Honnie's disappearance Adam kissed her goodbye, said that he expected to be back from work by five, five-thirty; perhaps they would see a film that night, eat out, whatever, "Okay?" he said. And she raised her eyes from her coffee and, without parting her lips, smiled tentatively at him.

Gabor was waiting for Adam outside his Montmartre office on the rue Coulaincourt, a fifteen-minute walk from Adam and Honnie's flat. Gabor was leaning against his old green Renault 4, smoking Camels and clearing his throat. When he saw Adam he said, "It's about fucking time."

"I'm ten minutes early."

"That's right."

Adam drove. Gabor sat beside him and rummaged through his battered old briefcase. The filmmaker had left Hungary in 1971 and, after some experience directing underground theater, had made two feature films, not to mention the uncountable anonymous others that could be shown only in cinema clubs or private booths in Clichy sex shops. His two major projects, quirky, violent, some said psychopathic, films, which quickly earned a large and appreciative audience, especially in London and New York, had become classics. He had hired Adam some years earlier because he required an assistant who spoke Hungarian and could drive a car. At first he was disappointed to see Adam Füst because in truth he had wanted a female assistant, preferably one without scruples, big busted and with long legs. But because Adam was the only applicant who replied to the advertisement, he hired him.

"Take the next left," Gabor said. He flicked down the visor and examined his face in the mirror, making a slight adjustment to the black leather patch that covered his left eye socket. Sometimes when he was drunk he would lift the patch and reveal a sunken wrinkled eyelid. He took out a red plastic comb and pulled it through his thick, curly hair. He parted his lips and looked at his teeth, removing from between two of them a shred of tobacco. Then he switched on the radio. For ten minutes they said nothing and listened to a symphony by CPE Bach. Then Gabor opened his briefcase and slipped a cassette into the slot provided on the car radio. A British rock group sang of death and despair and the dole. Adam hated rock music. He preferred, now that he thought of it, CPE Bach. In fact he rather liked CPE Bach, though given his choice he would have had some Coltrane or Anthony Braxton. He thought of Honnie lying in her bath, *Don't*, she was saying, *No.*

"How's Honnie?" Gabor asked.

"She's fine," said Adam, recalling what she had said to him that morning: "I'm not fine, because you are driving me insane, Adam."

"Turn right," said Gabor, gesturing with his knuckle. They were passing through Saint-Denis. Gabor asked Adam to pull up in front of a tobacconist. Gabor got out and bought some cigarettes. They got on the A16 and headed north toward Chantilly. Gabor took a folder from his briefcase. He showed Adam a glossy photograph. "This is the actress I'm thinking of hiring for the supporting role. These were delivered this morning." The woman seemed no older than sixteen, shaggy-haired, pouting into the camera. Gabor referred to an accompanying page. "She's done some television work in London, a few commercials, small parts in two legitimate films." He looked at Adam. "Of course if I hire her I'll have to change the character, I'll have to call Guy and have him do some rewrites. Can't have an English woman playing a Japanese wife, eh?" In another photo she was sitting in the middle of a low leather sofa, her legs spread, a paisley shawl draped strategically over her knees. Her breasts were bare. "What do you think?" Gabor asked.

"Very nice," said Adam. "Cute."

Gabor laughed and slapped Adam's knee. "Guess who I saw last night?"

Adam shrugged. "Depends on where you were."

"At a party for Isabelle Adjani at one of the clubs. Klaus was there, you know. And Jean-Michel. And Dany. But that's not who I'm talking about."

Adam shrugged. "I give up." It was difficult to hear, he lowered the volume on the cassette deck.

Gabor reached over with his carefully manicured fingers and raised it. "Nina."

"Really," said Adam. "How is she?" Nina was Gabor's ex-wife, an actress who had starred in his first film.

"Spaced-out as usual. But nice. Nice and mellow, you know. She spent the last six months in London, living with some independent producer. She said he was a real prick. I said, Why did you stay with him for six months, eh Nina? She said she liked him anyway, he had money, a car, he knew people, he didn't give a damn about anything. She said he wasn't at all like me, that's another reason she liked him."

Gabor ejected the tape in the middle of a song and let the radio play for a while, a Shostakovich string quartet, the eighth.

Adam referred to the directions the man who owned the *pigeonnier* had given him over the phone. Outside there was a heavy grey overcast and a light mist had begun to ride the breeze. He switched on the wipers and settled himself more comfortably in his seat. Gabor said, "Of course it had to rain today. How the hell am I supposed to know what this place looks like, eh?"

"You saw the photo."

"I'm talking about the light. I have to know how I'm going to light the place." He looked at the photograph of the building. "There are all these holes in the roof, right? It could be a fantastic effect, the sunlight blazing in through them, you think, yes?"

Adam nodded his head and Gabor opened the glove box and browsed idly through its contents: a half-empty bottle of Pernod, a wrinkled copy of *Playboy*, a cassette with half the tape hanging from it, a switchblade knife. "Tell me a story," said Gabor, as he often did when they went on long drives.

Adam told him about Honnie's first restoration job, the house in Alsógalla and the body. Gabor seemed interested. He said, "It sounds like a sex cult," then jotted a few notes in his pocket diary. "A costume drama," he murmured. "Candlelight.

A waiting carriage, an open window. The moon behind clouds. What does Honnie think?"

"We never talk about it," said Adam. "It's disturbing to her."

"Tell me another story."

Adam related a joke he once heard at a party. "Once upon a time there was an elephant named Fifi and her lover Ruiz the Flea. Ruiz flies over to her ear and begins to make love to her, 'Ah, my adorable, sweet Fifi, how I love your magnificent body, your breasts, your thighs,' you know, and sitting up in the coconut tree above them and listening in is Jumbo the Monkey."

"Jumbo the Monkey?" said Gabor. "What the hell kind of name is that for a monkey? For an elephant, okay, right, that's fine, but."

"Look, call him whatever you want, okay?"

"Never mind, just go on."

Adam said, "So Fifi begins to get excited, she stamps the ground and sweats and so on, and finally Ruiz the Flea takes off his trousers and mounts her and begins to make love in a more serious vein. He can hear Fifi sighing with pleasure. Did I mention that this took place in Fifi's boudoir?"

"I thought it was the jungle."

"Well it is, really, but it's funnier if you say it's her boudoir. Suddenly Jumbo the Monkey drops a coconut on Fifi's head. She cries out. Ruiz the Flea says, 'Oh I am sorry, did I hurt you, my delicate Fifi?' "

For a few minutes they rode in silence. Gabor looked at the paper with the directions written on it. "Make a right. It's the second road on the left."

Adam waited outside while Gabor and the Frenchman examined the interior of the *pigeonnier*. A fine mist continued to fall over the land. The earth smelled ripe and rich, earthworms twisted over clots of newly turned soil. He breathed deeply and gazed at the circular stone building and felt his spirits sink.

Seeing the photograph of it had depressed him. Close up, it seemed devastating. It was as if the structure itself carried some emotional power, as if, like some ancient site, it held within its core a form of magic, a protective spell. It was only days later, indeed a week after Honnie had left home, that he connected it to the Citadella Tool Works near his grandmother's house outside Skolnok. He recalled walking there when he was eight, being drawn to the building, which, in his memory, was not at all round; simply isolated. There was something elemental about it, he seemed to think, something that connected it to one's beginnings, or even to the origins of humanity itself, something prehistoric, perhaps that was it. It was the heat, of course, the great blast of infernal air that throughout the day and sometimes even the night shot out of the great square doorways; and naturally there was the sight of the fire, blinding orange forges against which could be seen the silhouettes of the men who worked there, kitted up in their boilersuits, steel helmets, smoked-glass goggles, protective earmuffs. The deafening sounds of metal being hammered carried across the valley to Adam's grandmother's house. She would nod her head eastward and say, "That's hell."

He was a child. He walked closer. In the light from the forges he could see black shapes hammering. Standing near him, in the doorway, was a demon in goggles and helmet, staring at a piece of paper in the hazy afternoon light. He looked up at Adam and smiled. Then he turned the page around and showed it to the boy: it was a photograph of a woman lying on a bed with her legs spread wide apart. When Adam finally returned to his grandmother's house he was breathless and in tears. He had been frightened, his mother could see that, and he knew it too, yet he never completely understood why. His grandmother suggested two tablespoons of fish oil.

On the day of Honnie's disappearance Adam returned with Gabor to the office on the rue Coulaincourt. It had been a successful outing: the locations would prove to be ideal. Gabor's secretary, LouLou, smiled as she sat behind her desk, one bare foot propped against it, painting the nail on her big toe. She told him there had been seven phone calls, three from people who had backed his last film and had been approached to do likewise with the new one. Adam stood by the window and surveyed a grey Paris. Gabor went into his office and shut the door. A radio on LouLou's desk played brash French rock music softly. She said, *"Ça va?"*

On the wall by the window was a framed poster advertising Gabor's most recent film, *Reparations*. Against a black background and toward the lower right corner a man in a suit was standing in a darkened doorway, lighting a cigarette. The flame from his match flared a bright orange. Filling the center of the poster were the titles and credits. The film had lost a lot of money, but after someone had published an article in *Sight & Sound* about Gabor's work, attention was once again being drawn to it. People who had condemned it were now beginning to say, "Actually I thought it rather interesting."

"Oui, oui, ça va, ça va," Adam said, turning to LouLou. "It went all right." She was smiling at him. He liked LouLou; she was kind, she was funny, she was pretty. She was always happy; even when her mother died she seemed to be happy. Sometimes this was infuriating to Adam, all this glee, this terrible merriment. She looked at her toenail and blew softly in its direction. Her leg was long and smooth and Adam could see under her skirt. She closed up the nail enamel and leaned back, stretching her arms above her head and revealing two gingery tufted armpits. "How's Honnie?" she asked.

Adam said, "She's fine."

When he got home the flat was dark. There was no note. Nothing seemed to have been taken. No keys had been left. He waited until half past eight and then began ringing their friends. No one had seen her that day. Madame Moreau, their concierge who lived with her husband and invalid mother on the ground floor, couldn't remember seeing her either.

That night, inexplicably, the clock radio snapped into life around two-fifteen, and until he gathered his wits about him Adam sat up in bed, gasping with fear and listening to some man singing "Waltzing Matilda."

2

I T HAD HAPPENED ONCE BEFORE, ABOUT EIGHTEEN MONTHS earlier. Adam and Honnie had had an argument that began as a slight disagreement in a Vietnamese restaurant on the boulevard Montparnasse, metamorphosed into an icy silence while they watched the latest Woody Allen film, then blazed uncontrollably into tears and recriminations when they returned to the flat in Montmartre. Honnie threw some clothes into her oversized shoulder bag and stormed out. She had said, "I'm off then, you bastard." And he had said, "Good, I'm glad, go."

She had stayed away for two days. She returned in the afternoon, while Adam was at the office. When he came home from work she said nothing, she was cooking chicken. Eventually he said, "So you are all right, you managed okay, then, yes?"

She shrugged and smiled. "Yes, of course," she said, as if Adam were a child or someone who had lost all sense of reality. She lit the candles and sat across from him and poured the wine. She looked at him above the flickering candles and smiled.

"You are certain everything is all right?" he said, and naturally she could only agree, everything was fine, wasn't everything fine with him? Now he found it difficult to respond, because although she had come back and everything at least in that regard was fine, he was not fine, uneasy is the word, because

Honnie had been away for two days and he hadn't the slightest inkling where she had been. And although he knew very well that if it ever came down to a question-and-answer session concerning this, she would have denied ever having been away, blaming it on a lapse of consciousness on his part. What he didn't want to admit, at least quite yet, was that he had made a series of frantic phone calls to all their friends, begging to know if Honnie was at one apartment or another. No one had seen her.

"You like the chicken?" she asked.

"It is delicious, very nice."

"Good. I bought orange sorbet for dessert. You have plans for tonight?"

He looked at her. "Plans. What do you mean plans?"

"Just plans. Plans. Ideas. Do you want to see a film, maybe, the new Tavernier, hmm?"

"Why, did you have plans?"

She lit a cigarette and shrugged. "Not especially. I just thought we'd stay in tonight. Listen to some music. Go to bed early." She paused. "That sort of thing."

Adam rose to put on a record. Honnie puffed on her cigarette and smiled at something that amused her. She said, "You know, I wouldn't mind going to Budapest to visit my parents this summer. Paris is beginning to drive me crazy."

Eighteen months later Adam recalled this and picked up the phone. He dialed the code, then the number at his in-laws' apartment on the outskirts of Budapest. After seven rings the phone was answered. Honnie's father sounded like a bath draining of its water: "Hullo?"

Then Adam remembered that it was an hour later in Hungary, half past one in the morning and long after their bedtime. "Shit," he said.

"Hullo?"

"This is Adam," he said.

"So late?" said his father-in-law. "I can't hear you so well."

The connection was poor. Overlaid on the conversation, like a thick curtain of noise, were numerous conversations conducted in various languages. Adam believed he could hear Edith Piaf singing "Je ne regrette rien" in the midst of it. "How are you?" he asked brightly.

"We were sleeping," said his father-in-law.

"I'm sorry."

"What, is something wrong with Agnes?"

Ah ... "No, no, everything is fine. Fine."

"You are drunk, Adam Füst?"

Adam quietly replaced the receiver and hoped the old man would wake up in the morning and say to his wife, "Last night I had the most curious dream. In it the phone was ringing ..."

The next day he would hear from Honnie.

"What is 'swagman'?"

Gabor looked up at him. "What?"

"'Swagman,' what is it?"

LouLou refilled their cups from a coffeepot. On Gabor's desk was a white cardboard box filled with croissants. The director was wearing an expensive, grey, double-breasted suit; silk Charvet tie; soft, shiny, leather boots. It was what he sometimes wore on opening day at Cannes. Later that morning he was scheduled to meet a woman from Paramount Pictures named Belinda. He stared coldly at Adam through his single blue eye. "What, this is a game, maybe?"

"It's from a song, 'Waltzing Matilda,' you know it. 'Once a jolly swagman camped beside a billabong,' dadada and so on, lalalee. I heard it last night. It frightened me."

"What's a 'billabong'?" asked LouLou.

Gabor munched on a croissant and reflected on Adam's question. Both of them spoke Hungarian, French, German, and

English, but neither could identify a "swagman." "But what's a 'billabong'?" LouLou asked again.

"Look, I've got to see this lady at one o'clock this afternoon," Gabor said. "She's flying in from London this morning and I'm supposed to have lunch with her at this place on the Champs-Élysées." He noted it on a slip of paper and passed it to Adam. "I want you to be available in case anyone important calls. If Victor in London rings, or that woman in Rome, whatever she's called, take the message. If they're still interested say I'm talking to Paramount but would be glad to speak to them. Then give them the number of the restaurant. Oh and do me another favor, Adam. Ring the guy in Chantilly and tell him we definitely want to use the *pigeonnier*. I've spoken to Blanchet, and he'll have the papers drawn up by Wednesday. If the guy wants to work through his lawyer, too, that's fine, it doesn't matter one way or another. Just tell him I'll have the papers sent along for his signature. And don't forget to remind him about checking the insurance on the building. And don't take any crap about money. We'll pay him his fee after the shooting is finished and give him a credit at the end of the film. Hello?" he said, picking up the phone before LouLou could get her hand on it. "Yes, yes, this is Gabor," he said in English. "What? Oh shit, you're joking …"

Adam and LouLou returned to the outer office they shared. She switched on the radio and searched the waveband for another station while he stood by the window, his hands in his pockets, unaware that the bright spring sun was turning Paris into a gem. He felt two hands touch his arms. LouLou said, "What's wrong, Adam?"

"Nothing," he said.

She smelled of Honnie's scent, L'Heure Bleue. That and the warmth of her hands made his skin tingle. He had never slept with LouLou. In fact he had never slept with anyone but Honnie since their marriage. Other women had appealed to him, of course, LouLou included, but the idea of betraying his wife was out of the question. And although Honnie was not of an experimental cast of mind, though she was not especially keen on exploring more adventurous sexual routes and byways, he found that in her own way she more than satisfied him.

Her sexuality was a subtle, ambiguous quality, an inner radiance, a collection of hints that only after long reflection added up to something more powerful, more potent, altogether more enticing, in a word more sophisticated, in another, perhaps, more mature. So that when Adam first met Honnie his first thought was that she was sexually inexperienced and indeed even a bit prim in her ways, imagining her fighting off hands reaching here, squeezing there, aiming for this and that, as if it were rush hour on the métro and one were frantically seeking a handhold.

It was only when he looked into her eyes, when he saw how confidently she moved, how gently, oh how seductively she caressed the hillock of her lower lip with her fingertip as she listened to him speak, and then smiled and crossed her long legs and showed him her slender neck ... it was then that he began to get an inkling of her more passionate side; then, and later when he finally made love to her ... And now she was gone ...

"Nothing?" said LouLou.

"What?"

"Nothing is wrong?"

He shook his head. He wondered why that when he thought of Honnie the first things that came to mind were her neck, her lips, her breasts, her legs. Was it because it was the only concrete way to summon up her presence, that part of her that remained indefinable? Was it that each aspect of her physical presence somehow corresponded to some spiritual quality, some abstraction that contributed to the wholeness of Honnie? Perhaps that was it. He missed Honnie. He missed her body and soul.

They could hear Gabor in his office, speaking a brash form of English: "What the hell, right?" he shouted. "Okay, great, far out, let's do that." Then he thanked his caller effusively, said goodbye more than once, "Right, 'bye. Right, 'bye. Right, 'bye bye ..." rang off and said, "The next time that fucking idiot from LA calls, I'm out, you understand, LouLou?"

"You picked up the phone," she reminded him.

After Gabor had left for his appointment, while LouLou was having lunch in a nearby bistro, Adam sat behind Gabor's desk and rang up all of his and Honnie's friends. The Kupkis hadn't seen her, and neither had Milosz, Jeannot Debray, Suzy Rinaldi, or Johnny Vodo, their Nigerian friend who played drums in various jazz groups based on the Left Bank.

Two nights earlier Johnny had briefly sat in with the pianist Mal Waldron at the Caveau de la Huchette and told Adam all about it. "And you didn't ring to tell me?" Adam said.

"Oh man, I wish I had, but it was just one of those things, spur of the moment, you know? I just got lucky. I also got paid. Come around tonight, bring Honnie and we'll go up there and see what's doing, all right?"

He told Johnny about Honnie. Johnny hadn't seen her. It was unlikely he would have seen her in any case, since he hadn't been out of bed since the night before. Adam rang off and had the strange notion to call his apartment. He let the phone ring fourteen times, as if he were attempting to travel down the wire, to imagine what his flat looked like while the phone was ringing: the remnants of his breakfast on the table, his records, his books, Coltrane's *Giant Steps* on the turntable; the Valloton print on the wall, *La Paresse*, that Honnie had fallen in love with and bought in the shop at the Beaubourg ("It reminds me of me," he remembered her saying, unrolling the print and showing him the nude woman lying on the bed, idling away an afternoon with her cat). Their unmade bed; her clothes hanging in the

wardrobe; the subtle, indefinable scent of her everywhere, glued
to the walls, the floors, the bedlinen, the memories.... And he
let his imagination journey even further; he pictured Honnie
sitting in the living room on the chair covered with the India
print, the print she had brought back with her from Budapest,
sitting with her knees up, in her black underpants, sitting and
smoking and staring blankly at the phone, he saw her clearly in
his mind's eye, he saw her frown briefly and reach her long slim
hand out toward the apparatus and he saw her grasp the receiver
and then LouLou returned from lunch and he hung up.

She came into Gabor's office and placed a paper bag on the
desk. Small slick stains had begun to appear on the side of it.
What's this? his eyes said, glancing up at her.

"I thought you might want it. And I think there's a bottle
of Orangina in the fridge, if you like."

"Thanks. I'm not hungry." He tore open the bag and
removed the contents, half a baguette slit and filled with remnants of chicken and a large portion of fried potatoes. Adam
examined the bony fowl, then picked at a greasy potato and ate
three more in quick succession.

"I saw Honnie," LouLou said, switching on the radio in her
office and then reappearing in Gabor's doorway. "Did anyone
call?" She approached the desk and smiled at Adam. "What's
wrong? What, I said something idiotic?"

"Where? Where did you see her, LouLou?"

"In a car, in the rue Lepic."

"You're joking. What kind of car?"

"A car. A red car, I think, I don't know, a car, just a car, the
usual sort of thing."

"What, a Rolls-Royce, a Renault, a Citroën, an MG, a
Cadillac, you must have noticed, what color did you say it was?"

"Red. A red car." She nibbled on one of his potatoes. "It's
gone cold."

"She was driving, then?" He was standing and holding tightly onto the collar of her blouse, twisting it and pulling her down toward the surface of Gabor's desk.

She stared wildly at him and tried to straighten her head, to regain her posture. "You're killing me," she cried.

"What the hell are you saying!" he screamed as her voice narrowed to a mere squeal in her constricted throat. Then he released her.

She backed away and tried to catch her breath and tried also to smooth out the collar of her blouse.

"What is wrong with you, Adam, are you insane?"

"Where are you going?"

"Back to my desk, you bastard."

It was the first time Adam had ever seen LouLou unhappy. "Look," he said.

"You look, you prick."

"Look, let's calm down and discuss this like two human beings."

"Go to hell, bastard." She slammed the door shut and returned to her office.

Adam remained standing behind Gabor's desk. He slid open one of the drawers. In it lay a .38 revolver and an imported glossy magazine devoted to photographs of Scandinavian women urinating on a pair of ecstatic Filipino gentlemen. Adam opened the door and watched LouLou, "Look," he said. "Forgive me, for a moment I lost control of myself." Still she said nothing. He was standing behind her when he reached out to rest his hands on her shoulders. At that moment she swung around to look at him and his hands fell into place around her throat.

"*Oh mon dieu*," she cried.

"Look," he said again.

"You are trying to kill me, is that it? Gabor goes off for an afternoon and you have nothing better to do than murder me?"

"Just tell me exactly what you saw today."

"You mean Honnie?"

"Yes, precisely; Honnie."

"I told you, she was in a car. Wait a moment, maybe you aren't supposed to know any of this."

"Tell me, LouLou."

"She was in a car. I already told you that."

"Alone?"

"No, there was someone else, a man I think. They'd stopped at a red light. Honnie was laughing."

He felt his anger once again rising to his throat. "Laughing," he said. "What do you mean laughing?"

"Laughing, just that, hahaha, you know."

"And what did the man look like?"

"I didn't get a good look at him."

"But she was laughing," Adam said.

"Yes, I told you, she was laughing."

"Did she look happy, was it a kind of devil-may-care laughter, or was it a more hysterical laughter, the kind of laughter someone in shock might make, did she seem hysterical is what I mean."

"It was just laughing, Adam. Hahaha laughing."

"As if she was laughing at a joke? Perhaps you misunderstood everything you saw. Was her window open?"

"I think so."

"And could it be that she wasn't laughing at all?"

"But."

"Could you be mistaken?" he went on. "Could she have been calling out for help, screaming for you, maybe, or the police?"

"But it was too quiet, Adam. Look, what is going on here between you and Honnie?"

"Or else maybe she was trying to pass on a message of some sort, perhaps she's in trouble and wanted you to know something, such as the name of the man who was driving, or an address, or something of the sort...."

LouLou looked at him. He was kneeling before her, resting his hands in her lap, gazing imploringly up at her. She stroked the side of his head with her fingers and smiled serenely at him. "Is Honnie in trouble, is that it, Adam?"

"I don't know. She hasn't been home since yesterday."

"And there was no note?"

He shook his head.

"Do you think there's someone else, is that it?"

He stood and stared down at her typewriter. "I don't know what to think." He pressed a key and the little steel ball jumped forward.

"You just typed on our letter to that guy in Chantilly."

"I'm sorry."

"It doesn't matter. Come, sit down and talk to me about this. You're in a horrible state."

He sat down. LouLou dragged her chair over and sat across from him. "Let me see if I can try to remember exactly what I saw. It was a red car, I'm certain of that. But I don't know what make it was. The car pulled up to a red light. Honnie was sitting next to her friend and quietly laughing."

"Wait a minute," interrupted Adam. "You said friend, I'm sure you said friend. Why did you say friend?"

"Because she was smiling and laughing. Just as I said before."

"So she seemed to know this guy, right?"

"That's what I thought, yes."

He stood and rubbed his chin as he leaned against the wall. "You know what the craziest thing about this is? Honnie didn't take anything with her when she left."

"What?"

"She didn't take a thing. Nothing. All her clothes are still there, her books, her makeup, everything, It's as if she walked out and decided to kill herself. People who walk out don't just leave everything, do they?"

"Not unless they intend to kill themselves."

"That's what I just said. Not unless they intend to kill themselves."

"Did you ring the police?" she asked.

He stared at her. "Why should I want to do that?"

"Because of what you said, that you thought Honnie might kill herself."

"The idea never crossed my mind."

"Then why did you bring it up?"

"Because now, only now does it occur to me. You see, when I got back yesterday Honnie wasn't home. I waited for her and then went to bed. I suppose I thought she'd come home sometime in the night."

"She's done this before, then?"

"Just once."

"And did she take anything then?"

He remembered the scene exactly: Honnie stuffing underwear and eye shadow into her big red shoulder bag. "It's odd," said LouLou.

"But you saw her in a red car, just today," said Adam.

"Do you think you should call the police?"

"Not yet," he said. "If you hadn't seen her I might, I suppose. But now things look different."

LouLou lit a Gitane and ran her fingers through her short, blond hair. The sun blazed against the windows. The room was airless. "But of course it may not have been Honnie in the red car. It may have been someone who looks like her."

Adam stared at her. "Now things seem different once again."

"Call the police," she said, lifting the receiver.

"No."

"You think she would kill herself?"

"I don't know," he said, an image of water coming to mind.

"Has she been worried about anything lately?"

He thought for a moment. He saw her sitting in the chair in the livingroom, smoking, her knees up, sitting in her black underpants and matching camisole, staring at the wall.

"Have you been getting on well then, the two of you?" LouLou asked.

"Yes, of course."

"No arguments, then?"

"No, not really, the usual."

"Do you think she's been seeing someone else, then, some other man?"

"No," said Adam, quite certain of it.

"But she hasn't been working ..."

"Not since that church in Argenteuil. And that was almost a year ago, eight months, whatever. She's put her name down, of course, she's," and then he let it drop.

"Hmm," LouLou hummed thoughtfully.

Gabor returned at half past four. He had clearly had too much to drink. His tie was loosened, his eye patch lopsided, his hair in disarray. There was a small damp stain on the front of his trousers. He threw open the office door, let it slam noisily shut, then staggered in and loudly broke wind. A distressing odor of rotten eggs, or sulphur, filled the air and lingered heavily between the walls of the office. It occurred to Adam that there was something hellish about the director. "Well?" he said. It was quite obvious the meeting had resulted in failure.

Gabor frowned and waved the question away. He stumbled forward and fell into one of the chairs before LouLou's desk. On the low table before it was a stack of recent magazines, an ashtray. Gabor idly picked up a copy of *Pariscope*, leafed through it as if to check on the time for a certain film or theatrical event, then flung the magazine against the wall.

"All right then, are you?" asked Adam.

"Go to hell," slurred Gabor.

"Lunch was enjoyable, yes?" said Adam. "You enjoyed yourself?" He sniffed the air. "A soufflé was it, or an omelette?"

Gabor pushed himself up into a standing position and began to make his way into his office. He walked as if his feet were mired in mud, or thick clots of manure. When he got halfway across the room he put his hand to his mouth as if to stifle a giggle and vomited copiously into it. LouLou and Adam watched as it overflowed onto the rug. He had eaten steak and onion soup. "Oh shit," LouLou said.

On the night of his first day without Honnie Adam stopped at a nearby corner market run by two Lebanese brothers. Adam and Honnie enjoyed shopping there because the brothers were honest and would sometimes procure hashish of a high quality for the couple. Adam found the shop unbearably depressing that night. Perhaps because it brought back memories of Honnie, or perhaps it was the way the overhead lights seemed to drain the color out of everything; he couldn't quite put his finger on it. He chose a frozen Italian dinner and a bottle of Evian water, and for dessert a chocolate pudding confection with whipped cream and a surprise on the bottom. Once before he had bought it and the surprise was a small round of shortbread that resembled a Communion wafer, and this startled him because nowhere on the plastic container was there any mention of shortbread or Host.

Had circumstances been otherwise he would simply have dined at a restaurant, at the Chartier probably, with a book or newspaper. But he felt it would be unseemly of him to enjoy a rare meal out without Honnie, to make, even on such a rudimentary level, even when he knew it was otherwise, a celebration out of his confusion and despair.

He returned home after stopping to buy a bottle of wine, and when he reached his flat paused a moment, his eye caught by a sliver of light by his feet, a tapering line that resembled the blade of a knife: someone was in the apartment. He lightly pressed his fingertips against the door, then placed his ear against the painted wood: silence. He slowly slid his key into the slot and listened as each of the tumblers was engaged in its turn. Then he pushed open the door and surveyed the room.

Then he remembered. The morning had been grey and gloomy, he had left the light on. He was beginning to become his own worst enemy.

He switched on the stereo and pressed the button on his turntable and after a moment's pause the first notes of Coltrane's "Syeeda's Song Flute" filled the air. He took the frozen dinner out of the bag and placed it in the oven, then went into the bedroom and changed into his jeans and a pullover. Then he stood back and looked around. Everything had changed. Everything. Nothing was the same. He returned to the living room, let his eyes become adjusted to his newfound solitude, then rubbed his forehead and sat in the chair with the India print on it. Nothing was the same as it had been. Nothing. Yet everything was where he had left it, nothing had been moved, stolen, or replaced. But without Honnie, with the knowledge that Honnie might never come back to this house, the significance of each object in it had drained away: book, record, lamp, chair, seashell, and photograph no longer carried any value for him, they had become blanched of their meaning, detached from their origins.

Yet something within him told him this was simply untrue, that it just could not be so. For Honnie could not have left, taken nothing with her and yet somehow, secretly, made off with the emotional content of an inanimate *thing*?

He made a tent of his fingers and gazed through it at the living room and mused over this conundrum. For surely he had invested these things with something of himself, certainly one could not destroy memories—shared memories, at that—with the simple shutting of a door. And yet ... yet there was something missing, something besides Honnie, something of great value. And because he could not at first find the word for it, it became part of the household, a great empty space around which he moved cautiously, respectfully; a focal point for cogitation, a conversation piece for one.

When his dinner was ready he turned over the record and listened to side one of *Giant Steps*. The music sounded ripe, coming through the speakers he and Honnie had saved for and bought only three months earlier. Coltrane's sax had a rich, delicious sound; one could never get enough of it. It was like a flame, nimbly flickering as it responded to the musician's breathing. He peeled the foil back from his meal and placed it on the rush mat before him. Wineglass, water glass, fork, knife, spoon; then a bottle of Beaujolais, his Evian water, an open book. The charade had come to an end. He shut his book and stared at his meal. He wondered why he had bought a frozen dinner when he was perfectly capable of preparing one himself. He examined the lasagna drowning in a sea of watery red sauce; he picked tentatively at a wan little green bean. The company had even provided a segment of bread, a wedge of baguette, not to mention a square inch of dessert; something yellow, stuck fast in a gel. Everything remained at the same infernal temperature. He looked again at the packaging: an obese Italian man with a moustache and chef's hat was kissing the tips of his fat fingers. Behind him a woman, not necessarily his wife, was stirring the contents of a steaming cauldron.

His appetite had fled him, had become incorporated into the terrible silent empty thing that stood invisible in the middle of the room.

He drank some wine. He drank some more wine, and more yet, and was still drinking when the needle had lifted from the last track of the first side of *Giant Steps*.

Then everything fell silent. Adam Füst slept in the chair, his legs outstretched, his head to the side, his hands folded in his lap. He slept for two hours and awoke only when the telephone began to ring. It took him a few seconds to understand what was happening, for in his dream the ringing had become something entirely different, something connected to a railway station, a journey, a departure, and when he quickly began to assess his circumstances, that he had fallen asleep in his clothes, sitting in a chair, and that the telephone was ringing, he suddenly awoke and ran across the room and picked up the receiver. He opened his mouth and tried to say "Hallo, hallo," but nothing came out. As he cleared his throat and wet his lips he heard Honnie say, through the atmospherics of a bad connection, "Adam, Adam, are you there, is it you?"

"Honnie?"

"I had to call you to tell you I'm all right. I just wanted to ring to say that everything's all right. And that I'm going to be fine."

And then there was silence. The dial tone returned. The operator said it was impossible to trace a number just like that, perhaps monsieur had been watching too many films, eh?

He hung up the phone and looked at his watch. It was just past four in the morning; an ungodly hour for anyone.

3

S HE WAS SITTING IN THE ARMCHAIR IN THE LIVING room—the chair covered with the cotton cloth imprinted with the India motif, elephants carrying maharajahs in a princely and unending procession—holding a cigarette, sitting in her black underpants and matching camisole, slowly exhaling the smoke in a slow coil of grey, her knees drawn up, her eyes staring at the wall. Around her there was silence. Nothing she was considering at that moment could be coherently shared with another person.

That is how Adam remembered his wife Honnie: a picture of a woman in repose, her thoughts turned inward; a kind of iconic portrait that continued to linger in his memory, and which struck him as particularly eloquent that morning. It was an image that his mind would retain and enhance, pick at and interpret, as if there was some clue there that might lead him to the answer.

For a week he did nothing. No idea he could commit to action could bring her back to him. She had left him, and soon she would return and explain all. That was what the phone call was about; to reassure him.

Six days after Honnie's disappearance Adam went to dinner at Johnny Vodo and his wife Eva's apartment near the Canal

Saint-Martin. They lived in a cramped ground-floor flat that could be reached only by walking through a covered passage that cut through the center of the building. At the end of it, to the right, was a red door. That was where Johnny and Eva and Johnny's mother lived. Johnny's mother was called Marimba or Miranda, Adam could never be quite sure, so that when he greeted her he simply said, *"Bonjour, maman de Johnny,"* a salutation that always made her bare her toothless gums and laugh. Johnny's talent had been recognized only a few years earlier, and now that people were willing to pay him for it, he had put money down on a larger apartment a few streets away. He hoped to have some work done on it when the summer came.

They drank some thick red wine and sat almost knee to knee in the tiny sitting room. Johnny had put a Sonny Rollins record on the turntable. Max Roach was playing drums. Johnny puffed on a joint and passed it to Adam. Adam said no, he wanted to keep his head clear. He wanted to keep his head clear because ever since receiving that phone call from Honnie he felt compelled to remain alert. Perhaps she had been kidnapped?

Or perhaps she had had good reason to take a kind of leave of absence, that would all be explained soon, when she returned. There was another option, of course, that being the possibility that Adam had dreamed the phone call; and when he considered this he thought too of the cruelty of the human subconscious.

He sipped at his wine and realized that even though he had refused to smoke Johnny's grass he had still inhaled enough of it in that airless little room to make him high. Johnny told about backing up Mal Waldron, and that after the second set he and Mal and the bassist went out for Chinese food and the bassist had come down with severe food poisoning and was still critically ill in the hospital. First he had felt a tingling sensation and now he was paralyzed. Because he was stoned Adam laughed until his sides hurt, and then Johnny began to laugh, too, even though he had hinted that the bass player might not ever play bass again, much less survive his twenty-three years. Eva held her wine glass between her fingers and stared into the bottom of it.

Adam didn't like Eva Vodo. He didn't like her because she didn't speak, although he disliked her somewhat less than did Honnie, who despised her. It wasn't that she was mute, or psychologically blocked from uttering noises (for if you tiptoed to the Vodos' front door and placed your ear against it you would hear her loud and clear, chatting away in her Swedish accent). It was just that, as Adam saw it, she was rude. When she wanted to say something she would whisper in Johnny's ear. "Eva wants to know if you'd like more chicken," Johnny would tell Adam. "Say thank you to Eva, it is excellent, and yes, I wouldn't mind that bit of thigh, just there." And Eva would lower her eyes and smile enigmatically to herself.

Her silence seemed almost to invite you to decipher a kind of esoteric code, as if the answer to all your questions were contained in the rhythms and anomalies of her bodily functions: her breath, her heartbeat, the light in her eyes.

Once Honnie said, "I am certain that Eva Vodo is a witch. My grandmother was the same way. She never talked; she was always silent. Do you know why? It was because she claimed she always heard voices. Voices of the dead, voices of lost souls."

Eva was originally from Stockholm. She was short, with long blond hair and a pretty if slightly heavy face. She wore cheap, baggy trousers that were three inches too short and, unless the weather was cold, oversized sleeveless blouses that made a display of her armpits. She bought her entire wardrobe at street markets, and once when Honnie asked her if she'd like to go shopping, meaning at Au Printemps, Eva, who said nothing, plucked at her sleeve and made her look at rags in the gutter for three hours.

Johnny had met Eva while sitting in for Dexter Gordon's drummer in Copenhagen two years earlier. She had been waiting in his dressing room when he finished his set. According to Johnny, she had been on holiday with a group from her school and wanted to settle down to marriage.

Adam watched Eva with interest. He wondered if when they were alone Eva would burst into raucous laughter and say things like, "Did you see that idiotic Adam? Christ, I make that prick uncomfortable, don't I, though?"

What he preferred to do at Johnny Vodo's apartment was listen to music and talk about who was playing where.

"So Honnie is gone," Johnny Vodo said that night. "I'm sorry, Adam, it must be tough." Eva smiled and took Johnny's huge right hand in hers. She traced the lines in it with her fingertips. "What do you think she's done?" asked Johnny.

Adam shrugged. For a moment, indeed for a long moment, there was silence in the room. Upstairs Johnny's mother was sewing on her ancient black Singer; one could hear the vibration in the walls, the furniture, the ceiling. The record had come to an end. Only Eva's eyes, large and clear and blue, looked up at Adam. Eyes that knew. *She's going to die,* Adam wanted to say, and he thought that were he to say it, Eva would nod her head with certainty and mouth the word *yes.*

"You haven't by any chance seen her, have you Eva?" Adam asked. He wanted to pick her up and shake her as one would a talking doll whose vocal mechanism had gone awry. She stared at the toes of her shoes and could not even bring herself to shed a tear for Adam and Honnie Füst. He said, "You'll tell me, though, won't you, Eva, if you ever see Honnie, or hear from her?"

Eva said nothing. *Cat got your tongue?* Adam thought, though he was too polite to say it.

As Johnny rose to get another bottle of wine a thought came to him. "You know, Adam, I have an idea. I know lots of people around here, people involved in one thing or another, you know what I mean. If Honnie's in trouble maybe I can get them to keep an ear out for any word, you understand?"

Adam liked the idea. He suggested Johnny broadcast a description of Honnie, then had a better idea; he took out his wallet and gave Johnny a photo of her, taken in Oberwil. She was wearing a black turtleneck jersey with the sleeves pushed up over her elbows. Her arms were crossed and she was holding a cigarette between her fingers. She smiled against the slanting rays of a setting sun. "I'm not much of a photographer," Adam said.

Eva took the photo from him and stared at it, as if attempting to invest the image with a kind of independent life. So intently did she examine it that Adam, and no doubt Johnny as well, for a moment believed that Eva might realize that she had seen Honnie, say six hours earlier, waving frantically for help from a third-floor window near the fleamarket on the place Monge. She placed the photo on the table and crossed her arms.

Even while Adam and Johnny tapped their feet to Sonny Rollins's lively calypso, "St. Thomas," Eva remained motionless. They ate barbecued chicken, which Adam found delicious, though Johnny explained it hadn't been properly barbecued on a grill. He had gotten the recipe while visiting New York the year before, touring with some backup group. For dessert Eva brought out a plate of pastries. Johnny made Moroccan coffee and put on another record. Eva seemed to have disappeared into thin air.

"She's gone to bed," Johnny said, as if it were the most normal thing in the world, leaving your husband and guest without even a goodbye or Nice seeing you, goodnight. "She's thoughtful," he added.

"Oh God," Adam moaned. "Oh God. Oh God."

Johnny sat beside him and took hold of his shoulders. "Look, man."

"Oh God, where is Honnie."

"You'll find your woman, Adam, don't worry, man."

He wept during the ride home on the métro. Other passengers stared at him and then turned away. It was a six-minute walk from the métro to Adam's apartment in Montmartre.

While he was waiting for the light to change on the rue Marcadet a car pulled slowly up to it and drifted to a halt. Adam wondered why it didn't proceed once the light had turned green. The driver of the car, a middle-aged man with a thin moustache and bags under his eyes and thinning hair, who in some odd way resembled François Mitterand, leaned over and looked at Adam through the open window of his red Citroën. Adam thought he was about to be solicited for directions. Then the man made some sort of gesture, a twisting of the hand, and drove slowly away.

The next morning he rang the police. They asked him to come and tell his story to Inspector Cuvillier. It seemed to Adam that Inspector Cuvillier resembled the musician Alfred Brendel, and it had perhaps been a bit thoughtless of him to ask the Inspector straight out, "Do you play the piano?"

Cuvillier listened to Adam's tale of woe, then sat back and gazed in wonderment at this young man. "And yet you wait— what?—six, seven days before reporting the disappearance of your wife? I find that odd. Don't you, Monsieur Füst, now that you think of it?" He smiled suddenly, brightly, and his face momentarily glowed like a flash camera. Clearly he enjoyed his line of work. "Well?" he said, "Don't you think so?"

"Yes, Inspector," said Adam.

"Yet you waited five or six days ... odd ... most curious ... Now kindly let me see your papers." Cuvillier held out his stained, calloused fingers, twitching them to illustrate his impatience, *tempus fugit* they seemed to semaphore to the young Hungarian. Cuvillier retired to another room with Adam's identity card. As Adam waited for him a large woman in what appeared to be a man's business suit, all pinstripes and sharp creases, badly stained in places, came over and stared at him. A thin line of drool began to overflow her bottom lip. Beads of perspiration appeared on her forehead, the smell of unwashed armpits repelled Adam. Then a gendarme rushed over and pulled her away by her handcuffs to an interrogation cell.

Adam listened to the cries and uproars of the criminal classes, the corrupt, the insane. The Naked City, he thought, ardent cinéphile that he was.

Cuvillier returned and handed back his card. "Everything seems to be in order. Have you a recent photograph of your wife?"

Adam felt for his wallet and recalled that he had given Johnny Vodo the snapshot taken at Oberwil. "Not on me," he said.

"Get one to me, will you?"

"Yes, Inspector."

He looked into Adam's eyes. "So your wife was an addict ..."

"What? No, not at all; of course not."

"Of course not," echoed Cuvillier. He thought for a moment, then: "You like living in Paris?"

"Until this happened, yes, very much."

"And you're a film director, you say."

"I'm the personal assistant to the director Gabor."

"Yes, of course you are. And when you're not working for Monsieur Gabor, what do you do? Do you walk the streets? Do you visit friends? Do you hang about department stores or go to the cinema or frequent prostitutes or linger in public lavatories—what do you do, Monsieur Füst?"

Adam did not know what to say.

"I'll tell you why I'm asking these questions, monsieur. It's because you waited six days after your beloved wife disappeared before reporting it to the police. Don't you realize how much you have hindered our investigations?"

"Yes. Yes, I do," said Adam.

"Then why did you wait?"

"Because I thought she might come back."

"Has she come back before?"

Adam looked at him. "Before when?"

"When she left you before."

"How did you know about that?"

"Because women don't just walk out forever on their husbands. They make practice runs; little daring attempts at freedom. Then one day something drives them to make a permanent break: their husband beats them, or is discovered in bed with some other lady. Or she simply runs off to some other man."

"Not Honnie. No, no."

"You seem certain of that, Monsieur Füst."

Adam stared with astonishment at his trembling hands. "I can't be certain of anything, Inspector. I just want you to help me find my Honnie."

Inspector Cuvillier smiled. "In that case we shall do our best. You understand, however, that the worst might have already happened."

"Yes, monsieur."

"In which case I want you to make me a promise."

"Yes, monsieur."

Inspector Cuvillier raised a finger to the air. "Just don't ask us why."

Later that evening there was a soft knock at the door. A gendarme with tired eyes and bad breath came to fetch a photograph of Honnie. He asked Adam for a glass of water. When

Adam returned to the living room he found the gendarme browsing through his and Honnie's record collection, classics cheek by jowl with bebop. The man displayed an album. "Who's this, then?"

"The late Maria Callas, a collection of her mad scenes."

The gendarme reinserted the record and took out another. "And this?"

"Yehudi Menuhin."

"Mad scenes, too?" asked the gendarme, clearly out of his depth.

"I don't believe he has recorded any mad scenes, Yehudi Menuhin, though he may perform them privately, at salons." Adam did not know what he was saying, he was half out of his mind over Honnie's disappearance.

Inspector Cuvillier rang Adam a week later. No one matching her description had been found, though the morgues were full of unidentified bodies, like so many unclaimed umbrellas, Cuvillier quipped, stacked in a corner of the lost-property office. He promised Adam they would continue to look for her, though the subtext of his statement was quite clear: tough luck, *mon vieux*, but your wife's having it off with another man.

Another man. Was such a thing possible? Not that he was much to look at, of course ... but it wasn't the sort of thing Honnie would do, fall in love with someone else and not inform him. Then Adam remembered what LouLou had told him: Honnie was laughing, hahaha, in a red car; a man was driving. A man was driving. A man. Hahaha. And when he thought of Honnie laughing he thought of just the opposite: Honnie not laughing, unhappy, standing at the bottom of a well of despair, staring up at a disc of sunshine ...

Which brought to mind their time in Oberwil. And when he recalled that period he seemed, too, to see into the future. A

41

corpse is pulled out of the Seine. It is a woman with long dark hair. Her eyes have been eaten by the fish.

They had lived in the cottage in Oberwil for only two months. It had not been their first choice, they would have preferred to live in the city. Zurich proved to be too expensive; Geneva too distant; Paris they would inevitably return to; Budapest was the city of their parents. They had traveled back to Hungary for a three-week stay, then took leave of their families and crossed the border into Austria and bought an old Fiat 124 in Mödling. They took a room in a guesthouse and each day drove into Vienna to see the sights.

From Vienna they drove to Munich, stopping at Salzburg for two days, then proceeding on to Zurich. They adhered to no itinerary; they would make their own leisurely way back to Paris. At first Honnie wanted to revisit some frescoes she had seen years ago in Tuscany. Then she thought she might want to travel down the Dalmatian coast. Then it dawned on her that her professor at the university had raved about the frescoes at a disused chapel near Zurich.

Honnie took the keys and sat behind the wheel. Adam rummaged through his shoulder bag and brought out a selection of cassettes. He had bought a little portable tape player at a discount department store in Vienna. He removed the Fauré *Requiem* and replaced it with Miles Davis's *Kind of Blue*. "Nice," said Honnie, turning to smile at her lover.

He loved her then, just as he loved her now. At the heart of his love for her lay the mystery that was Honnie, the unreflecting gemlike enigma that rotated slowly in the core of their relationship. He had met her by chance, one afternoon in Paris, in fact while having a beer with Johnny Vodo at a café near the place Saint-Michel. She had been sitting at the next table, reading a Budapest newspaper and laughing to herself. Adam instantly recognized the journal and said to her, "You actually like that?"

"No, no, my mother sends it to me sometimes, it's a lot of rubbish. What, you're a tourist?"

She was the first Hungarian he'd met since coming to live in Paris. She was taking some art courses and refining her work on frescoes with an authority on the subject named Corvin. She was sharing a room with two other students, Greek women. Adam made her laugh by reaching over and sliding off her sunglasses. She blushed when he told her she had beautiful eyes. He admired her long hair. He asked her if she knew some of his friends back in Budapest. She knew none of them, though one of the names seemed familiar to her; perhaps she had met a mutual friend, whatever. She said she had been in Paris for only a month. She laughed at his little stories and smoked his cigarettes and then looked at his eyes when he wondered aloud if she'd like to get together with him later. Dinner, he was thinking. A film, or a few drinks, if she'd prefer? He knew of a little place on the rue Saint André des Arts where you could get delicious ice cream. She said No, she couldn't, she had another appointment, and then changed her mind and Yes, that would be fine, perhaps an ice cream, and then she let herself get talked into having dinner with him as well.

They went to bed together that night. On her lower back was a large bandage. She said she had fallen down the stairs of the métro station near the Jeu de Paume. She'd been taken to the hospital. There were no stitches, just a bad bruise, a bit of a scrape. He noticed also the remnants of a bruise near her right eye, a faint bluish discoloration. She took his hand and moved it away from the bandage onto her left breast. Once again she told him she'd been in Paris only a month. The accident had occurred two weeks earlier.

Honnie moved in with him four days later. They had everything in the world to talk about: themselves. They spoke of their experiences back in Budapest, their work, their interests, their aspirations. But while Adam could talk for hours about whatever came into his head, Honnie spoke only selectively, touching upon certain subjects and avoiding others. She asked Adam repeatedly not to ask her about her previous lovers. "Did they touch you like this?" he would ask. "Did they do it this way?" And always she would allow a smile to form at the corners of her mouth and change the subject.

"How many were there, then?"

"Eighty-three," she would say, thereby effectively ending the discussion.

"I give you this much," she once told him, "I give you my full attention, I give you my love, I give you my body. You have me now, the way I am. But you don't have me three years ago or ten years ago or when I was a baby. Then I was someone else, there were other people. Be content with what I am."

And in three years, in ten years, would he still have her, would he have her love ...? He had never asked. She would never have answered.

Sometimes she would allow him a limited view of some past experience, such as the incident of the body found in Alsógalla. And sometimes she would be writing a letter to an old girlfriend back in Budapest and would read portions of it to him, occasionally illustrating them with photographs of her friend that she had taken from her parents' house during their trip home: another brief glimpse into the Honnie that predated their life together.

Thus she remained something of a mystery to him, much as the Citadella Tool Works did: each containing some knot of truth that he might never reach. It was only after Honnie's disappearance that he realized what a godsend it was, not knowing and yet wanting to know, this lusting after knowledge, this struggle with mystery, that lay at the heart of every profound relationship.

The chapel was located outside Oberwil, near the town of Jonen. Honnie had explained the significance of the frescoes there to Adam, but when he had begun to ask questions about them she fell silent. This was her interest; he was to mind his own business.

The chapel stood alone, about a hundred yards from the side of the road. It was obvious other buildings had once occupied the area, perhaps there had once even been a little village there; it was impossible to say. To gain access to the chapel one had to apply to a clerk in the town hall in Jonen. Honnie signed a ledger and was given a key in return for a refundable deposit. The clerk smiled genially and said that they were the first visitors to the chapel in eighteen months. Honnie and Adam drove there and parked the car just up the hill, on the side of the road, on the grass.

It was early spring, the sun was warm, and the air smelt green and fertile; but when they pushed open the door of the chapel they were forced to step aside and let the cold darkness of winter escape. Honnie shivered. Adam went back to the car to get her duffle coat. When he returned she was standing inside holding the big flashlight the clerk had lent her. At first she said nothing. She aimed the light at each of the walls, then focused it on a spot straight ahead of her, just where the altar would have stood.

"There was a chateau attached to this at one time, you see," she said, shining the beam on an undecorated wall that clearly showed the outline of an entryway. Her voice echoed slightly and decayed rapidly in the empty structure.

"It's cold," said Adam.

"It hasn't been used for years. There's no more God here. He's fled."

She stepped closer to one of the frescoes, a scene of Resurrection, and moved her fingers lightly about the surface

45

of the painting, as if she were seeking out a heartbeat. "Very late sixteenth century," she said, more to herself than to Adam. "Pretty average work, if you ask me. I don't know what the old man was talking about." She turned the light on Adam and looked at him. "It's funny," she said. He could hear something scratching at the wall in the corner, something desperate, large, clawed. "I'm cold," he said.

Honnie said: "Give me my bag." She reached inside and took out a stout palette knife, then began scraping gently away at a corner of the fresco.

"What the hell are you doing, Honnie?"

"It doesn't matter. No one will know. Go out and smoke a cigarette. I just want to check something."

Adam went outside and strolled around in the grass. Small purple flowers grew in clusters here and there on the lawn. Mournful little white blossoms, their heads dipped, were growing by the old foundation stones that lay alongside the chapel. A large striped cat, its shoulders hunched, stared uneasily at him from its corner by the chapel wall.

He sat in the car and without shutting the door listened to a tape. He realized that when he and Honnie reached Paris they would have to find another flat. He checked his watch: Honnie had been inside the chapel for nearly forty minutes. He shut the car door and stopped when he saw her walking slowly toward him. "Well?" he said, but she said nothing; she handed him the key and the flashlight.

They had lunch in a café in Oberwil. People stared at them, people with heads shaped like potatoes, with complexions resembling bruised vegetables. They seemed fascinated by the couple. Honnie smoked a cigarette and sipped her beer. After a long silence she said: "That fresco was comparatively recent, probably seventeenth century—at least later than I thought it was." She paused, seemed about to add something, then puffed on her cigarette and looked away.

A few weeks later Honnie fell into a depression. She ate only when Adam forced her to, and then only clear soups and bland puddings. She took to her bed and gave up smoking. She refused books, she wanted silence. Eventually Adam rang up a doctor from a phone in the village. The doctor had been recommended to him by the pharmacist. The doctor suggested he ring a specialist at a clinic in Zurich. Adam must have seemed helpless on the phone, for the doctor to whom he was speaking drove out and had a look at Honnie. When he saw her lying in bed he raised his eyebrows. She was asleep and apparently quite naked under the sheet that clung to her body. Adam roused her by touching her hip. Without opening her eyes she said: "Go away."

"There's a doctor to see you, Honnie."

"Go away. No."

"May I listen to your heart?"

"No. Go."

"Why do you need to listen to her heart?" Adam asked him. "Her heart hasn't anything to do with her mood."

"Ah, but."

"Go away," said Honnie.

"May I at least feel her pulse?"

"No," said Adam.

"Perhaps I could be left alone with the young lady?"

"No," said Adam.

"May I see your eyes at least, my dear?"

"No," said Honnie and Adam together.

The doctor took Adam aside. He said: "May I ask why you bothered ringing me if neither of you wish her examined?"

Adam didn't have an answer. The doctor wrote out a bill, a sizeable bill, and handed it to Adam. The doctor smelt of tobacco and beer. Adam handed him some money, then the doctor drove off in his old black Mercedes.

Honnie remained in bed for three days more. Adam lay cold cloths on her head when she seemed hot, and at night covered her well. When she had to use the toilet he would sit her on the chamber pot and afterward wipe her clean. On the last day of her illness she got out of bed, showered, dressed, and lit a cigarette. "I'm okay now," she told Adam. Her appetite returned. Although she hated living in the cottage with its pervasive smell of decay she tolerated it for the few months they were there. And though she never fell quite as ill again, sometimes Adam would come upon her sitting in a chair, in her underwear, smoking a cigarette, deep in thought.

4

LIKE AN ARCHEOLOGIST WHO HAS EXCAVATED JUST SO FAR, who has unearthed an entire civilization and then is unable to reach the one beneath, the conquered and assimilated one: that is how Adam felt in the shadow of the remembered Honnie.

It was futile explaining to someone like Cuvillier the complex nature of Honnie's personality; the secret motives that ruled her life; the various strata that constituted her identity; the fragments of her past that only rarely reached the surface. It was difficult enough explaining it to himself. He found that speculation over her reasons for leaving him only led to despair, to a kind of nausea in the brain, a disgust with ideas. He wished to descend into the earth, touch the grimy walls of the métro, let himself be rushed and jostled by other passengers; he wanted to feel the polished metal of the poles as he rode beneath Paris, to breathe the dust of the day, to seek out the answer in the design of a bridge, the random code of cracks in the pavement, the scrawls on the side of some forgotten building. He needed to live among facts, what he could see with his eyes and hear with his ears. He needed to search for Honnie in this solid, three-dimensional world of streets and buildings and cafés in which existed LouLou and Gabor and Johnny Vodo and crowds of strangers whose feet scraped along the pavements of the city, who gave off odors and made love and argued and shunned abstraction; feared death.

Now he was quite certain of it, the phone call was his proof: Honnie had left him for some sure purpose, and although he could not for the life of him even begin to comprehend what this was, he continued to examine his memories, as one traces a roadway on a map, until he might say with triumph: This is where it all began, this is why she left me.

He flattened his hands on the wood of Gabor's desk. The pattern of the grain brought to mind ripples in a pond. It felt cool against his palms. Gabor hadn't come in that morning, he'd said he might try to stop by in the afternoon if his meeting with a distributor was over early enough. Gabor's usual script collaborator, Guy Lanson, had that morning delivered a second draft of the screenplay for the as yet untitled new film. Adam had taken it from its envelope and left it on Gabor's desk. He glanced at the first page:

1. INT. PIGEONNIER. DAY.

In the obscurity of the *pigeonnier* we see SOLANGE, twenty-fourish, blindfolded, her hands and feet secured together with electrical cable. The light from the holes in the roof points up her near nudity. There is a hint of blood on her shredded clothing. Suddenly she hears a door scraping open.

Adam did not feel keen on reading more of it. He shut the cover and sat back in Gabor's chair. LouLou was sitting on the desk, letting her legs swing as she gazed out the window and hummed to herself. It was a warm day, spring was about to yield to summer, a light, pleasantly cool breeze moved like a ghost, silently through the room. Adam looked at LouLou's legs in a beam of sunlight and thought how unlike Honnie's they were.

Whereas Honnie's were just as long and slim, they were also duskier, for Honnie was naturally dark, and she once told Adam that back in grammar school in Budapest her friends used to call her Gypsy or The Greek.

When he looked up he saw that LouLou had been watching him. Her mouth slitted into a smile. She said, "And you say Honnie rang to tell you she was all right?"

He said nothing.

LouLou shrugged. "She'll be back, Adam. It's probably just something she needed to get out of her system."

On the portable radio in the outer office a small voice read the news. It spoke of terrorism. There seemed little else to discuss nowadays. There was an item about an earthquake in some other part of the world. The earth had swallowed up an entire village; nothing but a dog and an infant had been found. The infant was sitting on the ground, laughing and watching the dog writhe in agony; its back had been broken. Adam imagined a great crack in the earth, in the deep shadows of it nestling the remains of this small corner of civilization, houses, churches, cafés, a post office. One day the great crack would become a great seam. Eventually memory would die. In the local news a body had been fished out of the Seine earlier that day. Police were now attempting to identify the woman. The weather would continue to be fine, although rain was expected by the end of the week.

LouLou rested a hand on his shoulder, "Don't worry," she said, smiling frankly into his eyes. He looked at her face, at her short, blond hair and high cheekbones and tinted lips. Gabor had hired her as much for her secretarial skills and experience as for her slight resemblance to Isabelle Huppert, with whom at one time he had been enamored. Now that LouLou had cut her hair she no longer resembled Isabelle Huppert. In fact any resemblance between the two women probably resided within

Gabor's mind, for if anything LouLou brought to mind the actress in Truffaut's *L'Amour en fuite*, the pretty redhead; Adam could not remember her name. Sabine something, he thought.

Now a song was playing on LouLou's radio, every pop song sounded alike, Adam thought, everything seemed like lalala these days, he was sick to death of it. Suddenly he felt very tired, quite limp; washed-out. And yet his mind seemed completely calm, like the surface of a pond before the wind rises. LouLou rested a finger on his jawline and touched his lips with her mouth. He felt the damp warmth of it and smelled the fruity sweetness of her hair as it swung forward and grazed his cheek. He stared at her skin as she slowly withdrew, the curve and rise of her upper lip, the momentary flare of her nostrils, the pale, almost invisible hairs on her temples; his dark reflection in her eyes.

When Inspector Cuvillier rang that evening Adam recalled the news broadcast he had overheard in the office and his heart began to race. Cuvillier asked if he would like to go now to look at the body, or perhaps wait until after dinner. It was in the basement morgue of the Hôpital Boucicaut, not far from the bend in the river where it had been found. Cuvillier could meet him there, if he wished. Adam looked at the little meal he had prepared for himself: steak, rice, *salade verte*, a bottle of Stella Artois beer. "I'll go now," he said, then threw the lot into the rubbish, grabbed his jacket, left the flat.

It would be at least a thirty-minute métro ride, including a change of line at Madeleine and God knows what other delays that might occur. He stood on the platform and stared wildly at the tracks, unaware of the people around him, the people who were going to dinner, or to a film, or a party. As he sat in his car he thought of what Cuvillier had said, that a woman's body had been found in the Seine, and that he wanted Adam to have a look at it, and Adam remembered that he had given that stupid gendarme a photo of Honnie and that by now Cuvillier would have seen the photo, and that if the body fished out of the river had been of a platinum-blonde dwarf the Inspector would never have rung Adam. He lowered his head and held it between his hands.

There was an eight-minute wait at Madeleine for the train that would take him to Boucicaut. Adam stood by a wall on the platform and leaned against it and shut his eyes for a moment. When he shut his eyes he saw Honnie leaping from the quay into the cold river, and then after opening them and closing them again he saw her being thrown into it from the back of a van, her bruised and violated body falling like a rag doll into the murky Seine.

He sat in the carriage and watched the stations come and go. He looked at his shoes against the floor and noted the contrast. He rested his hands on his knees and made his knuckles turn white. A man standing near his seat, a heavy man in a raincoat, wore a ring on the little finger of his left hand. The ring bore a curious device, the image of a golden bee set in onyx. Adam stared at it and clenched and unclenched his jaw. His right foot tapped nervously on the floor of the carriage. He looked up at the man with the ring. The man wore dark glasses and thus Adam could not tell whether the man was looking at him or someone else, or was blind altogether.

When he got out at Boucicaut he stood on the avenue Félix Faure and looked around in bewilderment. He hadn't been in the district for so long, had rarely ever come there at night, when it seemed so different. Standing on the corner of the rue de la Convention and avenue Félix Faure were three gendarmes. Two of them wore machine guns strapped to their shoulders. Adam excused himself and was about to ask directions when one of the gendarmes requested his papers. Adam took out his wallet and removed his identity card. While one of the trio went off to examine it in the beam of his flashlight, another nudged Adam closer to the wall of a building with the tips of his fingers. He said, "Right there, okay?"

There was a crescent moon just emerging from behind a wisp of cloud. A man in a raincoat walked slowly down the opposite pavement, turned briefly to see what was taking place, replaced his sunglasses and rounded the corner. The gendarme returned his identity card, held it out to Adam between the knuckles of two fingers, blinded him momentarily with the light from his pocket torch. The men said nothing as they walked away. In the distance was the braying of a police Klaxon. Otherwise the city seemed silent, save for the low continuous hum that rose from underground. He still did not know how to get to the hospital. He looked at his watch in the glow of a streetlamp: he was already twenty minutes overdue. He thought of Honnie lying on a chrome table. He imagined Cuvillier had a short temper. He pictured the Inspector beating out a suspect's brains, watching gleefully as the grey matter spattered the walls and seeped into the rug, thirty, forty, fifty years of a life become a pattern of random stains, a spill, a roomful of waste. He saw Cuvillier on a misty Saturday morning at a gun club, dressed in a safari shirt, firing his revolver into the silhouette of a fleeing child; in his mind's eye he envisaged the Inspector shutting the door of an apartment behind him, his hands dripping with fresh blood. It was a scene Gabor had used in his first film. In those days it seemed shocking; now people laughed at it. The critics thought it brilliant, impressionistic, almost Gothic in its psychological depth. Gabor once said, "I did it because it disgusted me, not because I thought it was brilliant. I saw my own father murdered just that way," then dropped the subject.

A taxi pulled up to the curb and was about to discharge a grey-haired woman who glared at Adam as he hovered by her door, resting his hands on the roof of the car. The woman stuck a cigarette between her lips and leafed slowly through the compartments of her wallet. After she paid the driver she opened the door and before she could put a foot out Adam was leaning in and asking directions. "You filthy little bastard," she cried at him as he ran off to his destination.

Cuvillier was not there to meet him. The air in the hospital lobby was cool and dry. Adam went to the front desk and asked a nurse where the morgue was, and when a small bald man in a white coat was summoned to speak to him the nurse hid behind a partition and watched Adam with one terrified eye.

"Yes?" the man inquired, all smiles in a white jacket and stethoscope. A poster on the wall with a sketch of a grinning skull warned one not to engage in casual sex.

"The morgue, please," said Adam breathlessly.

The man stared at him and pulled thoughtfully at the end of his nose. He pushed his gold-rimmed glasses up against his face. He smelled of bay rum. "You have to find the … morgue? Now why is that, I wonder?"

"I'm supposed to meet someone there," Adam said, addressing the pink ovoid that served as the doctor's head.

"Ah. I see. You are supposed to meet someone there. A date, perhaps? Is this some new punk phenomenon, meeting girls at a hospital morgue?"

"I'm supposed to be seeing a police inspector there, I have an appointment, you don't understand." In a minute he would strangle the man in the white suit; I did it because he would not listen to reason, he would tell the magistrate.

The man in the white coat must have sensed his growing anger, for he retreated two steps and began snapping his fingers behind his back. Adam said fuck this and *merci* and turned on his heel. By the time he reached the lift there were two other men in white coats on his trail, and they joined him in his journey down to the basement, standing close by and staring him in the eye. "You don't understand," Adam said. "I'm not a patient. Inspector Cuvillier rang me and said I should meet him here. It's not a joke, I'm not a criminal, I'm simply going to identify a body." Tears began to course down his cheeks. He thought of a demented male concierge he once had who apropos of heartache used to say, "Tears ran down my eyeballs." The door opened. Cuvillier was sitting on an orange plastic chair, smoking a cigarette and reading *France-Soir*, its brash headline alluding to Princess Caroline seeming quite beside the point to Adam.

There was something distasteful about the basement of the hospital. They walked beneath huge pipes that slushed and sloshed with waste water, past rooms that contained heating systems, their walls adorned with wrinkled photographs of naked women, past the kitchen with its steam and stink and the shouts of those who plunged their arms into vats of cold mashed potatoes and porridge, who swore ferociously over the fruit cocktail and dropped cigarette ash into the puddings.

Cuvillier said nothing as he strode alongside Adam. The walls of the corridors were covered with graffiti, some of it in languages unrecognizable to Adam, and the bits that Adam could make out—for suddenly, in this unhappy walk, his senses took on an unaccustomed brilliance, an acuity, as if his mind and body had been brought into precision focus—spoke of death and sex and decapitation. He momentarily wondered if the surgeons who labored on the top floors, who explored the living innards of comatose patients and wrote papers for learned journals, who lounged about their luxurious offices and dined at La Tour d'Argent, sometimes came down here and expressed their true feelings about life with their marking pens, Kill All Women, one of them said; Cunts Die, said another.

Cuvillier muttered something to him, but Adam was lost in a sudden brief memory, LouLou's face receding into the near distance, the damp swelling of her lips, his reflection in her eyes. Afterward she had said nothing, done nothing, simply got down from the desk and returned to the outer office, to type, to answer the phone and say "Gabor Productions, good morning," leaving Adam trembling and uneasy.

"You're not listening," said Cuvillier.

"What?"

Cuvillier put out a hand and stopped Adam from proceeding further. A door before them bore the discreet sign Morgue in a tiny black rectangle. "Now I'm not certain this is going to amount to very much. In fact I haven't seen the body for myself." Suddenly life seemed bright to Adam. "All I know," continued Inspector Cuvillier, "is that the woman is approximately the same age as your wife and has long dark hair. Look, maybe I can spare you all this. Can you tell me if Madame Füst has any identifying marks, birthmarks, moles, that sort of thing?"

Adam instantly saw the brown spot, a large freckle really, high on the inside of Honnie's left thigh. Often he would seek it out and press his lips against it, much to Honnie's delight, her intimate laughter breaking the silence of his memory like a church bell at dawn. He opened his mouth and was about to inform Cuvillier, then decided against it. If the body was that of Honnie he didn't want to think of the Inspector parting her thighs with his crusty fingers.

"No," said Adam. "Nothing."

"Then you'll have to look for yourself, do you understand?"

Adam said "Yes." Cuvillier took his arm and led him aside. Adam felt a burst of cold air as a man in a white coat exited the morgue and lit a cigar before walking the length of the corridor with its graffiti and horror.

"Have you ever seen a dead body before?" the Inspector asked.

Adam shook his head.

"There's nothing to be afraid of, you know."

Adam said No, there was nothing to be afraid of.

"In my line of business you get used to them," said Cuvillier, and Adam remembered having heard precisely the same line in a film he'd once seen, the title escaped him—*Murder something* or *Dead on Arrival* or *Blood in the Gutter;* he didn't know. "It's cold in there."

"Yes," said Adam.

"Bundle up."

"Yes," said Adam.

"The body is on a table, covered by a sheet. The body is naked."

"Perhaps if I saw the clothing I might be able to ..." he began.

"The woman they pulled out of the river was nude."

"My God," said Adam.

"Yes," said the Inspector.

"How did she ..." Adam resumed.

Cuvillier shrugged. "Exposure, probably. There's evidence she'd been taking drugs, needle marks on the arm, traces of narcotic in her blood. There was semen in her vagina. Why was she naked? I haven't the faintest idea. You say your wife wasn't an addict?"

"Of course not, she."

"You seem very certain of that."

Adam nodded.

"I'll show you her face first, you understand? Just the face."

"The face," echoed Adam as Cuvillier pushed open the door.

Adam pulled up the zipper on his suede jacket and tightened the muffler around his neck. It was colder than he had imagined it would be; food could be kept fresh there for years. In prominent places stood two metal tables, each of them covered with a large, heavy sheet. Beneath the sheets there were bodies that caused the sheets to resemble models of natural formations on the earth: mountain ranges, possibly within the Arctic Circle.

The only exposed parts of the body were the feet. On the big toe of each left foot was looped a thin white string attached to a kind of cardboard luggage tag. Although it was quite obvious to Adam that one pair of feet was male and the other female, Cuvillier seemed to feel it necessary to check the tags carefully. Adam stared at the woman's feet. They looked simultaneously unlike Honnie's long narrow feet and yet hauntingly familiar. The nails were covered with chipped red polish. The shade seemed like one Honnie favored, *Caprice* something by Chanel. The tag read Unknown Female. Adam felt his heart beat stronger, he felt something in his stomach move. "Okay? All set?" Cuvillier was saying, as if about to start a race.

Adam felt his scalp tighten, Cuvillier took hold of a corner of the sheet, Adam saw long brown hair, he watched it lengthen as the sheet was withdrawn, he saw a white forehead, he saw two vacant eye sockets, he saw a nose, lips, he saw a chin and a long white neck, he saw and he didn't see, he felt suddenly blinded, and then Cuvillier replaced the sheet and looked at him. "You're absolutely certain?" he said.

Adam nodded, "Yes yes."

"Well," said Cuvillier, who seemed disappointed, "I suppose you know best what your wife looks like."

"It's not her. Not her. Not Honnie," Adam said, moving to the wall and leaning sideways against it, his hands in his pockets, his palms damp, his fingers uneasily clutching at coins, keys, nothing.

The Inspector pulled the sheet down again, this time letting it slide from the body onto the floor, so that when Adam turned he saw a naked corpse on the table. From the side it slightly resembled Honnie. The prominent hip bone; the tangled puff of pubic hair; the long thighs, flattened against the table. The Inspector passed his hands two inches over the length of the body, as if he were a conjuror attempting to levitate the poor woman. He said, "She was nice, wasn't she. A good body. A bit heavy in the hips, though. I kind of like my women like that, now that I think of it. Gives you something to hold on to when they're on top."

But by this time Adam was outside the room, he was running along the labyrinth of corridors, past the furnace room and the kitchen, past the laundry and the employees' cafeteria, past the graffiti that spoke of death and sex and decapitation, up the lift and into the lobby, and when he pushed open the glass doors and reached the fresh air he turned momentarily and saw a small bald man in a white jacket staring at this obsessed young man who had seemed so eager to visit death in the morgue.

That night Adam received a curious telephone call. It occurred late at night, long after he had returned from the morgue and was preparing to go to bed. Although the woman he had glimpsed wasn't Honnie and in truth bore little resemblance to her, the view of her unsettled him. Was a corpse a her or an it? Was one still oneself after death or did one simply assume anonymity? Was death then a kind of pseudonym or *nomme de guerre* for life? He put his feet on the floor and rested his hands on his knees. He felt like someone who has lived all his life in a desert tent and is suddenly taken on a journey over the mountains, "There is the sea, there," and he can't quite believe his eyes, all this blue wetness, this horrible endless unbroken expanse of reflection and wave, for until then the sea had been only a word in a book, a place in a fantastic tale, something that lay in the depths of nightmare. Something greater than oneself, like death itself.

Death was something that was mimed in a film, or on television, bodies accepting bullets, blades; falling backward, under and over, the rough and tumble of a violent end down a flight of stairs; it was something by Tolstoy in a novel, Prince Andrey dying as simply and decently as if he were excusing himself from a salon full of guests; or by writers of *policiers* and thrillers, to whom death was a sordid business, terror and blood and the sound of rending flesh, the crack of bone, the sleek slish of a blade, the shimmery sexy obscenity of expiration. Death was the death of the old man he was told was his grandfather: a distant soundless occurrence, a dot on the horizon of childhood, somehow unrelated to him; the tears of his mother, the way she pulled at her hair, as if to punish herself—but for what? The death of her own father? Was that not inevitable?

He thought of the stillness of death, the chill silence that surrounded it, and he felt too this abrupt stasis and hush in his apartment as he sat on the chair with the India print, his chest heaving, his breath attempting to escape him. He shut his eyes and then opened them; he could not get the face of the dead woman out of his mind. Perhaps that was why his mother had tried to tear her hair. Perhaps she only wanted to cause pain, to make herself aware not of the passing of her father but of herself, her own mortality, or even her own life, the fact that she would go on, would experience pain, and that her father would no longer experience anything. He shut his eyes and opened them once again. He became aware of his breathing and the rhythm of his heart. He thought of the fragile muscle pulsing within his chest. He wondered what the woman on the table had been like, and could only imagine her as a little girl playing in the park, when death hadn't existed. Perhaps that was the meaning of life: to discover death as the constant companion it is. He thought of Inspector Cuvillier making light of death, speaking of sex and procreation and pleasure in the presence of a dead woman, and he saw that Cuvillier had lied to him, that he was no more accustomed to death than was Adam, for Cuvillier was uneasy, edgy in the face of death, and was it not odd, Adam thought, that men joked and women wept when the subject came up?

But he had neither joked nor wept. He had neither joked nor wept because he was numb. Honnie was neither alive nor dead. She just wasn't.

At first he didn't hear the ringing, for he had been washing his face and listening to a recording of Coltrane's *A Love Supreme*, as had more than one of his now wide-awake neighbors. Because he wanted to fill the emptiness that he had brought back with him from the morgue, to drive away the silence that so cunningly teased him with its hints and indirection, he had turned on all the lights and switched on his stereo and now his flat seemed like the setting for a jazz festival, all light and saxophone and tone clusters and sheets of sound. So he thought the ringing was Elvin Jones's ride cymbal, chingching chingching, then realized it was the telephone. Without drying his face he made a dash to the living room and switched off the stereo and picked up the receiver. For a moment there was silence, or rather not pure silence, the white silence that one sometimes senses, not the absolute silence that can only be defined as the absence of all sound, but rather a kind of curious layering of static and hiss, as if the party on the other end had plunged the receiver into the depths of a subterranean cavern. The water from his face trickled down his arm and fell in small droplets on the floor. "Hallo?" said Adam. Then came certainty: "Honnie? Honnie, don't hang up, it's Adam, stay on the line, for God's sake, stay."

It was then he began to make a kind of sense of the seemingly senseless background noise, as if certain strands of it had begun to unravel from the chaos. There was a rhythmic ticking—a dull, repetitive sound that seemed to be tapping out a certain pattern: four short clicks, then a pause; then three short ticks; then two; then four; and so on. There was the sound of what seemed to be a flowing river, bubbling against rocks,

rushing through its banks. Ah: there was also the character-
istic noise of electricity, the high-pitched humming one hears
when standing beneath a pylon on a still summer afternoon.
And then—he could hardly believe his ears—he began to make
out in the most distant background of the hiss the sound of a
voice, a voice that seemed to be calling and in between calls
taking long pauses. "Honnie?" he said. "Honnie!" he shouted,
he repeated it over and over again until there was a knock at the
door and the dial tone miraculously returned.

It was the husband of his concierge. He was elderly and wore
a grey cardigan. He looked up at Adam. "The missus wants a
word with you."

Adam pulled on a sweater and jeans and slipped on a pair
of sneakers. He locked the door and followed the old man down
the stairs. The concierge did not allow her husband to use the
lift because once, a few years ago, he had done something to
the buttons or the wiring and had spent an afternoon trapped
between floors, drinking the Beaujolais nouveau he had bought
for their evening meal and then singing a vulgar sailor's song
about mothers-in-law. The concierge's flat was located just
behind the office, which was also the kitchen. There Madame
Moreau kept her keys and took in the mail and earned her living by keeping up with the gossip and sometimes sharing bits
and pieces of it with various of the tenants.

Adam followed the man into the sitting room. Madame
Moreau and her mother, whose name was unknown to him,
were watching a game show on television. A man walked about
the stage in his underpants while a middle-aged woman in a
bikini squirted whipped cream at his navel. The master of cer-
emonies, a squat man in toupee and tuxedo, mimed hilarity
and pointed to lighted numbers on a board. Madame Moreau
gestured toward the screen and said to herself, "Will you look
at that."

"Um, *chérie*," Monsieur Moreau said quietly.

Madame Moreau's mother did not respond because she had suffered some sort of massive stroke some years before and had since been condemned to a kind of shadowy half-life in a wheelchair. She would stare you in the face, and after twenty-three minutes of it you would realize she hadn't moved a muscle. Dead, you'd think, but according to her daughter she wasn't dead, actually she was very much alive. "She likes a good comedy act," Madame Moreau once explained to Honnie and Adam. "She likes comedy and sometimes she watches *Dallas*, and then she likes nature shows; she's fond, very fond, of tigers, you know."

But from watching her it was impossible to tell. She could be sitting in front of a Coluche special, her eyes open, stone-cold paralyzed, and her daughter would say, "She can barely contain herself."

"Oh it's you, Monsieur Füst," she said that night, switching off the television and wiping her hands on her apron. She stood and then took a few steps back; clearly she was not about to present him with an award.

"It's about the noise, you see," said Monsieur Moreau, and his wife turned to him and snapped, "Shut up, Marcel."

"Ah, *pardon, chérie.*"

Over Madame's shoulder Adam could see the old woman, her white hair, her face turned toward the blank screen. Then the phone rang. Monsieur Moreau answered it in the kitchen and told his wife it was for her. She excused herself and left Adam alone with her mother. There was the peculiar odor of age, a pungent, almost sour smell, like that given off by a trunk full of old clothes and mementos. He looked into the old woman's face; her eyes were fixed on his. He had the curious idea that she was neither wholly alive nor completely dead, but rather, as it were, straddling the cleft between the two states. He wanted to say, quietly, "Have you seen my wife, have you heard from Honnie?" and for a moment he quite seriously considered doing so.

Madame Moreau returned. She said, "It's about the noise, you see."

"Ah," said Adam.

"Yes," said Madame Moreau. "And how's Madame Füst?"

"Um," said Adam. "On holiday, actually. She's visiting relatives. An aunt. Her Aunt Anna."

"You see, it's about the noise," she said, and Adam remembered that speaking to Madame Moreau was like trying to examine a portrait by Rembrandt while riding on a merry-go-round, you only occasionally got a chance to face the subject head-on.

"Sorry," said Adam.

"It's the music, actually. The music and the screaming."

"The screaming?" said Adam, furrowing his brow.

"And the music. The screaming and the music."

"And the music …?"

"Yes," said Madame Moreau. "There's been screaming, too, according to some."

"According to whom, Madame Moreau?" Suddenly he wanted to set the apartment block alight and flee to the hills; humanity was beginning to disgust him.

"According to neighbors," she said. "Screaming and music."

Music he knew about, but the screaming was something new. Ah: "Do you mean the saxophone?"

She looked at him, as did her mother, who looked through him, rather, into the depths of some secret she was unable to share. "You mean you've got a saxophone now, Monsieur Füst?"

"The saxophone on the record, madame. On the record."

"No, they said it was screaming, a man screaming."

Adam remembered the phone conversation. Honnie Honnie he'd cried. "They must be imagining it," he said.

"Altogether I've had four complaints," said Madame Moreau, secure now that the specter of statistics had raised its ugly head.

"May I have the names of these people?" he asked.

Madame Moreau would have none of it. "Why, if I gave you the names of them who knows what you might do?"

"I assure you, madame," he said.

"I mean, I've got to protect the rights of the tenants here, you know."

"I understand that, madame."

He glanced again at the old woman. He stared at her so hard that Madame Moreau turned with terror toward her mother. "What is it?" she cried.

It was as if the light in the woman's eyes had changed slightly, as if she were attempting to express some emotion, and for a split second Adam wondered whether she had been able to read his mind and perhaps had a message from Honnie after all.

"What is it?" Monsieur Moreau said, entering the room and getting into the spirit of things.

"I don't know," said his wife. "Suddenly I'm talking to Monsieur Füst and then he stops and stares at Maman."

"I won't do anything," Adam said. "I won't do anything to the people who complained, I assure you, madame."

"What's that?" she said.

"He said he won't hurt anyone," said Monsieur Moreau.

Madame was still staring at her mother, then all three stared, for the old woman opened her mouth and, looking at Adam, made a noise, an ambiguous sound that could be interpreted in many and various ways. Sometimes when he thought about it, when he lay in bed at two in the morning, Adam was quite sure the woman had said "Agn," at other times he could swear it was "Agora" or even "Agony," while he tried to convince himself he was making too much of it all. And then he would turn on his side and try to reproduce the sound the old woman had made, *agn, agn, agony, agora, agon, angora, ago, aga, agnes, agon, again, aga;* he would repeat it over and over again until the sound became just a shred of nonsense, the noise of a throat clearing or a window rattling, and he wondered if this was a definition of insanity, the reduction of nonsense to the state of significance. He wondered.

5

TOTO ROGET, LIKE JOHNNY VODO, KNEW HONNIE FROM when she and Adam first began living together in Paris. In those days Toto was studying physics at the university and on weekends singing with a band at a club called Rose Bon Bon. His father, highly placed in the French embassy in Lima, was separated from his mother, who at that time was the mistress of a certain fashionable French film actor. In the warm weather Toto, who was half-Peruvian, would remove his shirt at the least excuse and show off his dark, hairless chest. He wore tight jeans that emphasized his small, shapely buttocks and would often make a display of himself, skipping like a child down the avenue Foch, or breaking into song on a café terrace. There was little doubt he would make something of his life, Toto Roget.

Now he owned an elegantly appointed shop in the Marais district that traded in electronic security and surveillance devices, all of them ambiguous in appearance, expensive, devious in the extreme. Soft electronically generated music of sorts wafted discreetly from hidden loudspeakers. Thick carpeting covered the floor. Leather armchairs were provided for customers. No cash register was in evidence; a small robot camera recorded every credit card transaction. Adam hadn't seen Toto in three years. Now he was standing in front of the counter while Toto, his mane of black hair flecked with grey, his body trim inside a Nino Cerruti suit, quietly explained what the tiny box in his hand could do.

"You simply place it in your pocket. If by chance you go to a business meeting, and your discussions are being secretly taped, this scrambles everything you say, and only what you say. Here, let me show you."

He dropped the box into his breast pocket, or rather gently nestled it among the folds of his silk foulard, then switched on a portable tape recorder that stood on top of the thick glass counter. One of Toto's employees was sitting behind a desk at the rear of the shop, murmuring quietly into the sleeve of his jacket. Adam caught sight of yet another camera suspended from the ceiling, its tiny red light pulsing, the lens following his every movement. Toto initiated a conversation with Adam. Adam disliked being compelled to carry on a conversation; he preferred to let things take their own course: *Bonjour*, how are you, what's new, oh really, oh smashing, oh great, oh how nice, oho!, see you then, *au revoir*. But considering the circumstances and the fact that at the moment he needed Toto more than Toto needed him, he tried his best to please the man. After a few minutes of this repartee, Toto rewound the cassette and pressed the playback button as he watched Adam through complacent, reptilian eyes.

"Thiydinroplino?"

"Well, actually, that's why I've come to speak to you. Normally I try to avoid this quarter."

"Honrityuposhbicum?"

"The problem, well the problem is, you see, if there is a problem that is, you'll probably think I'm making too much of it, the problem is, well."

"Noythsophonrolk?"

"Well, actually, she's gone. That's the problem. She's, um, disappeared, you see. Look, can we stop this bloody machine?"

"Mnopodoo!"

"Yes, I'm quite serious. She's just disappeared. That's why I looked you up."

"Forgleforgle!"

"It's not funny. I was wondering if you'd seen her. Walking by, maybe, or in a car or bus or whatever. A boat. Anything."

"Kisythrylukfukitcunjilkyu."

"Look, there's no need to get angry."

"Coksuklitkystthatha!"

"Look, fuck this, I'm only asking, no need to take it personally."

He was only asking because three years earlier he had quite by accident come across a letter that Toto had sent to Honnie and that she had left between the pages of a novel by André Gide. Adam had not forgotten a word of it, "My Darling Honnie," it began, the words were emblazoned across the horizon of his memory.

Would half past three suit you? I yearn that it will be so, for I know it will be a special day for both of us. How much I have anticipated it, you magnificent bitch! Just the thought of you lying beneath me, your long legs wrapped tightly around my back, your breasts bouncing against my hot chest, your burning slit sucking eagerly at my stiff cock! I want you to be my whore, you bitch, I want you to abuse me and debase me, I want to spread oil on your chest and knead your huge breasts, I want to sodomize you until you scream.

Perhaps afterwards we could have a drink and a bite to eat? I look forward to it eagerly.

Your slave,
Toto

"My darling," Adam had said to her the night of his discovery, "have you ever fancied Toto Roget?"

Honnie was lying in bed, reading a study of Giotto, occasionally referring to a huge *catalogue raisonné* lying beside her, both volumes having been borrowed from the library earlier that day. "Hm?"

"Toto Roget. The shirtless Peruvian."

"What about him?"

"Have you ever fancied him?"

"Don't be silly, Adam. I fancy you, my sweet."

Her reading glasses propped on the end of her nose, Honnie smoked a cigarette and leafed through the book. On the bedside radio Debussy's *Nuages* was playing, over it a woman's voice reciting poetry by Mallarmé. He remembered the words: "*Le vierge, le vivace et le bel aujourd'hui ...*" Adam stood in the doorway, the letter, wrinkled and folded, burning in his trouser pocket. He fingered it as he spoke, as if trying to divine the truth from the dried ink on the paper. "Tell me," he said.

She removed her glasses and stared at him. "No."

"What is this no? No, you never fancied Toto Roget or No, you will never tell me the truth?"

"Just No. N-O. No."

"But it is not enough, No is just not sufficient, Honnie. Perhaps I am putting it the wrong way. Perhaps I should reverse it, then. Does Toto Roget fancy you?"

There was a long pause. Adam looked into her eyes and for a moment felt he was watching a peep show, all he could see in them was a lurid drama of Honnie being oiled and sodomized, her breasts bouncing against Toto's hot chest, sperm like fireworks spraying over her body. "I couldn't care one way or another," she said. "Besides, I think he's gay."

"Handy little thing, isn't it?" Toto was saying, removing the device from his breast pocket. "But I suppose in your line of business things like this are irrelevant. Security doesn't much matter in the film industry, does it. Gabor's been stealing ideas for years and nobody's batted an eyelid." He smiled coolly at Adam. "Would you like to see something else? A bit of fun, really." He reached under the counter and brought out a black box, from which emerged a small flexible rubber appendage, a high-tech sex organ, Adam could not resist touching it. "That's the aerial," said Toto. "Now listen carefully."

He pushed a switch on the side of the box, then turned off the music coming from the hidden loudspeakers. Filling the shop was the sound of echoing footsteps, then a door-latch being slid shut. There then followed what sounded like the rustling of sheets, or clothes, then a tinkling noise and a sigh. Toto smiled. "We've planted a bug in the ladies' toilet in the restaurant next door. Just for demonstration purposes, of course. You should only know what we sometimes hear. And we also carry a line of specialist photographic equipment, including the latest devices for taking photographs undetected at night."

"No one is safe while you're around, Toto," said Adam, and Toto smiled, for he knew that his erstwhile friend had spoken the truth.

"So Honnie's left you," Toto said. "Pity. Who's the lucky guy?"

"She hasn't left me, Toto. She's disappeared."

"Oh come on, Füst. People don't just disappear."

"I bet they do in Peru, just like in Argentina," and Adam was beginning to regret he had ever decided to approach Toto Roget; now he was about to get into a heated political discussion and because at that moment he hated Toto Roget, anything even vaguely associated with the man also became loathsome, like Machu Picchu and bananas and the cha-cha-cha. *I want you to be my whore, you bitch*, Toto had written to Honnie.

Toto checked his watch. "Look," he said, "let's have lunch together and talk about this, all right? There's a nice little place just around the corner in the place des Vosges."

Now Adam felt at a disadvantage, for he suspected that their conversation was not only being taped, as they sat at a table in the little restaurant, but also overheard by all and sundry, Marguerite Duras and Bernard-Henri Lévy and whoever else patronized Toto's fashionable boutique. Even when he went for a pee he felt certain the sound of his urine splashing into the ceramic device was being heard with interest elsewhere, and perhaps even undergoing analysis, and if the night before he felt as if he were going out of his mind, he now had the sudden and enlightening and somehow even comforting notion that he was not mad: everyone else was.

"No one just disappears," Toto was saying as he sipped his third martini. "To talk of people disappearing is like trying to have a rational discussion about alchemy and wood nymphs. The age of magic has long passed, Adam my friend. That was two thousand years ago. This is today. What would the ancient Greeks make of what we have now, hm?"

"Ah, to listen to a woman having a pee, now that would have taken Plato's mind off his caves, eh Toto?"

"You joke, but you still don't follow me. Look: everything is connected to everything else. It's like one vast electronic circuit, a kind of monster computer: one action sets off another, and so on, all across the network. All you have to do is follow the effects and causes and trace them back to their origin."

The words *big bang* sizzled into life in Adam's mind: that was the origin, a ball of gas the size of your fist, a big wind, a soundless pop in the eternal night and *voilà*, here I am sitting with the shirtless Peruvian in a Marais bistro. "I'm talking about Honnie," said Adam, "I'm talking about my wife, not some bloody, ah, I'll have the escargots, I think, do they come with bread? And another one of these." He wiggled his glass and smiled dully at the waiter.

"Yes, yes, I know, I've heard that argument before, Füst, we're dealing with people; you can't reduce them to a series of digits, treat them like objects, but that's a load of rubbish," he declared, sipping his drink again. "People don't just disappear. You only think that because you're lacking the knowledge of a first cause. The notion of a solid object dissolving into thin air is insane. First of all, because of the atomic structure of a solid object."

"Why did you ask me out to lunch, Toto?"

Toto Roget smiled, he had an answer for everything, but he was like an oracle, all his replies were couched in riddles and delivered with enigmatic smiles. "I don't dislike you, Adam. Actually I've always been rather fond of you. And Honnie."

"We used to be great friends, you know, you and I and Honnie," reminded Adam.

"In the old days." He opened his hands as if to point up the cut of his suit: "Before this."

Adam nodded, he felt the martini coursing through the byways of his brain, one thought triggering off yet another, *I want you to abuse me and debase me, I want to knead your huge breasts*, and suddenly he was thinking about something else, LouLou's kiss, the scent of her hair as it grazed his cheek, "Which is really what I want to discuss with you," Toto was saying, sober as an archbishop's wife, as Adam's old granny used to say.

"Sorry, what?"

Toto smiled, he lit a king-size Dunhill cigarette, two thin streams of smoke shot from his nostrils. "The old days," he repeated. "Do you remember the old days, Adam? Ah yes, the old days. Recall them at all, Füst? Ah, you think you do, but you don't. The old days. When I first came to know you. And Honnie. And here's our lunch, thank you, Louis."

The waiter Louis deposited the plates and called Toto *monsieur*, while Adam, who appeared to be a perfectly reasonable and normal member of the human race, was not addressed as anything at all. "The point is," Toto continued, "the point is, really, that there's so much one doesn't know. It's the sort of thing I try to explain to my customers. Often I'm called in as consultant to a large company. All they're worried about is security, which is a reasonable concern these days, believe me. So I have a sweep of their offices done and we either remove the bugging devices or, if this is impossible, if, you see, the devices have somehow been incorporated into the fabric of the building, we install scrambling devices and other forms of circuitry which negate the planted bugs. Do you follow me?"

"It'd probably be cheaper simply to blow up the building, I should think," suggested Adam as he made light work of his little gastropod.

"Very amusing. At the same time," Toto went on, "at the same time I try to show these companies how important it is not only to keep one's premises clean of surveillance devices but also to ensure that you are always monitoring the activities of your competitors, either through standard bugging devices, microphones and the like, or with more sophisticated instruments, such as those which can read the vibrations caused by voices on an office window. Or even tell you what a typewriter is typing."

"That seems a little unfair," said Adam.

Toto smiled his smarmy smile, *I want to spread oil on your chest*, his lips seemed about to say. "Like Argentina, I suppose you'll say. Like Poland or Chile or Russia or America or wherever. Come on, Adam, grow up and join the real world. Nobody really gives a damn about those people. And worrying about them doesn't do them any good, does it?"

"Only those whose windows vibrate to your profit, eh Toto, is that it?" It was time to eat up his escargots; he was about to make a scene.

"My point is," Toto said calmly, "that if you knew Honnie better you'd know where she is. That's why I asked you out to lunch." It was a statement that seemed to pierce Adam through the heart, *if you knew Honnie better, if you knew Honnie better* … I have had eighty-three lovers, she once told him. Now he didn't want his snails, the waiter could shove the lot up his backside for all Adam cared. He looked up at Toto. "Tell me, Toto. Toto Roget, the great. Tell me, you bastard."

"You're drunk."

"Tell me, Toto."

"You're drunk, Adam, be careful."

"Let me finish, Toto. Let me finish, tell me if you've seen Honnie recently, you slimy Peruvian."

"Don't be silly, Adam. I have my own women. You know, it's a funny thing. I've always wondered what a beautiful creature like Honnie could have seen in someone like you." He reached over and plucked at the long hair that fell over Adam's collar. "You're not bad looking, really. You're actually quite attractive. And somewhere up there is a mind."

"Tell me, Toto."

"Oh Christ, not that again."

"Tell me, Toto."

"People are staring, Adam."

"I've got a gun."

Toto's eyes bulged from his head. "You're joking …"

"Yes, Toto, I'm joking and now you can feel relieved and tell me what I came to find out. Did you knead my wife's breasts? Did you sodomize her, you oily ponce, did she scream?" Adam did not know what he was saying, but it must have been good, for Toto was now sitting at a slight angle, as if driven aside by a powerful wind. He waved his American Express card in the air and the light reflecting off the gold caught the waiter's eye; he was beside Toto in a flash, "Monsieur is finished?" he was saying, and plates were being whipped off the tablecloth. People at neighboring tables began to speculate on this man who was accusing the other man of having done something to his wife's breasts and there was also chitchat about sodomy, certainly not the proper subject to go along with your sole *meunière*, and although Adam couldn't give a damn about what they were thinking, Toto had a reputation to protect and wanted to get the hell out of there but fast.

While the waiter went off Toto stared at Adam. "Now listen to me, Füst. I haven't seen your wife in years. But I knew all about her back then, I knew everything; there are things about her you'd never imagine. And I remember how she acted around you, I remember it very well. It was as if she had a second personality, she was a great actress, she was fantastic, Honnie."

"What, what are you saying, Toto, tell me."

Toto shook his head. "No. Oh no. No no. Nothing. Get yourself a detective. Then ask her. Ask her about Versailles. And Fontainebleau. And that night in that warehouse in Nanterre. Ask her why Borrel had to die. And why she ran off so soon afterwards." Toto signed the chit and said *merci*, the meal was delicious, *merci* Louis, see you tomorrow, *merci au revoir*, "and then perhaps you'll know your wife better, Adam. But don't count on me to tell you about it. The old days mean nothing to me. I'm only interested in the day after tomorrow."

Adam remained at the table and watched Toto as he walked past the window of the restaurant toward his shop. Although he had had too much to drink Adam could remember those names as if they had been engraved on the wall of his skull: *Versailles; Fontainebleau; Nanterre; Borrel*. It sounded almost like highlights from the memoirs of the Duc de Saint-Simon, grand

fêtes at Versailles, all fountains and Rameau and naughty esca-
pades with Madame de Maintenon. But it wasn't something out
of Saint-Simon.

No. It was something out of the life of Honnie.

Adam returned home just before the sky broke open.

He leaned against his door and waited, breathless, his head
aching, in the unnatural darkness of his flat. Over all of Paris
was a terrible stillness, colored dark green. A chemical, gaseous
odor, not wholly unpleasant, filled the air. An early heat wave
lent an edge to the air; it lay heavily on one's breath, it tasted of
uncertainty. The world had become a still life.

Adam sensed that something was about to happen, as if
this world were made of glass, two crystal hemispheres bonded
together that might shatter at any moment, at the least sound.
Adam looked around the room. For a moment it seemed that
only shadows of things remained, smoky phantoms that seemed
to gaze back at him who stood framed against his door, unmov-
ing, uneasy, waiting.

The pain in his head had grown more intense, it burned. It
burned and swelled because whenever a storm was impending
his body became a kind of barometer, the fluids within it acted
in sympathy with the atmospheric pressure, and it burned and
swelled with especial intensity now because he knew things could
never be the same, would never be.... He pressed his hands to
his face and listened to his breath as it was caught in the palms
of his hands. His eyes continued to survey the ghosts of books,
chairs, candlesticks. Even the echoes of memories lingered there:
a shimmery Honnie sitting in her armchair, her knees up, a
cigarette between her fingers, thinking. They hovered against
the wall, these shades of memory, neutral afterimages of less
ambiguous days. And as he looked about this museum of the
living and the dead he began to sense a new presence in the flat;

he saw that the old presence, that of Honnie's absence, had been joined by a new one, Honnie's infidelity, and suddenly it seemed that the apartment had become too crowded: someone would have to go. *Draw lots*, a voice seemed to whisper, but it was only the wind returning, and then the sky cracked in half and the city exploded and the rain fell in heavy sheets across the boulevards and the Bois and over Montmartre and into the Seine, the river that yielded bodies, over Balzac's house and his tomb in Père-Lachaise, over the rich and the poor, sheets of water that billowed like silk curtains as the winds rose, and Adam felt the pain and pressure trickle away to nothing. Nothing had changed. Nothing would change.

Nothing has changed: Honnie's words, spoken after she had left him that first time, eighteen months earlier. Now he remembered it: *Nothing has changed*, she had said, the words decaying in the heavy silence and leaving behind only the chalky residue of meaning and significance.

She hung up the phone and looked at him. "You surprised me," she said.

He stood in the doorway, resting one bare foot atop the other. He said, "Who was that?"

"Wrong number." She lit a cigarette, brushed the hair from her eyes, scratched her arm, busied herself with this and that.

"Wrong number. You tell a perfect stranger that nothing has changed? I don't understand."

"It's just," she said, then let it go.

"Just. Just what?"

"Nothing. Just nothing. Put on some music, will you. That Ornette Coleman thing, that piece, that thing I like, that piece, you know."

He put the disc on the turntable and pressed the button and watched her as she shut her eyes and lay her head back against the India print, the maharajahs and elephants, the endless meaningless antique procession of princes going nowhere in particular, and as he watched her he tried to read the signs in her profile, in the slope of her nose, the rise of her lips, the curve of her chin, and he felt as if he were instead looking at an ancient sculpture in the Louvre, something white and enigmatic, carved from marble centuries earlier, its meaning forever lost, its beauty eternal. He looked at the skin on her bare arms, no longer smooth but rough with gooseflesh, and he speculated on the subject of her thoughts, he wondered if what she had done for those two lost days was returning to her, and then she opened her eyes suddenly, her stare turned to meet his, and she smiled and began to laugh and held out her arms and pressed his face against her breast, and from that day forward everything was fine. Nothing had changed. Nothing would change. Those two absent days had become just another locked room in an old mansion, inviolable, half-forgotten, its secrets hidden in the dusty corners, enmeshed in webs spun by spiders. Now he was standing in the corridor just outside the door, his ear was pressed against it and he could hear someone calling him: *Adam, Adam*, it said, the voice harsh and jangling, his hand was on the doorlatch, he felt it give way, he pushed it open and peered into the darkness, and then the voice said, "Have you heard anything, have you any news for us, Monsieur Füst?"

Adam rose out of sleep, gasped for air, looked around him: unending darkness. Sweat dripped from the ends of his hair. The voice said, "Monsieur Füst."

"Yes," said Adam.

"It's Inspector Cuvillier."

"My wife has disappeared."

"You haven't by any chance heard from her, have you?"

"No," said Adam. He reached out for the light switch on his bedside table and grasped nothing. "What time is it?"

"Half past ten. Something like that."

Behind Cuvillier's voice Adam could hear other voices, laughter, a glass breaking. He said, "Have you found Honnie?"

"No. Have you?"

"My wife is not dead," Adam said.

"You seem very sure of that," said the Inspector.

"I'm certain," said Adam. "Find her."

Adam extended his fingers first in one direction then another. All the landmarks of his domestic life seemed to have disappeared. He held the phone away from his ear and listened to the light pattering of rain on the street. Someone in the distance, on the pavement, shouted, "Go to hell, you blind bastard!" and then laughed the laughter of the drunk, a low, growlish, depraved laugh, punctuation mark of the nocturnal city.

"I was dreaming," Adam said. "I was dreaming about a house. I——."

"Yes?"

"I——." and then he found the light switch and opened his eyes wide and saw that he had fallen asleep in the living room chair with the India print over it. He looked at his watch: it was not half past ten; it was nearly two in the morning. Adam pressed the receiver tightly to his ear and listened to Cuvillier's heavy breathing, the sound of breaking glass, a woman's uncontrollable laughter. Then he pulled it away from his head as if it were a dangerous weapon, a loaded revolver, and quietly replaced it. Then he picked up his jacket and left his flat.

He spent the night in the office, too agitated to fall asleep until just before dawn. He had fled his apartment because during the course of his curious telephone conversation with Inspector Cuvillier something seemed monstrously wrong with his surroundings, as if during his luncheon with Toto Roget something intangible had taken up residence there, something malign, discolored, putrid. And then there was Cuvillier himself, at a party perhaps, or some low bar in the northern margins of Paris, telling tales to Adam. Half past ten, he had said, when it must have been obvious to him it was considerably later. There was the sound of breaking glass; a woman laughing hilariously.

Adam had sat at his desk from half past two until he had fallen asleep, his head resting on a cushion, on the carpeted floor. He had sat in the dark, staring out the window onto a deserted rue Coulaincourt. At three the rain came to an end and within fifteen minutes the moon and stars began to appear between the rips in the overcast, scudding, dirty clouds that moved eastward toward the German border.

It was then that Adam saw a man walk to the corner by the streetlight. For a minute or two he stood with his hands in his pockets, gazing at the sky, the gibbous moon. He touched his forehead with his fingertips, withdrew them as if greeting someone, walked away. Adam switched on LouLou's radio and listened to a music program on the BBC World Service and then switched it off when he saw a Citroën glide to a stop before the building across from the office, and then, a moment later, move away and turn the corner. After a few minutes the car reappeared, precisely as before, repeated the same routine and then returned a third time, just past four o'clock. The headlights and motor were switched off. That seemed to bring to an end the absurd ritual of arrival and departure. Adam realized some ten minutes later that the driver still had not left the vehicle. He wondered if a man and woman were inside it and if they were making love on the back seat, but he saw a face appear against the window of the driver's side, its pinkness against the glass, as if the man were in distress, or attempting to sleep. The face withdrew into the shadows; then the door swung open. A man somewhat older than Adam, heavyset, slowly extracted himself from behind the wheel and slammed the door shut, locking it with his key. Then he stood still and looked up at the moon.

Until then the windows in the building opposite had remained dark: now one of them blazed with light as a slim man in a dressing gown switched on a lamp in a living room, walked behind the sofa, and took a cigarette from a box on a table. The flat looked perhaps too lavish for the quarter: the sofa was clearly covered with black leather and there were a number of framed paintings on the wall, whether originals or reproductions Adam could not tell. The man walked to the other end of the sofa and sipped from a glass. Adam felt as if he were watching a play, or a film, and although nothing of great interest had yet happened, an atmosphere of expectation, of the linking of disparate elements at this late hour, had been established.

Adam moved closer to his window, indeed rose from his chair and almost pressed himself against the glass, when Honnie entered the room. He caught his breath and felt his stomach churn and then relaxed when he realized it wasn't Honnie. Or at least it appeared not to be Honnie. Certainly the woman's hair was as long as Honnie's, and the way she flicked it away from her face was familiar, but there was also something quite alien about the woman, so that although at first he had felt about to cry out her name and run across the road to rescue her, now he felt himself once again detached from the scene, a voyeur, an observer. The woman, too, was wearing a dressing gown, and when she sat on the sofa she put her head back and laughed, and before moving away the man stood behind her and slid his hands into her gown, parting it as he did so and exposing her breasts to Adam. For a moment she looked straight ahead, right at Adam, but it would have been impossible for anyone to have seen him, standing in the darkness of his office. He wiped the condensation from the window with his sleeve and felt his heartbeat quicken: something was about to happen.

The man returned to the room and stood behind the woman, a curved ornamental dagger secured beneath the belt of his dressing gown. He, too, looked straight before him, as if the couple were posing for a professional photographer, a formal portrait. Then, apparently playfully, the man reached down for her hand. She refused, slapping his, and laughed. He took hold of the belt of her dressing-gown, slid it away from her body and wrapped each end briskly around his fists. Then he pulled it between her jaws and knotted it behind her head. He removed the dagger from its scabbard and pressed the blade against the woman's throat. She lifted her knees and parted her legs. Then, for a moment, they both looked straight ahead, at the window, at Adam's window, at half past four in the morning.

In the east, to the right of the building, Adam could see a faint shimmer of light just forming. Soon it would be daylight. It was then Adam remembered the man in the Citroën. He glanced down at the deserted car and then again at the lighted room. The scene seemed to have become frozen, as in a tableau: the woman exhibiting herself at the moment of death. Adam looked at the woman's breasts. They were round and heavy, the nipples large and dark, like Honnie's. It was Honnie and yet not-quite Honnie. The man from the car, the man in the raincoat, the heavyset man, suddenly appeared in the living room. For a moment or two he stared at the couple, then walked toward them and stood before the woman. Then he, too, turned to Adam. His hands were in leather gloves. When he turned back to face the woman the light went off, only darkness remained.

Adam stood by the window for perhaps fifteen minutes more, and the next thing he knew he was being awakened by a startled LouLou, who crouched down and rubbed his shoulders until he roused himself, and pressed her lips against his neck and then opened her blouse and made him kiss her breasts.

After LouLou pulled up her underpants and buttoned her blouse she smiled and knelt beside him. She helped him fasten his trousers and ran her fingers through his hair and once more kissed his neck. "I was afraid," he said. "I couldn't stay in my apartment." She pressed her finger against his lips, and then the palm of her hand. When Gabor arrived a few minutes later they were both at their desks.

"It was a dream," she told Adam. "All a dream."

A few minutes later he was driving out to Orly Airport in the green Renault 4, Gabor beside him. Adam could barely keep his eyes open. Little by little certain highlights of the previous night returned to him. He saw a woman sitting on a sofa, her breasts bared, her knees raised, her legs parted. He saw LouLou straddling him, her body silently rising and falling, her smooth muscular thighs, her hands pressed to his chest. He saw a man standing and staring at the moon at an ungodly hour. "It's funny," he said to Gabor. "I spent the night in the office."

Gabor sat back in his seat, his arms folded, his eye shut, listening to the radio. A voice frantically announced the results of some sporting event, *"Deux et deux et deux et deux,"* he seemed to be shouting, he was driving Adam insane. Adam switched it off and found the knob lying in the palm of his hand. He wondered if Steven Spielberg was driven about in a twenty-year-old Renault 4. "I saw something strange," he said. "You know that building across from ours, those apartments?"

Gabor looked at him. "Yes, so?"

Adam described the events that took place between 3:00 a.m. and perhaps ninety minutes later. Gabor listened to him and then lit a Camel. He said, "Do you know how my father died? I was four years old. I was sitting on the floor of my bedroom in our flat in Budapest, playing with my toys. From my room I could see into the living room and also into my parents' room, both rooms were connected to mine. So that when I was in my room, you see, they could watch me and I could watch them, it was an arrangement we all liked, it made us all happy. There was a knock at the door. My mother answered it and then some man pushed her backwards, through my room and into my parents' bedroom. It was a continuous movement backwards, and it took maybe all of half a minute. Then he shut the door. Just my mother and him in her bedroom. Just the two of them, you understand? Another man shook hands with my father. I can still see him. He looked like a doctor, he had a grey moustache and nice eyes, kind eyes. And he seemed so old to me, so much older than my father. He wore a hat, a much better hat than my father could ever afford. He wore a dark overcoat. He said something to my father and shook his hand again and then he reached into his pocket and took something out of it and the next thing I knew my father was in my room, lying on the floor, with all this blood pouring out of his throat onto this game I was playing, a puzzle I think it was, onto my toys. His eyes looked at me as he died, I was the last thing in the world he saw, he blinked and then he was dead. Then the door to my parents' room opened and my mother was alone, but she was half-naked, her dress and underpants had been taken off, and she was bleeding down her legs."

He opened his window and threw his cigarette out into the slipstream of the A6. "When I got older, when I was thirteen or fourteen, I became very curious about this memory of mine. Of course I was curious before, but I could never tell whether it was just a recurring bad dream or something I had seen. I began to think there was something I should know about my father's death, some secret. I kept asking my mother what happened, what had happened to Papa. Of course I barely remembered him. But there was always the blood, the blood on the floor, the blood on the walls, where his hands had been, red fingers and palms: this I never forgot. Mama told me that Papa had died peacefully in his sleep of pneumonia and that everything I remembered was just a dream, a figment of my imagination." He looked at Adam: "And the critics say I revel in cheap sensationalism." He pointed to a highway restaurant and Adam pulled into the parking lot. They took a table and drank coffee and ate croissants. Adam drank three black coffees and felt not so much awake as having risen temporarily from the dead.

Gabor was wearing an expensive leather jacket and pink tie; Adam looked ruffled and sickly in the trousers and shirt he had slept in. Some people in the cafeteria recognized Gabor and stared at him. A fat woman with a Midi accent came over and requested an autograph. She asked him if he was acquainted with Brigitte Bardot or Johnny Hallyday.

Back in the car Adam wondered aloud if he should hire a detective to find Honnie. He told Gabor about Cuvillier. He mentioned Toto Roget and what he had said about Honnie. Gabor laid a hand on Adam's arm, seemed about to say something, then took his hand away and sat back in his seat. After a few minutes he took a cassette from his briefcase and slipped it into the tape deck. It was Julian Bream playing the second Bach lute suite. Adam looked at Gabor, whose eye was shut.

When they arrived at the hotel just outside the airport Gabor and Adam were met by the manager, who led them up to a suite on the top floor. On a long table were a pot of coffee; a plate of sandwiches; a platter laden with croissants, brioches, rolls. Gabor asked for a large vodka. While he and the hotel manager spoke quietly in the corner, Adam laid out his work in the adjoining room, designed to resemble an office: a desk, a few chairs, even a bookcase filled with books. When Adam went to examine a volume of Balzac's *Comédie Humaine*, a strip of false spines came away in his hand, revealing an empty space dominated by a spider in its web. The corpses of moths and beetles, sucked dry of their lives, lay scattered in the dust.

On the desk he placed the two files, the photographs of the actresses to be interviewed; some other material Gabor would need, including some photocopied excerpts from the script; a synopsis of the film; and a list of questions LouLou had typed for him the afternoon before. Adam set a chair off to the side and left his notebook and pen on it. The hotel manager asked him if he and Monsieur Gabor required anything else, a typewriter, word processor, even a secretary to take dictation. Adam asked if the telephone were hooked up and if outside calls could be made without having to go through the switchboard. The manager nodded and smiled and oh-yessed Adam and then went off to ogle the actresses. A woman knocked lightly on the door while she looked at Adam. She identified herself as Dominique something, from the newspaper *Libération*. Adam examined her identification card. Through his work he thought he knew all of the journalists covering cinema. She was blonde, with dark roots. She seemed tense, her palm was damp as he held it in his. He said, "Are you new?"

She didn't seem to understand the question.

"I mean are you new to *Libération*, have you just begun work there?"

"Ah, yes, that's right. My editor sent me out, he said he'd heard that Gabor was auditioning for a new film. Are you his press liaison?"

"In a manner of speaking," Adam said.

The woman looked at his face, then at his clothes. He looked like a tramp. She said, "Oh."

"I'm afraid Monsieur Gabor is giving no interviews at this time. Information concerning the new film will be released when all the details have been finalized. I'm sorry you've wasted a trip."

"You're a prick," the woman said, wiping tears from her eyes and walking away.

When Gabor came into the office the woman was following him. Gabor said, "All set, then?"

Adam nodded. In Hungarian he said, "That woman is a journalist. She called me a prick."

"Ha-ha," Gabor laughed. "Hahaha."

"I told her you weren't granting interviews."

"That's right, Adam."

"She doesn't believe me."

Gabor turned to her: "I'm sorry, no interviews at this time."

"Please," she begged.

Gabor walked away: he was a star, he could afford to do so. The woman stood and stared at Adam. She said, "He's a prick, too."

Adam laughed and took her arm. He accompanied her to the lift, pressed the button, and stepped inside with her. He said, "I'm sorry you wasted a trip to the airport. I told you that before, but Monsieur Gabor has nothing to say at this time."

"It's my first assignment," she said.

"I understand that," said Adam.

"What am I supposed to say to the boss?"

"Tell him that Adam Füst says he should know better. He knows Gabor, he knows how he operates. No interviews until everything is definite. Do you want me to get you a taxi?"

They stepped out into the lobby. A man lay on the carpet, his body trembling violently. Three or four people stood nearby, staring at him. A small amount of blood had gathered at the corners of his mouth, bubbling and then subsiding. The man said, "Thna-thna-thna-thna."

Adam said to the journalist, "This man is an epileptic," but when he turned to look at the woman she was running out through the glass doors, her hands to her face. A loud American woman with bluish hair standing near Adam said, "This guy's having a fit. Stick a pencil in his mouth. Stick a spoon in his mouth. Stick a shoehorn in his mouth."

The other people in the lobby looked at the American woman. Nothing she was saying made any sense. A man in a safari suit pushed his way through and knelt beside the man on the floor. He felt his pulse and then began going through his pockets. The man on the floor stopped trembling. His face turned bright red and the front of his trousers darkened as he lost control of his bladder. If the man were epileptic, Adam once heard it said, probably by Johnny Vodo or Suzy Rinaldi, who managed a bookshop near the place Saint-Michel devoted to the occult and the black arts, he would be in touch with a higher level of existence during the time of his attack: angels and winged devils and the spirits of the ancients. To Adam it seemed a pathetic sight, terribly sad. The man in the safari suit said, "I am a doctor," browsed through the man's wallet, then removed the money and some cards before disappearing. Someone suggested he was going to buy some medicine at the hotel gift shop. Adam saw him walk out of the hotel and into a taxi. Adam picked up the wallet and looked at the man's identity card. The man was named Jacques Borrel.

Ask her why Borrel had to die, Toto Roget had said to him. *Ask her.*

Adam placed the wallet beside the man's body. Another man in a blue suit joined him and felt the man's pulse. "Does anyone know this man?" he asked.

Adam said: "His name is Borrel. Jacques Borrel."

The man in the blue suit stood and adjusted the cuffs of his shirt. He said, "Well, Jacques Borrel is dead."

The man in the blue suit identified himself as a police inspector. He asked Adam a few questions, took down a description of the thief in the safari suit, then told Adam he could return to work. "That man in the safari suit," he said to Adam as they parted. "If I ever catch him I'll cut his throat."

Gabor was sitting by the food table sipping his vodka. He looked at Adam. He said, "There's been a delay in the flight from Vienna. We'll start in half an hour, okay?"

"Do you need me now?"

Gabor shook his head.

I just saw a man die, Adam was about to say, but it seemed an irrelevant statement in the light of Gabor's story. *He blinked and then he was dead,* Gabor had said. *There was blood all over the puzzle.*

Adam went back down to the lobby. A black woman was vigorously scrubbing the spot on the carpet where the man had died. Hanging from a chain around her neck was a red plastic charm. She looked up at Adam, stopped scrubbing for a moment, then returned to work. Beyond the smoked glass of the windows he could see a brilliant day forming, jet planes defining sharp angles as they pressed upward into the sky.

Adam went to the newsstand and leafed through some magazines. In one of them a voluptuous woman lay back on pink satin sheets, her fingers spreading apart the lips of her vagina. The magazine was American in origin, the woman was called Cindi. "I love cowpokes," the caption read, and because Adam did not know what that meant he presumed it was an American obscenity. *You cowpoke, you. I want to cowpoke you.* The woman was making the kind of face no woman on earth ever makes during the act of lovemaking. Or at least no face that Honnie had ever made. Sometimes when the position was right, when he knew Honnie's eyes were shut, Adam would watch her as she climaxed. Her mouth slightly open, a vague smile about to form, she seemed simultaneously composed and excited, as if she were privately considering something amusing: nothing dramatic, for pleasure was undramatic in nature, it required no false histrionics, moans and the like. And by nature Honnie aspired to stillness.

It just occurred to him: a state of perfect repose, like a pond. And although this in itself did not bring her back to him, though through this notion he had not discovered her whereabouts, her motives, he felt somehow more certain: Honnie was alive and she knew that he knew. By uncovering various hidden aspects to her nature he was also drawing closer to her. He smiled to himself, lost in his thoughts, he continued to leaf through the magazine. He read a letter from some man named Luke. Luke said he had a big problem; he was hoping the editors might help him out. Luke, who was from someplace called Encino, said he had the urge to pierce a small hole in his scrotum and by means of a rubber tube fill it with air; he'd heard it was the turn-on of the century. The editor suggested he have it done by a certified doctor and not by his girlfriend, as the man had suggested.

In another magazine there were more photographs of naked lovelies, some of them not so pretty, Adam saw, and in some cases the ladies were fellating their gentleman friends, and at other times the act of cunnilingus was being performed, the men looking as if they were gorging themselves on pomegranates. In the rear of the magazine were hundreds of small advertisements for dildos and enema gear and leather garments and strange rubber gasmasks with tubes that attached lower down on one's body. There were also advertisements for hunting knives and cheap revolvers and semiautomatic rifles and Nazi memorabilia, as if there was some pertinent connection between the sex act and cold-blooded murder. A small notice gave an address in Manila, where for a fee one could write and procure a list of available women. Adam suddenly had the sick feeling that Honnie had been kidnapped. He thought of her chained to a bed, left to be abused at the whim of four or five men. Adam quickly put the magazine back when he realized the woman who managed the concession was staring at him, trying to read his mind, his undoubtedly lubricious thoughts. He smiled and asked what time it was. The woman told him he had a watch of his own. He said Yes, of course, how silly of me, then stepped outside and watched the planes take off. He thought again of the scene he had witnessed the night before. He felt rather ridiculous, now that he thought of it. There was something of the quality of a performance about it, and it was clear it was being staged for some reason, as a rehearsal for a play, or a film, or even as a commissioned scene for someone with odd tastes who lived a few floors beneath the offices of Gabor Productions. He thought of the woman with the gag in her mouth. He thought of himself, how at that moment he had not been moved to pity or anger, but had been aroused by the scene, put almost in a trance. He saw the dagger pressed against the woman's throat; the man who raised his face to the gibbous moon. He wondered if he would have remained in a trance had the woman been murdered before his eyes. He blinked and watched a plane circling overhead, the sun glinting off its wings. Honnie had once told him that men were visually aroused, while women preferred words. "We can make up our own fantasies, you see. But you need us to create the image," and she laughed and lay back on the bed and stuck her tongue out at him, miming a magazine model, holding her breasts in her hands.

He looked at his watch. He still had ten minutes left. He phoned LouLou. "Any messages?"

"Yes," she said, "I want to make love to you again."

"No calls?"

"How are the interviews going?"

"They haven't begun yet."

"Will you spend the night with me?"

He thought of Honnie. "I don't know," he said, though he felt like the loneliest man in the world. "I don't know," he repeated, then rang off and for some reason dialed his own number. He listened to it ring: once, twice, three times: then there was an unexpected clicking sound and a brief pause and the ringing resumed. Then the phone was answered. There was silence. Adam said, "What?"

But there was no one there. Clearly he had rung the wrong number, perhaps even Johnny Vodo's by mistake and had reached the effervescent Eva. He tried his number again and this time the phone rang ten, twelve, thirteen times without being picked up. He rode up the lift to the suite. In the room with the food two women and two men, actresses and their agents, stood sipping coffee and laughing and eating sandwiches. Gabor strolled in and out between the reception room and the office. There was the sense of celebration in the air. Adam smiled and was introduced to the two actresses. Adam recognized both women. The more petite of the two, a German, was quite famous. She had appeared in Gabor's second feature, *Reparations*, and had been romantically linked to the director during filming. Romantically linked was perhaps putting it mildly, for at the time it was Adam's job to correct the rumors of sadomasochistic orgies. The Italian actress, also short but with a strikingly voluptuous figure, had had her breakthrough four years earlier in a costume drama set in *fin-de-siècle* Paris. Adam remembered the way the director of the film had lingered over the nude scenes, the camera highlighting the texture of her breasts in the afternoon sun. It was so aesthetically pleasing that one found oneself not so much sexually aroused as astonished by the objective beauty of the woman's body, the sheer satisfying elegance of her curves, the smoothness of her skin.

Adam smiled at her and released her hand and then looked again at the German woman. After *Reparations* had been released Gabor told Adam that she had gotten her start seven years earlier in underground films, many of them overtly pornographic. Since then she had been seen as a talented and serious actress. That was Gabor's great gift: to take an unknown actor and reveal the brilliance beneath the surface.

Adam recalled having seen the German actress in Zurich. It was during their first week in Oberwil, when Zurich was still exciting to them. They'd looked through the newspaper listings and found a film they hadn't yet seen. It was billed as a psychological drama. Adam and Honnie sat in the front of the cinema and ate ripe pears while the German woman removed her clothes and kissed the chest of the Englishman with whom she had fallen in love. The film contained absolutely no psychology. She lingered over each kiss, as if she were calibrating a compass on the man's hairless chest. When they returned to their stinking cottage in Oberwil that night Honnie put up her hair like the German actress had and kissed Adam on the chest: protractedly, her lips slowly withdrawing themselves from his flesh, their damp imprint a cool O, a silent exclamation, on his skin. And it occurred to Adam, as he stood exchanging small-talk with the actresses and their agents, that Honnie had in some way been preparing him for this moment in the future, when she was no longer with him and his quiet grief was driving him out of his mind.

6

EVERY MOMENT HAS ITS COUNTERPART, EVERY VOICE ITS echo: each a faded version of the first, an afterthought, a ghost, a ringing in the ear, a torment.

The auditions concluded as expected; the German actress had won the part, as everyone knew she would. Gabor was known to use his favorite actors from one film to the next. He told the Italian woman that he would certainly consider her seriously for the next film. The only reason she hadn't been chosen for this one, he convincingly explained, was because he didn't want to waste her in a supporting role. She smiled at the German woman and wished her well.

Gabor and Adam, the actresses and their agents, stood by the table and ate hors d'oeuvres while a waiter in a white suit dispensed drinks from a small bar that had been wheeled in after the interviews. Adam stood slightly apart from the group. He felt sour, strange, unamusing, irrelevant. Gabor was in his element. Astonishing: he was like a chameleon, he adapted to any crowd, he was accepted by all; only to read, some time after this or that party or gathering, the unrevised litany of his reputation, that he had been his usual repellent self, drunk, abusive, flatulent, sexually forthcoming, deranged. He drank vodka and smoked Camels and gestured with his hand, "You see," he kept saying, and "It's like this, you understand?"

The agents stood together drinking whisky and staring edgily over their shoulders, speaking bitterly in undertones. Gabor was saying to the ladies, "So Ruiz the Flea unfastens his trousers and lets them fall to his ankles. Then he mounts Fifi the Elephant...."

A second waiter was about to remove the leftover platters of brioches and croissants and rolls. He looked at Adam. Perhaps he believed Adam was somehow unconnected to Gabor's party: a servant, a bodyguard, or else a trespasser, some maniac who had crashed the little affair in hopes of assaulting one of the beautiful actresses, pressing her up against the bathroom door, interfering with her clothes. Quietly he said to Adam, "Some guy he die downstairs, you hear?"

Adam found it difficult to understand the waiter. His accent, Spanish or Maltese or Greek, was too thick; it stuck to his tongue like undigested cheese. Adam said, "What?"

"Some guy, he dead. Some guy, he lose control, he bite tongue, he shit his pants, he dead."

"What?"

The waiter beckoned to Adam with curled fingers. The man's breath stank of drink, a small pimple by the corner of his mouth appeared green in the brash light of midmorning. He said, "You want to buy some shit, some good shit, yes?"

Adam still could not understand the man; nothing was making sense. Or rather certain words were perfectly comprehensible, but it was as if he were listening to them on some distant radio station beset by enemy jamming and a barrage of atmospherics. He shook his head tentatively, squinted at the waiter. Gabor was saying, "Oh my Fifi, did I hurt you, *chérie?*"

Everyone laughed. Even the agents laughed, though they hadn't heard a word of the joke. Gabor could have been talking about the lingering and painful death of his own father and everyone would have laughed, that was what being a star meant. In three days the rumor would be abroad, however, that Gabor had insulted one and all by telling disgusting jokes at the expense of certain endangered species.

"Listen," the waiter whispered to Adam. "This guy who dead, you know, this guy, he die strange death, he shaking and shitting in his pants. That why some guy he come and rob him, no? That why. Because of the woman. The sexy woman in the room. The woman, she all fucked up, she crazy, she screaming. Everyone been fucking her, this woman, everyone been fucking her everywhere, she do anything you like. You want a piece of this, maybe?"

Adam felt disgusted. Looking at the magazines had depressed him. He understood precisely what the man was saying to him, he walked away and laughed because everyone else was laughing and Gabor was beaming stardom to the four walls of the suite.

Every moment; every voice: what is an echo but the ghost of a sound? The cryptogram of Honnie's life: every moment another echo, a phantom, a plume of ectoplasm, the dying syllable of a significant word. Bits of the puzzle: *Versailles, Fontainebleau, a warehouse in Nanterre; Borrel who had to die.* Honnie, sitting in the chair with the India print, her knees up, the swelling of her black underpants, her long slim fingers holding the cigarette to her lips. An unending procession of maharajahs going nowhere in particular, smiling Eastern princes happy in their insouciance, a still life on a timeless summer afternoon before the rainy season. *Borrel, who had to die.*

This guy, he die strange death. This woman, she crazy.

Adam caught up with the waiter at the end of the corridor. He was wheeling his trolley before an open door. Inside the room a robust grey-haired man, an Englishman, was looking at himself in a mirror. He passed a silver-backed brush over his scalp. An elderly woman, evidently a bright young thing in her day, stood behind him, her hand resting on the back of a chair. She said, "Henry, you disgust me," then caught sight of Adam and walked over and swung the door shut.

Adam said, "What do you mean this man died a strange death? What do you know about it?"

The waiter looked at Adam, he said, "It was set up, see? That guy he rob the dead man. He take evidence. That woman, she too fucked up to say nothing."

Adam said, "Have you seen this woman?"

"Twice I fuck this woman. Two times." He moved his fist through the air: two quick jabs.

"What does she look like?"

The waiter smiled. He tore off a piece of stale half-eaten croissant and chewed slowly on it. His teeth were yellow. The whites of his eyes seemed stained. Everything about him seemed corrupt. He said, "You pay me a little something, then maybe I take you to her, okay?"

"First I want to know what she looks like."

The man cogitated briefly. "Hundred francs up front."

Adam removed the money from his wallet and gave it to the man. Where the photo of Honnie had been was now just an empty slot, nothing. The waiter said, "Follow me."

Adam found it difficult keeping up with the man. He walked briskly to the end of the corridor, turned right, then entered a service lift. Adam squeezed in with him. There was an odor of unwashed bodies, stale cigarette smoke, urine. The man looked at Adam and smiled as he finished his croissant. He sipped cold coffee from a cup stained with lipstick. On the middle finger of his right hand was a large gold-plated ring with an image of a horned man on it, his eyes two small garnets. When the lift reached the basement the waiter stepped out, rounded a corner with his trolley and disappeared. Adam stood in the darkened corridor and looked up at the pipes that ran the length of the ceiling. He listened to the hum of some vast machine, a pump or a boiler. He remembered the man who had died, Jacques Borrel. He recalled the noise he had made, *Thna-thna-thna*. He walked along the corridor until he came to a room. He felt in vain for a light switch and stepped inside. Lining the walls were metal lockers, ranked tightly together. At the end of the room was a large wastepaper basket, overflowing with crumpled papers, orange peels, half-consumed sandwiches. A small, dirty skylight provided scant relief to the gloom. On a long trestle table in the middle of the room were newspapers, some magazines devoted to sport, motorcycling. Metal chairs were pushed unevenly into the table. Adam opened a locker. Within it was nothing but a long cardboard tube. Taped to the door was a colored postcard from Zurich. He shut the door of the locker and realized he was standing in a puddle of some liquid. He saw too that he had been cheated, the waiter had taken his money and disappeared, he now became aware he was being watched, he turned, he said, "Sorry."

A man in a raincoat stood in the doorway. In the darkness Adam could not see his face. The man said nothing. A sense of fear spread out to the four corners of the room. Adam said, "I'm lost, I'm supposed to be in suite 12." It was an absurd thing to say, here he was in the basement of this huge hotel and suite 12 was all the way at the top. Adam shut the locker and turned to the door. The man was no longer there.

He began to move along the corridors, some of which were plunged in utter darkness. For a minute or two he heard a radio playing a nocturne by Fauré, then silence, then what sounded like a news report, or lecture, it was difficult to say, but a man was speaking of Pascal and his view of the universe. Adam felt along the wall until the wall stopped. He placed his foot inside the cavity and felt the floor and then realized he had been standing inside the service lift. He indiscriminately pressed the heel of his hand against the buttons and stopped at various floors until he emerged into the sunlight of the top floor.

When Adam returned to the suite he stood in the bathroom and mopped his brow with a damp towel. He felt unwell, fatigued, overheated. He wondered if he had actually met a sinister waiter with stained eyes and bad teeth or had dreamed it. Perhaps he had imagined it or had supplied the mental picture to some obscure story Gabor had been relating to the actresses and their fidgety agents. Adam returned to the room and looked at the German actress. She was looking at Gabor, smiling, her eyes sparkled. She looked like a million bucks. It was what he had said to Honnie that night in Oberwil, after they had seen that film with the German actress. You look like a million bucks, and Honnie pressed her lips against his chest, around his nipple, and sucked lightly on his flesh. Gabor turned to Adam and joined him by the door, holding his arm in a gentle grip and smiling. The Italian actress suddenly glanced up at Adam, as if she just then recognized him from somewhere. He remembered her last film. He saw her breast in the afternoon sunshine. Gabor said, "I'm not returning to the office. I'm off to a party. A few of us are going. You don't mind driving back by yourself, do you?"

Adam could see Gabor was in for an evening of pleasure. He gathered up his notes from the interviews, collected the various other papers Gabor had needed, signed copies of the contract and so forth. He swung onto the highway and opened the window and tuned in the jazz show on the radio, an Ornette Coleman piece; Adam could not quite place the name of it, it bothered him. He rested his elbow on the window ledge and smiled as he picked up speed. He listened as Ornette and Don Cherry traded fragments, fours, eights, then twelve bars by Ornette alone. He listened carefully to Charlie Haden's bass solo. It was astonishing how someone could make such an unwieldy stringed instrument so resemble the human heart, pulsing in time, exuding such love. He thought that when he got back to the flat he would treat himself to a bottle of wine and listen to Ornette Coleman records. But he couldn't do that. He couldn't do that because Ornette Coleman reminded him of Honnie. It was difficult enough dealing with the uninvited thoughts that came to mind, the terrifying scenes he could not repel, Honnie being tortured, screaming out for him, Honnie in a dark cellar wondering when her husband would arrive to free her. He thought that perhaps there was still much to learn about the mind, that there were unexplored areas of it that seemed to have a life of their own, that tormented you with pictures and thoughts, leaving an aftertaste of guilt and hatred. He looked in his rearview mirror and saw a red Citroën quickly approaching him in his lane, then he shifted into the right lane as the car seemed about to drive into him. When he switched off his directional light and looked up he saw the Citroën far ahead of him, nearly out of the range of his vision.

When he walked into the office he saw Cuvillier sitting behind his desk. LouLou gave him a significant look and said, "This man is Inspector Cuvillier."

Cuvillier smiled and extended his hand. "You don't mind, do you, Monsieur Füst?"

"May I speak to my secretary for a moment, please?"

The Inspector swept the air aside with his hand. "By all means."

"In private."

Cuvillier rose and walked into Gabor's room. Adam said, "That is Monsieur Gabor's office. Would you wait outside in the hallway, please? I'll only be a moment."

When Cuvillier stepped out LouLou was astonished to see Adam follow him. Adam grasped his arm and said, "Have you found my wife, is there any word?"

"No, monsieur," said Cuvillier. He sucked merrily on a breath mint.

Adam excused himself and joined LouLou. She seemed upset, she pressed herself into his arms. She said Cuvillier had been there some forty minutes, he had looked through Adam's desk and asked her questions, some of which she found upsetting, "He asked if I was having my period. Now what does a cop need to know that for?"

"Did you ask him?"

"Bloody well right I did. He said he was just trying to make me uncomfortable. He told me a story about some case he'd been assigned to, the conviction hinged upon some woman having her period. That guy's out of his mind. He asked if you and I were lovers."

Adam looked at her.

"I told him you were married, that I don't go to bed with married men."

Adam caught a whiff of something sour. He said, "Do I smell bad?"

LouLou opened her bag and took out her cigarettes. Adam went to his desk and looked through the drawers. Nothing had been taken. Nothing in his office pertained to his life with Honnie. He was about to walk out to the corridor when he turned to the window. He saw Cuvillier crossing the road and entering the building across the way from the office.

It was Johnny Vodo's idea that Adam should have a notice inserted in the personal columns of whatever newspapers Honnie was inclined to read. The phone was ringing just as Adam returned from work. It was Johnny, with his idea. Adam stretched the telephone cord as far as it would go and sat on the floor, against the wall, pulling various items out of his plastic shopping bag as he listened to Johnny speak: a tin of sardines, two tomatoes, bread, a dessert with the little unadvertised surprise on the bottom, a box of breakfast cereal. On the back of the cereal box was a child who did not look French. In fact there was something completely alien about the scene, the little country kitchen, the bright sunshine, the mother, the son, the bright smiles, the glut of innocence. It all seemed to add up to something American. The boy was looking at the cereal heaped on his spoon and saying, "Mama, look, I can fly!" But the boy was not flying, he was eating cereal out of a large bowl. Beside the bowl was a glass of orange juice and a glass of milk. The mother was putting dishes into a dishwasher, even though the dishes were perfectly clean and gleaming in the artificial sunshine. The woman was garbed for exercise. The boy was claiming he could fly, was indeed at that moment aloft. Either the boy was dishonest or unbalanced, that was the only conclusion one could reach. A liar or a madman. Adam realized what the problem was as Johnny continued talking to him, "Today I was rehearsing man, and this and that and this and that and blah blah blah," the problem was that he had bought the wrong cereal, he had not picked up the cornflakes but had instead and by mistake taken something called Astro-Nuts. Mama, look, I can fly.

"So what do you think, Adam?"

"Okay," said Adam. "Okay. That's fine."

"Eight-thirty all right?"

"What?"

"Eight-thirty. At the club. That okay with you, Adam?"

Adam reviewed the past few minutes in his mind: insert a notice in the newspapers. *Mama, I can fly, look!* Then he remembered that Johnny had suggested he come to watch him play at a club that night. "Okay," said Adam. "That sounds fine, great."

He hung up and continued to look at the box of breakfast cereal. He wondered why there was no father in the picture. Perhaps Papa was still asleep. Perhaps he was in Sing Sing or Alcatraz, serving time for bootlegging, or else on the run, in Indiana like Dillinger. Or perhaps he had simply disappeared and the mother was putting on a brave face for her son who had grown imaginative in his grief.

By the time he was finished with dinner it was half past seven, and although it was spring and by rights the sky should still be light, a heavy overcast lent the appearance of premature night. He switched on some lamps and removed his clothes and went into the bathroom. Above him, in the toilet belonging to the woman who lived on the next floor, he could hear voices, a woman's laughter, some water sloshing about. He imagined the woman and her lover were having a bath together. He had spoken to the woman on only a few occasions, a greeting, a smile, a comment on the weather. She minded her own business. He and Honnie sometimes did that, have a bath together. They would soap each other and press their bodies together, in Switzerland, in Oberwil. In Budapest and Zurich and Mödling and Paris. He stepped into the shower and let the hot water run down his face and immediately he felt better. Indeed, when he returned to the living room he felt much invigorated as he thought of Johnny's suggestion. How excellent! Put a notice in the papers. *Honnie Füst: Please let me know that all is well*, it would read. That's all: *Just please let me know.* No demands, no conditions or recriminations, nothing more than a desire to know that nothing was amiss. He would have his phone number printed beneath, just in case someone had come across the name, had seen her laughing, speeding by in a stranger's red car. He was certain Honnie was still alive and perhaps even in danger. This way she would know Adam was looking for her, waiting for her, remembering her.

It was when he went into the bedroom and opened the wardrobe he and Honnie shared that he realized some of her clothes were missing. Not everything, certainly, but a few items: her duffle coat, her black nightgown, a dress. And from her drawers, too, some pieces had been taken, underpants, a camisole, some tights. He pulled on his trousers and buttoned his shirt and ran his fingers through his hair. He was both elated and distressed, elated because this was a sure sign that Honnie was alive and had stopped in at the flat; and distressed because if this were true, if she had stopped in, she had done nothing to allay his fears.

He stood in the middle of the living room and held his breath. If Honnie had returned sometime during the day or previous night ... if this was true, had she come back, even for five minutes, just to grab a few things, perhaps under duress, meaning gunpoint—something slightly out of the ordinary, something shifted from here to there, something significant to them both would stand out in his eyes, would say things that only the two of them would understand. He could almost see her doing it, leaving a drawer half open, or a book lying on the table: something simple and inconspicuous that would indicate the state of her life and mind. He stood and he looked. He sought out the sign, repeated the ritual in the bedroom and likewise in the kitchen and bathroom. But there was nothing he could see beyond the disappearance of her clothes. Her duffle coat, her black nightgown, a dress. Underwear, tights.

He sniffed the air. He looked out the window. A figure was standing in the doorway of the *tabac* on the corner, across the road. It was impossible to say whether the figure was waiting for a bus or a woman or for him, indeed it was impossible, in the increasing gloom, with a threat of rain, even to see whether the figure was looking at him, at his window, his flat; and yet Adam had no doubt it was Cuvillier: a fact confirmed when he moved from the doorway of the tobacconist to the terrace of the Café Picard.

Johnny Vodo was playing at a club on the rue des Lombards, which for Adam meant only a twelve-minute ride to Châtelet followed by a short walk. Châtelet was a madhouse, there seemed to be thousands of people there, crossing through the warren that constituted the vast exchange of métro lines, people lost, people begging, addicts, tourists screaming in English to each other. "Give me the goddam umbrella, Selma!" some man was shouting, his face red, his hands angrily gripping the thin air of gay Paree. There were Japanese tourists snapping photos of each other's cameras, old people who rarely saw the light of day and lived out of old shopping bags, criminals and exhibitionists, people drinking from bottles of cheap wine, Dutch girls with golden hair and innocent smiles, jugglers, Russian émigrés, musicians, even a man playing an accordion whose eyes met Adam's, who said, "I am blind."

When he reached the club there was a short queue outside the door, maybe fifteen or sixteen people. The headliner that night was Sun Ra and his Arkestra. But Johnny was only sitting in with the opening group, a quartet led by an old friend from Lagos, an alto sax player whose fame beyond the frontiers of his native land was celebrated only by his fellow countrymen in exile. Johnny had played Adam the man's five records, and although his style seemed somewhat derivative, he had successfully incorporated elements of Nigerian folk music into the bop idiom.

Sun Ra was something else altogether, a living legend, a musician Adam had always wanted to hear in the flesh. He went to the head of the queue and knocked on the thick glass door. The man who had been heading the queue tapped Adam on the shoulder and told him in no uncertain terms to go to the rear of the line. Adam claimed friendship with one of the musicians, Johnny Vodo. The man left him alone and spoke quietly to the woman beside him, he said that Adam was a prick and a fucking idiot and a snob, and the woman said that it was an insult having to endure this kind of naked assault on their status as first in the queue, and Adam endured this with a measure of dignity as the man inside the door opened it and stared at him. Adam explained that he was a guest of Johnny Vodo. The man pushed the door shut and just missed severing Adam's fingers. Adam knocked on the door again. He explained to the bouncer that he was a friend of Johnny Vodo and that Johnny Vodo had invited him to listen to the group he was playing with. The man switched on a small flashlight and aimed the beam into Adam's eyes. Adam blinked and heard the man behind him in the queue say that in a few minutes the police would come and take him off to the cells for the night, and he was just about to add a few more insults to injury when the bouncer double-checked his list at the door and admitted Adam.

It was good to hear live music again. It was good to see Johnny tapping away at his cymbals and drums and smiling to Adam with that contented, feline look assumed by jazz musicians on a good night. They led off with a version of Coltrane's "Giant Steps," and this suited Adam fine; he like Coltrane, he liked the tune, he thought they played it well, with all those difficult chord changes and intervals. He looked around for Eva, then remembered that Johnny never brought her to his gigs. Perhaps he never brought her to his gigs because she was so controversially silent. Some visiting tenor sax player, a big man like Sonny Rollins, for instance, might take a strong dislike to her rudeness and pick her up and throw her against the wall. He looked at his glass and tried to remember how many daiquiris he had drunk. He wondered why he was drinking daiquiris. He had never before drunk a daiquiri, and although he had originally requested vodka he was now drinking one daiquiri after another, grinning to himself and plucking at the waiters' coats, *Encore un daiquiri*, he was saying, Just one more, I beg of you.

Now Johnny's group was playing Horace Silver's "Song for My Father." Adam tapped his toe as he thought of Gabor's papa, the blood streaming out of his jugular vein, red palm prints all over the walls. He thought too of what had passed through his mind vis-à-vis Eva Vodo. He pictured Sonny Rollins casting aside his sax and flinging Eva against the wall, *Say hello*, he would bellow, *Say something*. He smiled stupidly to himself and wondered what she was doing. Was she terrorizing Marimba or was she chattering away to herself, or even to the television screen, hurling insults at the characters in *Dallas* or the authors who had come to push their books on *Apostrophes*. Perhaps she went into a kind of trance and allowed others to speak through her, to use her body and vocal organs as a channel for their thoughts and opinions. He saw her writhing on a bed and heard Honnie's voice swirling about in the back of her throat, "Adam, they are killing me," he imagined her saying, "Adam, I am dying."

He drank half of his next drink and his thoughts turned to another subject, the subject of LouLou. He revisited that scene which seemed to have taken place so long ago, replaying it again and again, LouLou unbuttoning her blouse and pressing her freckled breasts against his face, "Kiss them," she was saying, undoing his trousers. Now he was thinking about the waiter at the hotel, who claimed the dead epileptic man had been connected to some woman who was allowing herself to be abused by all and sundry. It depressed him, this thought, it depressed him because he had been raised to think the world a bright

place, and all humanity essentially good, and his thoughts took
a profound turn as he came to the conclusion that his entire life
had been a gradual stripping away of illusions, that the world
was a dark and dismal place and humanity a hateful and brutal
species. Now he was no longer happy, he was drunk and miserable, he did not even notice that Johnny was taking a solo,
ditditditcrashsmashditditboom said his drum kit, he was looking
straight at Adam, he was playing drums for Adam, he was making a special moment for Adam, and Adam was staring into the
bottom of his empty glass and thinking about Honnie and the
nature of the human race, his moment of glee had passed.

Now even the music sounded bad. The famous Nigerian
alto player was sweating out one cliché after another, Adam
wished to God Sun Ra would come out and throttle the sax
player and get on with his own music. Even Johnny seemed to
be marking time, *ching-ching, tap-tap*, Adam was in despair.

Now he looked around the room. It was a cellar really, decorated the way jazz clubs always used to be done up, their walls
covered with record jackets, and all Adam could see was a grinning Gerry Mulligan, his hair *en brosse*, peeking out at him over
Johnny's left shoulder, and if his mood didn't pass in a minute
or two he knew he would be compelled to storm the bandstand
and tear the image from the wall. He forced himself to look at
the other record jackets, many of which duplicated those in his
and Honnie's collection. Odd how nostalgia was so much a part
of the musical experience... And as he thought about this, as
he looked over the record jackets and traced the high points of
his and Honnie's relationship, he began to recover his wits, there
was a strange warm feeling forming in his chest. He looked
at the cover of a Mingus record, and although it wasn't one of
Mingus's best efforts it was one of Adam's favorites, for he had
bought it the day he had met her on the café terrace, indeed
an hour earlier, when he was simply a single man with the odd

girlfriend or two, who had expected to spend the night alone in the flat listening to the record and going to bed. Odd how the world seemed to shift a degree or two when his eyes met hers. He recalled sitting at the café table with Johnny Vodo, the Mingus record in its red plastic bag under his arm as he turned his head and looked at the beautiful woman reading the terrible Hungarian newspaper. And thus this memory was still alive inside him, it burned with a special intensity, it told him that Honnie was alive in absentia, that love still existed.

And look there: Miles's *Kind of Blue;* that chapel near Oberwil, the frescoes, Honnie's depression, the doctor who stank of tobacco, who wanted to touch Honnie's body; an entire chapter of their life blossoming out of a handful of tunes. He remembered holding Honnie in the bath and moving the cloth gently over her legs, her breasts, her arms. He remembered her sitting in a chair, her knees up, holding a cigarette to her lips; very still.

The sound of hands meeting hands woke him from his reverie. He joined hands and joined them again and looked at Johnny and raised his hands slightly and continued clapping and smiling. Johnny looked at him and indicated that Adam should join the group in the dressing room. Adam left some money on the table for the waiter and made his way around the bandstand to the back stairs. Trying to keep up with them he passed a dressing room where Sun Ra was sitting with some of his musicians. Sun Ra said, "I do declare," and then laughed.

Adam told Johnny Vodo and the other musicians how much he'd enjoyed listening to them, citing as memorable the sax player's solo in the opening Coltrane number, and the pianist's big moment in their version of "St. Thomas," even though the pianist hadn't an original bone in his body; one moment he was imitating McCoy Tyner, the next he was Hilton Ruiz imitating McCoy Tyner. The bass player, a lanky taciturn man from

Port Harcourt, filled a pipe with hashish and puffed slowly on it, drawing the thick fragrant smoke into his lungs and staring intensely at his calloused fingers. Johnny opened a small metal box and formed lines of cocaine on the top of the dressing table. Adam said no, he didn't want any coke, but the hash smelled good. The bass player was not in a generous mood, however. Johnny gave Adam a joint, and then a waiter came and asked if anyone wanted a drink on the house. Adam requested a daiquiri and even the bass player laughed at him for his folly.

Johnny snorted some cocaine and slapped Adam on the knee. "Any news?"

Adam shook his head. He didn't feel like discussing the scene he'd witnessed in the flat across from his office, or recounting what had taken place at the hotel earlier that day. Johnny said, "Look, I gave that photo to some friends of mine, some people I know." He frowned. "Nothing, man, not a word; nothing yet anyway."

Adam asked for the photograph. Johnny said, "It's making the rounds, man, the more people who see it the better your chances are of getting your woman back."

Adam liked Johnny because Johnny was honest and sympathetic and a good friend, even though his wife was not a good friend or sympathetic. Now Adam was feeling considerably jollier; he could not keep from smiling as he reviewed in his mind the absurd notion that had come to him that night, Sonny Rollins beating out Eva Vodo's brains against the wall of the dressing room, "He-he-he," he giggled, holding his hand over his mouth. Johnny had the bright idea that they get something to eat and show the other musicians something of Paris. The sax player said he wanted a woman, in particular a white woman, and the pianist concurred, a woman would be just the thing, a Chinese woman, however; he had a weakness for orientals. Adam suggested they therefore stop for Chinese food and a waitress or two, it would save them time. Everyone laughed as they stood outside the club in the mist and drizzle of a spring night.

The McDonald's on the boulevard Saint-Michel was packed to the doorway with tourists and Parisians alike, and it was Johnny who spotted Keith Richards and some blonde standing in the corner with cigarettes hanging sleazily from their lips, surrounded by fat bodyguards and paparazzi. Adam and the band stood at a counter eating their hamburgers. Adam looked out the window onto the wet pavement, his eyes meeting those of a sullen young woman wearing a military coat and fingerless woolen gloves. Her dyed pink hair was moist from the rain. Her mascara had been smeared, she looked tired, unwell, abused. He thought that she had perhaps the bitterest expression he had ever seen, it was a look that destroyed desire. He could barely taste the food in his mouth, it had the texture of papier-mâché. Now and then he would imagine Sonny Rollins swinging Eva Vodo against the wall, though he found the humor of it growing more obscure each time it came to mind. What began as whimsy had become a bloody and pathetic scene of animal brutality, one unworthy of the saxophonist, undeserving by Johnny's wife. He thought of Honnie, and his heart went out to Eva as she lay at the feet of the great improviser Sonny.

Now they were on the métro. Now he could think of nothing else but Honnie. He felt like a scrap of paper carried along by the wind, a fragment of detritus, a plaything for the elements, and had Johnny and the boys suggested he leap onto the tracks he probably would have done it gladly, anything for a laugh, anything to make time move forward, to help him grow more intimate with the truth about Honnie.

They alighted at the place Pigalle, the last place on earth Adam would wish to be on such a night, but the band wanted women and *voilà*, so be it, women they would have. There were women, all right, lots and lots of them, all standing in doorways and clicking their tongues and flashing their thighs and saying *Hallo, big boy.* The alto player went into a shop called Sex à Gogo and of course everyone followed him, the bassist, the piano player, Johnny, and even Adam. The shop resembled the McDonald's they had just left, save that here there were no hamburgers and pickles. The band stood around a long table and leafed through glossy magazines. Johnny read one entitled *Back Door.* Interleaving a novella of some sort were full-color photographs of couples in sexual nirvana. Adam caught a glimpse of the text: *Would you like to buy some insurance? Bill asked as Sheila parted her thighs.*

Adam plucked at Johnny's sleeve and said that he was tired, he wanted to go home. He had the funny feeling that at any moment the cops might kick down the door and arrest the lot of them for the unchecked luxuriance of their indecent thoughts and fantasies. Along a wall of the shop were cupboards of some sort, closets or booths, it was difficult to tell. Coming from them was unintelligible conversation, a low rumble of words occasionally broken by dramatic moans and sighs. There was a small commotion as the boys in the band began to occupy the booths, and suddenly Adam found himself inside the confines of the little room with only a dim light to allow him any sense of its dimensions. He moved his hands along the walls, one of which seemed to be a pane of thick glass. He tapped on it with his fingernails. A woman's tired voice said, "Oh God, would you sit down please?" He cupped his hands around his eyes and tried to peer through the glass and it was then he discerned the outline of a woman. He sat back on the small wooden chair and stared at his ghostly reflection in the window. Now the light was switched off and a brighter light in the other room revealed a woman sitting in a plush armchair. She had long dark hair and was wearing a leather bustier and high-heeled shoes. She sat perfectly still, her knees together, allowing Adam to feast his eyes. Covering her hands and wrists were black leather gauntlets. From the adjoining booth he could hear Johnny's voice, "Show it to me baby," he was saying. The woman indicated a small slot in the wall. She said that the more he paid the better the show would be. She told him that credit cards were acceptable and pointed at a little machine and a stack of receipts on the table beside her. Now Johnny was saying, "Come on baby," and Adam could not keep himself from smiling at the thought of silent Eva getting wind of this, oho!

He should have walked: out of the booth, the shop, the district. But he felt compelled to remain, as if he were meant to be there. His head throbbed as the happier effects of the alcohol evaporated. He reached into his wallet and passed a fifty-franc note to the woman. She looked at it with disdain and put it in a little steel cashbox that sat beside the credit card machine. She stood and unhooked something and the bustier came away from her body. Adam blushed as she slowly rotated in front of him. He wondered what she expected him to do. Or rather he knew what she expected him to do. The words of the song suddenly came to him: *I know a dark secluded place, a place where no one knows your face.* She peeled off her gloves and slipped off her shoes and sat back on the chair, her eyes staring at his. She was an attractive woman with a slim figure. On her right thigh was a small tattoo of a death's-head set against a red rose. Her eyes watched as he looked at her breasts and then moved farther down. She raised her feet to the edge of the chair and parted her legs. And for a moment, a significantly long moment, he was reminded of a woman in an apartment; inevitably, of Honnie. He felt certain the woman was trying to tell him something, pass on a message. He said, "My wife has disappeared, her name is Honnie, she resembles you, have you seen her?" And it was difficult to make himself heard for Johnny Vodo was nearly screaming "More more more," and there was the sound of furniture being rocked back and forth and the walls were shaking and the woman with the parted legs suavely continued stroking herself with her fingers and said, "What? What do you want me to do?" and Adam asked her again if she knew Honnie Füst and if the name Borrel had any significance for her and then suddenly she looked at him in horror and switched off the lights and all was still.

7

S IT DOWN. SIT AND REFLECT: THINK.
He quietly shut the door and secured the lock. Sit. Reflect.
Think.

Five minutes past one.

He waited by the door and let his eyes grow accustomed to
the darkness. Slowly the topography of the room murkily began
to take shape: record shelves, bookshelves, the stereo system;
Honnie's Portuguese vase, her ceramics, a small bronze statuette of Aphrodite she had bought somewhere. He walked to the
window and looked at the figure in the doorway of the *tabac*.
And when the Inspector struck a match and lit his cigarette the
sudden orange flare endowed Cuvillier with a curious cinematic
unreality. Tough guy: it was like a scene from a film, a melo-
drama set in some seedy border town, monochrome crime committed by big shots, rough talk over bourbons and beers in a bar
with stuttering neon sign. A faded blonde looks sourly into her
cocktail; the hair bristles on the back of the fall guy's neck; the
man in the doorway shifts his feet.

Adam pulled the curtains shut and switched on the lamp
beside the chair with the India print. He rubbed his eyes and
looked at his fingers, then at the base of the lamp, a vase Honnie
had adapted to hold a light fixture. Four dusty tracks ran deeply

across it, gouges in the accumulated grime of lost time. Within the shade a small beige spider with spindly legs huddled in its web, raising a tentative foot as Adam disturbed it, settling into a light sleep as he went off to the kitchen.

Nothing more had been taken; nothing moved.

Adam put on the kettle and made himself a cup of tea. He sat in silence for a few minutes, holding the cup between his palms, warming his fingers, listening to the rain patter intermittently against the windows. A car passed down the street, its tires screeching as it just survived the corner. Then there were no sounds. He swallowed two aspirins and washed them down with scalding tea; tears came to his eyes.

He sat and reflected and thought.

Although the naked woman in the booth had not said anything to him, the look in her eyes at the last minute was worth a treatise or two: she had reacted to the name Honnie, to Borrel. Piece by piece the puzzle was beginning to take shape. Was a puzzle still a puzzle once you'd completed it? Did it not then lose its identity as a puzzle and, as a butterfly cannot in good conscience be called a caterpillar, therefore not retain such a title? Once you had completed a puzzle it was a picture, not a puzzle. Half a puzzle completed was thus something of a mythological object: half puzzle, half picture, a kind of Sphinx of the game world. You only saw the whole picture once the puzzle was completed. And once the puzzle was finished it had then outlived its reason for existence, there was only one fate left for it, to revert to the state of puzzledom, to be broken down, destroyed. He thought of how Honnie had parceled out small facts of her life, names of friends, trips she and her parents had taken, the fresco at Alsógalla. And sometimes there were lies: I have had eighty-three lovers. Perhaps she felt that by keeping about her a cloak of mystery she would remain alluring, desired, loved. Yet now that something had happened, now that she was in what he was certain was danger, he had no way of reaching her. Describe your wife, sir? No problem, she looks like this and that, here's a photo. Occupation? Fine, she does this, she does that. Anything in her past, sir, that might indicate she was at some risk?

Silence.

The answer to Honnie was silence.

Or had she been all along protecting someone, some-thing...? *Versailles, Fontainebleau, a warehouse in Nanterre. Borrel, who had to die.* And if she had been protecting someone, what was Adam's role in all of this? Was he, an innocent man, a form of protection for her?

He set down his cup and took off his clothes and stepped into the shower and thought. Honnie had been taken by some people for some illicit purpose. And more, perhaps. As retribu-tion for some act she had committed in the past? Perhaps she was staying in that hotel near the airport. Not staying: being held. By whom? Jacques Borrel, who was now dead? And who was the man in the safari suit who had robbed Borrel? And what role had the waiter with the stained eyes and yellow teeth? And then there was the nude woman in the booth. Was she connected to the people in the apartment across the road from Gabor's office?

Toto Roget: *Ask her why Borrel had to die, why she ran off so soon afterwards....* Yet Borrel died after Toto had mentioned it to him. *Thna-thna-thna*, he had said, and then died. Had there been another Borrel? Was Toto capable of seeing into the future?

He stepped out of the shower and rubbed himself vigor-ously with the towel. Could it be that Honnie led a life apart from theirs, a second life governed by a separate personality? He thought of the nonchalance of her last flight eighteen months earlier. He thought of what Toto Roget had told him. He thought of Oberwil, the frescoes in the disused chapel; Honnie's stillness, as if she had retreated into the sanctuary of more profound thought. And as he seemed to catch a fugitive glimpse of the entire picture he heard the noise. He held the towel against his face and listened.

Streams of water ran down his torso, his thighs. Something thumping, banging, stamping in the other room. For a moment he recalled a man in dark goggles in a black entranceway displaying a picture, a dark labial mystery against a square of fire, the sound of hammering incessant in his ears: someone was in his apartment. He thought of the waiter with the yellow teeth, he saw a flashing blade intersecting a stained smile, he felt the heat of blood. Adam quickly patted himself dry and began to dress, one silent limb at a time, *I am blind*, a beggar at Châtelet had said to him. *Ask her why Borrel had to die. Why she ran off so soon afterwards. Why she ran off so soon. Why she ran. Why. I do declare*, said Sun Ra, *I do declare, I do I do I do declare.*

Cuvillier.

Adam could hear him walking about the living room, sliding drawers open and shut, poking into things that possessed no relevance for him, things of a sentimental nature, things that lived close to the skin, the small intimate satellites of the lives of Honnie and Adam Füst.

He silently pulled open the door and stared at the man's shoulders, hunched, bureaucratic, sinister. He seemed to be examining something small, something that demanded close scrutiny. The lock on the front door had been bent away from the jamb. Utterly unsurprised, Cuvillier turned to him, an ashtray in his hand; he said, "So you went to that marvelous sex shop. I often go there myself. Did you try the booths? Fantastic, no? There's a girl there named Gabrielle...."

His gaze drifted toward the bedroom. He was wearing an old trench-coat and brown suit. His tie had been loosened, his collar button undone. He moved unsteadily toward the bedroom

and disappeared. Adam heard him opening drawers. He imagined the cop going through Honnie's underpants, her tiny black
lacy ones, he saw the man's greasy fingers rubbing the material,
feeling it for evidence of the subtlest degree, hair, dried semen,
blood. He appeared in the doorway, Honnie's camisole dangling
from his hand as if it were some obscene thing pulled from a
murderer's pocket. He held it to his face and slowly inhaled its
scent. He said, "I'm like a bloodhound, monsieur, I like to know
the scent before I go hunting."

He looked at the spines of the books ranked neatly along the
shelves, the record sleeves, the prints on the walls. He lifted his
arms slightly and stared up at the ceiling, at the flowered globe
of the light fixture that Adam and Honnie never used. With
his eyes he inspected Adam's face and demeanor. He said, "Sit
down, Monsieur Füst, make yourself at home." He said, "I suppose you haven't heard anything about your wife. Or even from
her. Otherwise you would have contacted me, wouldn't you?"

"Nothing," said Adam. "Not since the phone call."

"So we can continue to say your wife remains at large. Did
you hear the news, though? We found the body of another
woman. Just yesterday. Up near the railway lines in Saint-
Denis. Impossible to establish a positive identification, her face
had been disfigured beyond recognition. From the marks on
her arms we've concluded she was a drug addict. She used a
needle pretty regularly. Your wife ever dabble in dope, eh monsieur?"

Adam pressed his hands to his head and realized his hair
was dripping wet. He didn't know what to say.

Cuvillier went on: "All we know is what we can deduce
from a small tattoo on the victim's hand. Her name was there,
you see, her name was Agnes." When he saw Adam's expression
he laughed, he said it was all a joke, he puffed merrily on his
cigarette and tipped forward, trapping Adam within his chair

by two powerful arms. He said, "Where is your wife, Monsieur Füst, let's get this sordid business over with, all right?"

The heady sourness of drink had spiced the Inspector's breath. His right eye was bloodshot, as if he had recently been struck. Adam said, "Someone's been in my flat. Someone took some of Honnie's things."

Cuvillier's face remained close to Adam's. He looked at the pores on the Inspector's cheeks. They seemed large, discolored from the grit of the street, the filth of the police cells. The man's face was unnaturally white. His hair was patchy and brittle, flakes of dandruff were visible on his clothing. It was odd. It was odd because in a funny way Cuvillier really did resemble the pianist Alfred Brendel, and although Alfred Brendel did not look as if he would hurt a flea, Cuvillier had about him an air of violence, as if it were something you could hide in your pocket and bring out at any unexpected moment, a fistful of brutality to toss in your adversary's eyes.

"Someone's been in your flat," Cuvillier mocked. "Someone's taken some of Honnie's things. Someone's taken Honnie, my fine lad, someone's taken your wife, and all you can talk about are things? You know, I'm beginning to think you've been messing me about, my sweet boy, I'm standing here thinking you're laughing at me inside that calm exterior of yours. You probably think I'm drunk, don't you. Say yes."

Adam said Yes.

"You probably think Inspector Cuvillier is insane, breaking in here at this miserable hour and stinking of drink. Say yes."

Adam said Yes.

"You probably think the police aren't supposed to do things like this, don't you. Say yes."

"Yes, I think," said Adam, his mouth going dry.

Cuvillier stepped away from Adam, cleared his throat, wiped his lips with a handkerchief. He lit another cigarette and coughed into his fist; he said, "I'm off duty." He dragged a chair away from the table and sat in it, his knee pressed against Adam's knee, and to Adam it was like an electrical shock. Very quietly the Inspector said, "I think you know where your Honnie is. I think you know and I think one day you will tell me where she is. I think you're a clever man, Monsieur Füst, I think many things about you, but most of all I think you're playing a smart little game with Inspector Cuvillier. Say yes again."

Suddenly Adam could envisage it. Dawn: four men in rumpled suits gaze down at the body of a mutilated young Hungarian male, approximate age twenty-eight. A wisecracking police photographer takes a few snaps for the file. Suddenly the inspector assigned to the case enters, everyone greets Cuvillier: *Bonjour, boss, bonjour.* In the doorway, Madame Moreau in her apron. *Such a nice young man,* she says, *but I'd always known Monsieur Füst was mixing with dangerous people.*

Cuvillier said, "So someone's taken your wife's things."

"Just some of them," amended Adam. "Just."

"Do you know what I think? I think your wife is dead. I think your wife is dead and I think someone wants you to believe she's still alive. I think someone wants you to believe she's still alive so you can try to convince me that she's still alive. And if I'm convinced she's still alive I'll stop looking for her."

Adam watched Cuvillier as he rose from his chair and approached the far wall. He stood beneath the Valloton print of the nude woman on the bed playing with a cat and tapped the wall lightly with his knuckle and smiled at Adam. "But there's also a little voice inside me telling me a different story. Do you know the case of John Christie? An English murderer. He hid the bodies of his female victims behind the walls of his house."

He tapped the wall once again. Adam was afraid his neighbor might get the wrong idea. Cuvillier said: "He gassed them first, then strangled them, then placed their bodies in the cavity behind the wall. Clever chap, as the English say. Then they hanged an innocent man in his place. Then," he added, his smile radiating beams of justice, "they hanged Christie."

To himself Adam thought: Alsógalla.

Cuvillier went to the window and parted the curtains slightly with his fingertips, as if handling human flesh. He breathed deeply the clean air of the dark morning.

"I've seen Honnie," Adam said. "Someone very like her, I mean."

The Inspector showed Adam his face. "But it wasn't your wife, of course."

"No, no, I'm sure of it. I was in my office one night. The night you rang me. I went to my office, I sat in the dark."

Cuvillier said nothing. He moistened his lips with his tongue and listened. Adam said, "I sat by the window." He described the rest of the scene, the man in the Citroën, the little play that had been performed, the curved ornamental dagger, the moon. Cuvillier shut the window and stood by the table. Somewhere in labyrinthine Montmartre an alarm began to ring, probably another robbery. Adam said, "I saw you going into the building, that day you were waiting for me. The day you spoke to my secretary." Then he realized he shouldn't have said it. He thought of decomposing bodies pressed up against the thin walls of Paris.

Cuvillier stared at him. He unclenched his left hand and looked at his palm. He said, "I went there on a tip. I was told I would find a dead man in one of the apartments. What you claim to have seen has nothing to do with the case. Nothing. There was no dead man. It was a hoax. The apartment was empty, apparently no one had lived there for three or four weeks. That's why I came to see you tonight, you understand, Monsieur Füst." He approached Adam and hovered over him. He wiped his fingertips with his handkerchief; he said, "There wasn't a stick of furniture to be seen, nothing. As a matter of fact, the previous tenant, a Monsieur Borrel, had left without even giving a day's notice."

Adam looked up at him, his hands trembled, he could not find the words to express his fear. Cuvillier said, "Perhaps it's nothing more than coincidence, but Monsieur Borrel's brother disappeared just the same way almost two years ago." He shrugged, he said, "It's just another mystery," then took something from his pocket and tapped it nervously against the edge of his fingernails. "All we found in the apartment was this photograph. It was lying on the floor, in the dust. Look at it, see if it means anything to you. None of us at headquarters can make any sense of it."

Honnie, standing before the cottage at Oberwil: the photo he had lent Johnny Vodo. Honnie, a cigarette in her hand, in her black turtleneck jersey with the sleeves pushed up. Honnie, with her long slim fingers and thick long hair; Honnie, alive.

Honnie, whose face had been burnt out of the photograph.

Honnie swimming.

Now it all came back to him.

There was a lake, he recalled, a small lake located halfway between Oberwil and Jonen, where the disused chapel stood. She had spotted it as they were driving back to the cottage, she had touched his arm and pointed. Adam slowed down, then pulled the Fiat onto the shoulder. He switched off the ignition. They sat in silence, looking at the still water, the landscape and sky inverted in it: small puffy clouds against a deep blue background; trees. Honnie said, "I wish I'd," and lapsed into silence.

Adam had never learned to swim. Deep water terrified him, in some curious way reminding him of childhood. Honnie loved to swim. He knew what she had been about to say: *I wish I'd brought my bathing suit.* She opened the door and stepped out. Adam watched her through the curved windshield. A week earlier a pebble had been thrown up by a truck's wheel and had left a tiny notch in the glass. Now a crack had begun to develop, each day snaking farther across his line of sight until, by the time they had reached Paris two months later, the entire windshield had become a work of delicate tracery that collapsed into a thousand pieces as they entered the city.

He joined her by the edge of the lake. She picked up a pebble and tossed it in and watched the ripples radiate away from the impact. A wooden sign indicated that it was forbidden to swim there, prosecutions were inevitable. He watched Honnie's eyes trace the limits of the lake, the woods around it. A cluster of chalets had been built across the water from them. It was impossible to tell whether they were holiday cottages or year-round houses. It was difficult to say whether at that moment they were inhabited. He saw Honnie gazing at them, he saw the skin on her bare arms prickle and toughen in the cool breeze, the hairs on them sticking straight out, her eyes squinting in the bright sunshine. She had lost her sunglasses and had yet to replace them. She was worried that they might not be able to afford new ones, she rather liked the black Vuarnets she had seen in the department store in Zurich. She thought aloud about them, she suggested that she steal them somehow.

In the distance a fish momentarily broke the calm of the lake, plucking an insect from the mirrored surface. In the distance was the sound of a door slamming shut in one of the chalets. Overhead a plane chalked two puffy lines across the sky. Honnie pushed her sleeves up over her elbows. She was wearing her jeans and black turtleneck jersey. She fingered the button on her trousers, rested her hands on her hips, thrust them into the tight pockets. There was no sound now but the songs of the birds. They walked back to the car, Adam and Honnie, touching only once as she lost her footing and extended her fingers toward his arm.

She said little about the frescoes. She gave Adam the impression that in themselves they were unimportant. Yet he sensed that something else had happened inside the disused chapel. Perhaps she had merely had a fright. Or something had reminded her of something from her past, something she had until then forgotten. Perhaps what she had discovered there was somehow mirrored within herself. During the time of her depression Adam considered all of these possibilities. He felt it imprudent to question her about them. If she wished to speak of it, she would. This time he would respect her silence. But he would not allow himself to stop thinking about it.

A week after her recovery Adam woke up one morning to find himself alone in the cottage. He thought she might have driven to the shops to pick up some bread and milk. Yet the car was parked where they had left it the night before, after they had returned from seeing a film in Zurich, the keys still on the table. He showered and dried his hair and pulled on his jeans and sweater. Still Honnie had not returned. He stepped outside the cottage and breathed the air. He looked around, he listened, he thought she might have gone for a walk. Twenty minutes later he was in the Fiat, slowly patrolling the roads around Oberwil. He pulled the car off the road and put on the brake. He wondered.

At first he had driven past the chapel near Jonen, then thought twice and reversed direction. He got out and knocked on the door of the building, pressed his ear against it: listened. He could feel the winter within pushing against him, trying to force him away. He could hear something scratching, the sound of claws grazing the stone floor. He returned to the car and rolled up the window and for a few minutes remained parked outside the chapel, tracing the crack in the windshield with his finger as if planning a journey with the aid of a road map.

Honnie was still not back at the cottage. He wondered if she had left a note for him somewhere. He wondered if she had left a clue for him, something that might indicate where she had gone; perhaps even why. He waited a half hour longer, then set out once again in the Fiat.

When he arrived at the lake he found Honnie's clothes neatly stacked beneath a pine tree: her jeans, her turtleneck, black panties, sandals. He looked at the surface of the lake and only saw her when a cloud passed over the sun: Honnie, naked, floating on her back, her arms extended; absolutely still in the silence of the morning.

He again read the sign that forbade swimming. He looked at the chalets and their shuttered windows. He heard a door slamming in the distance, in one of the houses.

He followed the curve of the lake until he could be seen by Honnie. Her eyes were open. She blinked. He said, "What are you doing here, how did you get here?"

After a moment she said, "I hitchhiked."

"You should have woken me."

He looked at her body as it gently bobbed on the surface of the water: her breasts, her thighs, her knees, the palms of her hands as the sunlight returned to them. He thought: *the mystery of her.*

He remembered the chapel. He wondered what had died there. The little faith that remained within her? Her fear, her caution, her hopes, her dreams? Her heart? She would never speak of it. The mystery would remain, a third member of their marriage, a shadowy hooded figure in the corner.

And now, as he woke up on that morning exactly four weeks after her disappearance, he thought of it again. He gazed into the empty bath.

Every moment has its counterpart, every voice its echo.

8

NOW A GREAT CALM DESCENDED UPON ADAM FÜST. He sat in the chair with the India print and listened as "Lonely Woman" came to an end, and then reached over and lifted the needle from the record. He sat back and touched his lips with his finger. Honnie was dead. Now he was sure of it. Now came the serenity of certainty. Soon would arrive the anguish of loss, the emptiness of days, the terror of the night.

There had been no more phone calls, no replies to his newspaper notices, no word from her at all. He thought of the photograph Inspector Cuvillier had shown him and pressed his hands to his face. He hoped Honnie had not suffered. With his eyes shut and his hands pressed against them he saw the image of a subterranean room. Hidden in the shadows was a kind of platform with iron clamps attached to it. He saw two iron doors. He sensed intense heat, heat that melts.

The image had come from nowhere. Or perhaps that was not quite true. Perhaps it came from some dark recess of his imagination, his store of fears. Or from one of Gabor's films, he could no longer be sure of its origins. It didn't matter. It didn't matter what he saw when he shut his eyes. It was just another level of unreality. He had lived without Honnie for one month. Now that he knew she was dead she was all that seemed real to him. Everything that was not sucked into his grief remained transparent, irrelevant. Words became nonsense, mere noises repeated over and over, echoing within his brain, mocking interpretation. All that remained coherent were his guilt, his regrets. Honnie had died in the midst of life. Their life. Unfinished, like a sculpture still emerging from its block of marble, its final image unknown to him.

When he arrived at the office he went up to LouLou and gripped her arms until she winced and cried out. He said, "My wife is dead, LouLou," and she took him to her and pressed him against her body and cradled his head to her shoulder.

Gabor sat behind the closed door of his office. He was with the cute English actress whose photos he had shown Adam. Adam could hear their voices. Gabor was saying, "Now turn around. Now lift your arms." And the actress, ticklish, giggled, "Tee-hee."

LouLou said, "I'm sorry, Adam. I'm so very very sorry." She sat and lit a cigarette. Her eyes were moist. She had never much cared for Honnie. She'd thought she put on airs. She'd envied her her dusky, sensual looks. She'd envied her her husband, Adam Füst. She sniffed, she said, "What happened?"

Adam looked out the window onto a city lying beneath charcoal clouds. A few drops of rain dotted the windowpane. He looked at the window of the building across the way, the window that had framed the curious scene he had witnessed that night. He wondered if it was there that Cuvillier had found the mutilated photograph of Honnie. The memory of the photo disturbed him, it gave him a physically ill feeling. It was like a kind of rape. He said, "What do you mean?"

"I mean what happened, how did you find out, how did it happen, I mean Honnie."

He turned to LouLou. "Nothing's happened. I didn't find out anything. I just feel it's what's happened. I know she's dead.

She's been murdered." He continued to gaze at the window across the way.

"My God," said LouLou. "My God, my God."

He could just discern Gabor saying, "Now let's try it this way." He wanted to force down the door and confront the director with the news of Honnie's death, he wanted to destroy the gaiety of the moment, he wanted time to stop. "I never really knew her," said Adam. He looked at LouLou and thrust his hands into his pockets. "I never really knew my wife."

"When my mother died," LouLou began to say.

"That's the worst thing," he went on. "It's the worst thing, isn't it, not knowing. Not finishing. Never seeing it to the end. She was so ... private, you know, so withdrawn."

This came as a surprise to the extrovert LouLou, who considered everyone to be as candid and happy as she was, although now that she thought of it she realized that what she disliked most about Honnie was her silence, in her mind a form of childish moodiness. "It's a funny thing," she said. "When Mama died," she began again.

"And the worst thing is that I have to live with this. I have to live with these moments, these ... memories, I don't know, these times when I remember I could have been kinder, I could have tried to understand her better."

"Oh you're just blaming," LouLou started.

"And then I keep feeling that all along, all during these weeks she was suffering in some way, I don't want to talk about it, please, I cannot go on."

"Shh," said LouLou. After a moment of silence she said, "When my mother was dying I thought the."

"Fuck. Fuck fuck," he shouted.

"Shhh, Gabor's holding an interview."

"Fuck Gabor. Fuck his interview. Fuck the film. Fuck the whole fucking world. Fuck you, LouLou. Fuck you with your smiles and your I don't know, just fuck the whole bloody fucking thing. The fucking streets, fucking cars, the fucking city."

"You're overwrought," she suggested.

He turned to the window and then retreated through the door. He approached the building opposite and was stopped by the concierge, a woman surprisingly like Madame Moreau, but with an elderly crippled father instead. She said, "What do you want here?"

"Fuck you," he said, moving toward the lift.

"Oh, *mon dieu*," she said, tearing at her hair.

He found what he was certain was the door to the flat. He tried the latch. He applied his shoulder and with a newfound strength tore the lock away from the jamb. A stocky, middle-aged woman wearing a hairnet and underwear was walking through with a pot of coffee. She looked at Adam. He couldn't quite find the words, he said, "Ah, *pardon*, do you know what time it is?"

The woman stared at him. A man's voice from another room said, "Who is it, *chouchoute*?"

"How long have you lived here?" Adam said. He thought he might lie and claim he was taking a poll.

The woman said, "A week, monsieur."

"*Merci*," he said, shutting the door and racing toward the stairs. The concierge was waiting for him outside her office. "You wait here, monsieur," she said. "You just sit yourself down and wait right here for the police."

He walked around her and dashed out into the street, just missing getting run down by a red Citroën. When he returned Gabor and LouLou were in the outer office. The cute English actress had left. Gabor and LouLou stared at him. The radio was on. Mick Jagger was singing "I see a red door and I want to paint it black."

Gabor said, "I'm sorry, Adam."

"Yes," said Adam. He looked out the window just as the police pulled up at the building opposite. The middle-aged woman in the hairnet looked down at them from her window. From the flat in which Honnie had been tortured and murdered. "LouLou's told me about it," Gabor said.

Now she was not being so charitable, she remembered the curses Adam had rained down upon her, she said, "But he hasn't any proof, you know. He still isn't sure."

Adam sat and caught his breath. His mouth tasted like electrical current, there was a ringing in his ears. His hands were damp with perspiration. He said, "I," and then dropped it.

LouLou looked at him. She waited for Gabor to leave for his luncheon appointment. She said, "Come home with me tonight and have dinner. I'll make you whatever you want. I'll do anything you like. You need some comfort." She was pleased he allowed her to finish her sentence. He looked at her and pulled at his lower lip. Distractedly he said, "All right," then picked up the phone and dialed a number and asked for Inspector Cuvillier. Cuvillier was eating something; it was difficult to make out his words. He said, "Fumpfga," and Adam identified himself, he said, "My wife is dead, isn't she, please tell me the truth."

And Cuvillier said, "She's not dead until we've found the body. Personally I suspect your wife is no longer alive. That's just my opinion, you understand."

"But do you feel it inside?" asked Adam.

There was a pause. Cuvillier sounded like a cow as he chewed his sandwich. "Your wife is dead," he said, ringing off.

LouLou looked at him. Twenty minutes later he was walking along the Seine, under a light drizzle. A tourist boat plying the river came slowly abreast with him. Through the large glass windows of the cabin area he could see thirty people sitting around a long table. They were drinking champagne. A man in a dinner jacket and ruffled shirt held out his arms and sang,

"I love Paris in the springtime, I love Paris in the fall." Adam thought of throwing himself in front of the boat and leaving these people with a memory of Paris they would never forget. Paris, they would think, and instantly would come to mind the broken body of a distraught young Hungarian, the Seine running red with his life's blood.

He thought of LouLou. He thought of her bending over him that morning in the office, after he'd spent the night there. He recalled her unbuttoning her blouse and letting the pink tips of her breasts touch his face, he smelled her scent, Honnie's scent, L'Heure Bleue; he remembered the sunlight on her strong thighs as she knelt over him, shifting her hips gently from side to side to ease him into her, "Hallo, LouLou?" he said into the phone.

"I've been so worried," she said. "Where are you?"

"I've just gone for a walk. What time do you want me at your place tonight?"

"Come home with me."

"I'm not returning to work."

"But Gabor."

"I don't care."

"But Gabor said."

"Fuck Gabor. What time?"

"Seven?"

"Yes, okay, fine."

"I'm sorry, Adam. I'm so very very sorry."

"I know," he said, hanging up. "Hallo?" he said again after he redialled.

"You don't know where I live," she said. "I forgot to give you the address. Do you have a pen?"

"Yes," he lied. She told him the address. He traced it invisibly on the window of the phone booth with his fingertip. Then he hung up. He went into a café and asked for pen and paper and a cognac. He wrote down the address. He had forgotten the phone number she had also given him. It didn't matter. He drank his cognac. Beside him stood a film actor he recognized. His name escaped him, but his face was familiar. In an earlier film the actor had kissed Catherine Deneuve. He wanted to tap the man on the shoulder and question him closely about this encounter. Adam was strongly attracted to Catherine Deneuve, physically very unlike Honnie. The actor was talking to another man. The actor was saying, "So I told him he could take his lousy part and shove it. I said I don't work like that. I told him You come up with a better offer and then perhaps I'll consider it. And I won't work opposite that fat American bitch. No. Never."

Adam would try to remember this little exchange and pass it on to Gabor. Within six hours the news would be common knowledge throughout the Île-de-France. By this time tomorrow it would be the headline in *Variety*. He smiled and finished his cognac. When he returned home the phone was ringing. The voice said, "I saw your notice. I have your wife. I want six million francs by tomorrow at noon. Otherwise she dies."

Before hanging up the man left instructions as to where Adam should leave the money. Adam rang Cuvillier. Cuvillier said that it was undoubtedly a hoax and that Adam was an idiot for having had his telephone number printed in the newspapers. "You'll get every crackpot in town calling you. You won't know a genuine response from a fake one."

An hour later the same man rang. He said, "Your wife is naked on my bed. I am standing over her and looking at her body. Do you want to know what I am doing while I am looking at her?"

"Describe her," said Adam. "Tell me what she looks like."

"Long dark hair," said the man, and Adam felt his heart race. "Big tits," the man went on, "big huge full ones. Juicy ones," and Adam told him to go on, keep going, "Do you want to know what I'm doing?" the man said, and Adam said he would very much like to know but that he would like to hear more about his wife, he hadn't seen her in so long he wished to be reminded of what he had lost, and the man said, "She has a hairy pussy," and that was very unhelpful, for most women were graced with this very attribute; and then Adam had a bright idea, he said, "And the birthmark?" and the man said that she had a mark near her cunt, and Adam began to feel sick to his stomach, he remembered the freckle, and he said, "What is my wife's name?" and the man said "Her name is Barbarella," and he began to tell Adam what he was doing while he was talking and Adam laughed and hung up.

Cuvillier laughed, too, and reminded Adam he was an idiot.

LouLou had an apartment near the Beaubourg that she had inherited from her mother. Before then they had lived together in what Adam imagined was a golden age of harmony and smiles. By the time he was due to leave for LouLou's he was in no mood for her. He knew what she would do. She would try to make him forget his troubles. She would try to bolster his spirits. She would tell amusing stories and have him drinking cocktails until midnight. She would put on Jacques Brel albums. He shut the door and ensured it was locked and heard the telephone ring. By the time he had unlocked the door and picked up the receiver the person had hung up. He waited five minutes, then prepared to leave the flat. Then the phone rang again. It was an unfamiliar male voice. The man sounded serious, solemn even. He asked Adam how long his wife had been missing. Adam said, "One month precisely, monsieur."

The man said, "I am very sorry to hear that. Do you need comfort and prayer?"

"I need my wife," said Adam.

"I understand that, monsieur, and I hope and pray that you find her well and alive. But in the meantime you must be in need of comfort and prayer." He asked Adam if he had seen the Bright Light of the Fifth Heaven, and Adam said no, he didn't think so, not lately anyway. The man said, "Would you like to see this light, would you like to make contact with the Guardians of the Light?" Adam said he needed to know more about this, and if he proceeded with this plan, would the Guardians be able to help him find his wife?

"The Guardians know all," declared the voice. "They see all, they sense all. They are the beginning and the end."

Adam did not know what to say. After a pause the man, who seemed very friendly, said, "If you wish comfort and prayer you can join the Supplicants of the Guardians. We will pray on your behalf to the Guardians of the Bright Light of the Fifth Heaven. The sooner this commences the more quickly your wife will be beside you, safe and sound. If you delay we cannot guarantee success. Do you understand? Please send as a token of your faith a check in the amount of," and then Adam rang off.

On his way to LouLou's he had the funny idea to stop at Toto Roget's shop in the Marais, not far from LouLou's apartment. He stood across the road and saw Toto going over the day's receipts, pressing buttons on a computer keyboard. He crossed the road and tried to open the door. It was locked. Toto looked up from his work. He shook his head. He forgot to smile. Adam began shaking the door. Toto waved his hand as if to say No, no. Adam gave the door a friendly tap with his foot and the heavy glass slid a few inches downward in its frame, tilted away from him and shattered into a thousand slivers inside the shop. Adam smiled. He hadn't felt so good in weeks, he said: "Just stopped by to say hello."

"You bastard," said Toto. "You fucking little turd."

"Toto, the shirtless Peruvian. Tell me the truth, Toto. Did Honnie really know someone named Borrel?"

"You're drunk, you diseased prick."

A crowd began to form. Adam turned to them and indicated Toto. He said, "That is the famous shirtless Peruvian."

"You're crazy," said Toto. "He's insane, he's out of his mind. His wife's run away and he's gone off his nut."

Adam did not know what to say, suddenly he didn't feel on top of the world, "Toto, the shirtless Peruvian," he repeated. "The pimp of Lima, the arsehole of the Andes. Did you sodomize my wife, Toto, did she scream, did you have a bite and a drink afterwards, eh? Did you oil her big breasts, eh, Toto, the shirtless Peruvian?"

The crowd grew larger. Toto was on his knees, gingerly picking up the splinters of glass. Adam looked at the people looking at him. He didn't know what he was doing there. He worried for his sanity. He grieved for Honnie. He said, "The man who did this ran away," and then walked quickly off.

He was half an hour late for LouLou's party. He did not know why he thought of it as a party. He didn't expect anyone else to be there but themselves, and there was no reason for a party, not on a day like this.

LouLou must have been waiting inside the door, with her hand on the latch, because no sooner did he reach the door and lift his knuckles to knock than it swung open to reveal smiling LouLou with a cigarette in her hand. He stepped in, she kissed his cheeks, he said, "I just destroyed a man's door," and she laughed because she thought he was making an erudite joke. When she had first begun working for Gabor she immediately found herself attracted to Adam because he seemed to take the world so lightly. He was so unlike the people she met every day, in the supermarkets or *boulangeries*, people who went into a rage if their soccer team had lost, or who became melancholy at the first sign of rain.

Adam took off his jacket and looked around and then had the odd sensation that a piece of his mind had suddenly become detached from the rest of it, he felt his identity stretch for a moment and then spring back. He said, "My God," and then felt better. He thought, This is grief. This is what loss feels like. There is a space in my life and I will never grow accustomed to it. He imagined the rest of him, the part that could not fathom grief, attempting to fill the space. First it tried crime, at Toto's shop. Now he was at LouLou's.

LouLou's apartment looked as if it belonged to a seventeen-year-old. Unframed posters had been tacked to the walls, travel posters, reproductions of paintings, a brash advertisement for some musical comedy, happy smiling people dancing and sing-ing and mocking his misery. On the mantel was a small collec-tion of birthday cards. Adam said, "Happy Birthday, LouLou," and LouLou laughed; she said her birthday had been three weeks ago.

Adam pitied her. He pitied her because he suspected she was a lonely woman, and contrary to appearance not terribly happy. LouLou said, "Would you like a drink?"

Adam said Yes, a drink would be nice, something strong, perhaps strychnine, haha.

He sat on the sofa and felt two emotions battling within him. On the one hand he felt like settling into a profound inac-tivity, akin to an animal's period of hibernation; he wished that his heart might slow down, two beats an hour, perhaps, and that his entire physical system might go into a state of sus-pension. On the other hand he felt like snapping into a violent rage, tracking down Toto Roget and throttling him, watching his eyes bulge from their sockets and the blood run from his ears; and for a moment he even felt like murdering LouLou and Gabor, and it was only when he realized this was perfectly normal as long as one didn't actually carry out these misdeeds that he began to settle into an intermediate stage that some call normalcy. *"Merci,"* he said to LouLou, smiling wanly and accepting his Campari and soda. She sat beside him and touched his hair. He had never seen her outside the office. Gabor had never invited her to the parties he threw for his cast and crew, and though Adam was sometimes in attendance at these she never complained about having to sit in the office, answering the phone and typing letters.

She laid a finger on his wrist and looked into his eyes. She said, "I'm sorry, Adam. I'm sorry again, I really am. But you said the police hadn't found any evidence, so you can't give up."

"I don't want to discuss it," he said, and he recalled that he would have to return to his flat that night and, for the thirty-first night since Honnie had disappeared, sleep alone.

LouLou said, "That actress was a bit of a bitch, that English girl. Too young for the role, I thought. Gabor was all over her. By the way, he said it was all right that you didn't return to work, that he understood."

He looked at LouLou. She had changed her clothes since that morning. She wore a loose grey silk blouse and cream trousers that moved sensuously when she did, folding and uncurling as her legs cut through the air. He could see her breasts whenever she leaned toward him. She asked him if he wanted to hear anything special, she had lots of records. He said, "Whatever," and she insisted on his being specific. He asked if she had anything by Albert Ayler; he requested Olatunji and his Drums of Passion; Glenn Gould playing *The Well-Tempered Clavier.* She laughed and said he was being silly. Finally they together decided upon an album of Chopin waltzes her mother had sent for by way of a magazine advertisement and which had arrived three days after her burial.

She said, "I'm making chicken paprikash." She blushed and said, "It's Hungarian, isn't it," and he said if you put paprika on an old umbrella it would be Hungarian also, and perhaps rather tasty, mmnn, and they both laughed. He had another drink. He asked if she knew what constituted a daiquiri. She told him she thought it was made of cotton. He said he was referring to a drink, and she said she'd heard it was also a kind of shirt, or robe, something North African.

LouLou was sipping gin. She'd once had an English boyfriend who taught her how to drink gin, among other things. He had a degree from Cambridge. She had had to have his baby aborted. She had waited too long and something had gone wrong and one day while she was sitting on the toilet the fetus had fallen out. Adam set down his glass and began to wander around the apartment. Honnie's scent, L'Heure Bleue, lingered in the corners, subtle, elusive, as if she knew Adam would be there tonight, eating chicken paprikash and being seduced by LouLou. The bedroom was a fantasy of pink, and Adam felt instantly depressed; he wanted to seek out greys and whites and the coolness of a blue. Calmly, as he glanced out the bedroom window, he thought, *My wife is dead*. He repeated it once again, this time silently moving his lips, *My wife is dead*, and he pressed his hands against his face and cut off the light and this time saw a woman with a bloodied bandage strapped across her eyes and electrical contacts clipped to her nipples. LouLou touched his shoulder, she said, "Kiss me, please kiss me, Adam."

He pressed his lips against hers and felt her arms entwine around his neck, and he pulled away and steadied her body with his hands. LouLou frowned and shook her head, as if she didn't comprehend him. She said, "No, Adam, it isn't that, it isn't what you think. I want to comfort you. I want you to know you have a friend. Do anything you want to me. I don't care. Do anything. Hurt me, if you like, I'm your friend, Adam, I'll do anything for you."

He thought of the phone call: comfort and prayer. Now that he was certain Honnie was dead he wondered if he could somehow communicate with her soul or whatever it was that remained of a person afterwards. Perhaps he could speak to Suzy Rinaldi and get in touch with a medium. He would draw up a list of questions and put them to Honnie, and then he would say a few words, apologize for whatever wrongs he had done her, and wish her well in her next life, and when he realized what he was thinking he gasped for breath and stared at LouLou and then grabbed her and pulled her mouth against his, "I'm going insane," he said a moment later, "I'm losing my mind."

She held him and sat beside him on the bed. She wiped his tears with her sleeve. On the wall was a pastel drawing of a clown's face. It was an ambiguous face, it could be either hilariously innocent or insidiously sinister. LouLou said she had drawn it when she was fifteen and had given it to her mother and hadn't taken it down after her mother's death. The clown's name was Coco, she said, she'd learned how to draw him from a book she'd received one year for Christmas. *Coco*, thought Adam. *Coco the Evil. Coco the Angel of Death.*

LouLou looked into his eyes and unbuttoned her blouse. She unbuttoned the sleeves and tossed the garment over a chair. Adam looked at her breasts. He liked the fact that they were freckled. He thought of Honnie's breasts and remembered once telling her that the three stretch marks on the side of each one were like tribal scars. LouLou took his right hand and placed it on her right breast. She held him by the wrist and made his hand move in a circular fashion. He gently hefted her breast. She stood and removed her trousers, and when she was naked she looked at him and took his hands. He could smell something burning in the kitchen. He felt his shirt being unbuttoned and his trousers opened. Nothing mattered anymore. He let LouLou undress him. She got onto her knees and took him in her mouth. Nothing mattered, nothing ever mattered, the notion that life possessed meaning was a delusion. He rested his fingers on her shoulders and stared at Coco. *Coco the Clown. Coco the Crazy. Coco the Slasher.* Now LouLou was facing him, she said, "Forget the past. Just for tonight forget everything. Look at me, Adam. Look at me. Look at me, at me, damn you, look at me, me," and then she slapped him across the face with all her might and he looked at her and seemed to awaken from a dream. "Love me," she said quietly. "Love me. Please love me. Love me, Adam, please."

But his love had died with Honnie. While hers might have fled weeks or months or even years earlier, his was a recent loss. Love could not exist because life had no meaning. Life existed merely to be destroyed. He could not love LouLou because he had no love to share. No love, no hate, no passion, no hope. His love had died forever. He pulled on his clothes and looked at LouLou standing naked and shivering beside her pink bed. He looked at her breasts, at the roseate circles around her nipples, the gingery hair between her legs. He looked at her freckles and her tears. He wished LouLou had never existed, for then there would be no LouLou to weep because of his coldness. He shut the door behind him and walked slowly home, all the way to Montmartre.

9

GABOR HAD BEGUN TO SPEAK OF GEARS. IT WAS A HABIT HE had picked up from American colleagues. He would say, "Now we are getting into gear," which meant that shooting would begin within six weeks. Second gear alerted one to the fact that shooting would commence within ten days. After that it was all overdrive. "Ach," he would say after a hard day's work, "I'm burning oil."

The whole of the next day was devoted to getting into gear. Various people connected to the production came and went. They left messages for Gabor, sometimes thick envelopes. The phone rang often. Gabor had been out revisiting locations since half past six that morning. Adam sat in Gabor's office and began to organize the distribution of the latest script revisions. He placed them in their envelopes and carefully printed the names of the actors and their addresses on the labels. He rang up the messenger service. Adam watched his fingers as he smoothed down the gummed flaps of the large brown envelopes. He looked at his knuckles and the ring Honnie had given him when they were married. He held up his hands for a moment and flexed them.

Adam was astonished that life could proceed without Honnie, that people could go about their business, commute to work, dine in restaurants, shop in department stores, walk and talk and watch television and play drums and beg for coins and make love and take baths and move to new apartments and pray to God and write books and have babies and grow old, while for him there seemed no purpose to it, life itself had been sucked dry of its significance. He thought of Honnie dead. He did not want to know why she had died, or even how, because then he would have to concentrate on the moments leading up to it, the suffering and the agony. He wondered only where her body had been abandoned; it was becoming an obsession with him. The river would have been charitable enough to give her back to Adam. Perhaps she had been taken out of Paris, to some wasteland beyond the eastern suburbs. He imagined her body hastily buried in eight inches of loose soil. He thought of what would happen when the dogs discovered her, their slimy pink tongues swinging from their chops, their claws tearing at the dirt to get at the flesh on her arms, her breasts, her thighs. He wondered if her eyes were open and then he went into the toilet and wept into his hand.

This was the worst thing of all: watching life go on when your own has come to a halt. The death of Honnie was death in the midst of life, it was the demise of a part of himself. He thought of her sitting beside him that first night they had met, sitting beside him in his apartment and listening to Mingus and laughing at his jokes. He saw the way she looked at him, the way her eyes darted from his mouth to his eyes, the wonder in her gaze, the joy, the way it reflected his own in that moment of certainty. That too was a function of love: flattery, the sublime recognition of oneself by another. He remembered his own happiness as he took her hand and felt her fingers as they rested on his palm, he saw her lips as she parted them and sought his, he recalled the fresh musky scent of her hair, the feel of her skin. He washed his face and blew his nose and returned to Gabor's office and the life that would continue without Honnie.

The actors who were not already resident in Paris had taken hotel rooms or were staying with friends or in rented apartments. Adam brought the envelopes to LouLou's desk. She said nothing, her eyes looked elsewhere. For the third time that day he said, "I'm sorry," and still she said nothing.

He had left her apartment the night before in a state of despair. Despair and longing. Although he hadn't been aware of it at first, LouLou had excited him sexually. She had excited him because she had offered to give herself to him unconditionally: *Do what you like with me*, she had said. Honnie would never have said such a thing, she abhorred the idea of complete surrender, of yielding the last scraps of control to another person. He wondered what he would have done had he not left LouLou's. He imagined the scene; saw it going slightly out of control. He saw the pink flesh of her thighs and the tears on her cheeks. He heard her voice: *Do anything, do anything, love me, love me, do whatever you like*. But it wouldn't be love. It would be gratitude. Thank you for coming under my power. Thank you for letting me do this to you and that, and the other thing as well. He wondered why she was so desperate to give everything away, to destroy the mystery.

He had shut the door to the sound of her weeping. He had slept fitfully. He dreamed he was in bed with two women, that while he made love to one of them the other caressed his body. The women seemed to be twins. Their voices were alike and physically they were identical: to each other and to Honnie.

He lingered by LouLou's desk and read a bit of what she was typing. It was a brief summary of the plot of the still-untitled film. Eventually it would be distributed to members of the press and other interested parties; once Gabor was in overdrive.

Solange, an unsophisticated young woman from a village in the Pyrénées, comes to Paris to work at a large department store. Various male employees attempt to seduce her, none successfully. Her life in the city awakens a taste for freedom and risk. She begins to steal merchandise from the store; small objects at first, then larger, more expensive items. One day she is caught by a member of the security staff, a quiet, retiring man who in the past had shown her much courtesy. She begs him not to report her. She says she will do anything for him.

Adam could not easily forget the rest of it. Gabor and Guy Lanson had written a diabolical and horrifying script about the nature of freedom and license. He knew there was to be a prolonged scene of sexual torment in the *pigeonnier*. He knew that in the end Solange would triumph over the man and woman who had attempted to turn her into an object. An object: just like those she had stolen from the store; useless things, like the cheap little statuette of the reclining nude woman that had first dropped into her handbag.

Adam was aware that Gabor would be accused of exploiting women, of stepping over the line of propriety, of manufacturing pornography and manipulating his audience's emotions. That was a favorite one: controlling people's emotions. "But that is what it is all about," Gabor would rage, throwing his newspaper reviews against the wall and leaving them for Adam and LouLou to clean up. Adam looked at the last words LouLou had typed: *She says she will do anything for him.* He read it and blushed, for it was what LouLou had said the night before. For a moment his body shivered, he again imagined what that might have meant. He saw her satisfying his darkest fantasies in her pink bedroom, beneath the unsparing gaze of Coco. He touched her shoulder and then took her chin between his thumb and forefinger. He said, "You must understand what I'm going through, I am sorry for you," but she averted her eyes and snapped away from him and returned to her work, the little steel ball racing across the paper, *Then begins the humiliation of Solange at the hands of Henri and his young English wife Julie*, it typed.

At half past two the director returned from his meetings with his technical crew. They had visited the locations chosen for the film, the *pigeonnier* in Chantilly, a farmhouse on the out-skirts of Beauvais, the Bois de Vincennes, an apartment belong-ing to a friend of Gabor's in which some of the interior scenes would be shot. At four o'clock Gabor looked up at Adam with his one eye and said, "Now we are really getting into gear," then sat back and stretched his arms and pulled open his drawer and unscrewed the cap from a bottle of vodka. He offered it to Adam. Adam shook his head. "So you are okay?" asked Gabor. "I mean about Honnie, everything is okay now?"

"No one knows anything. No one's seen her. The cops haven't learnt a thing. She's dead. I'm certain of it, she's dead. I just want to," but Gabor was already nodding his head to the left, to the right, he was saying "Look, look," and then he tilted the vodka to his lips.

He had nothing more to say. Adam knew that Gabor hated unpleasantness, that he was uncomfortable even when watch-ing a news report on television dealing with a plane crash or a house fire or the death of a child. It was another reason why he had hired LouLou; merry LouLou with her unceasing smile. Gabor dropped the empty bottle into the wastepaper bas-ket and left the office, stopping briefly to say goodbye to his secretary. Adam heard her ask him what he had planned for the weekend. There was something about a party for Jeanne Moreau at some nightclub, then a flight to London to speak to the UK distributors. Adam remained in Gabor's office and lis-tened to the sound of her typewriter as she resumed work. He stood behind the desk and looked through the drawers. The .38 revolver. The magazine with the incontinent Swedish women and their delirious Filipino friends. Glossy photographs of the actors who had been hired for the new film. Sketches for proposed shots: the *pigeonnier* standing in terrible isolation against a barren field. It brought to mind the Citadella Tool Works. Adam slid the drawer shut.

He listened as LouLou finished typing and organized her desk. The radio was shut off. The answering machine was switched on. Adam felt sorry for LouLou. He said, "LouLou?"

Then he heard the door shut. He stood by Gabor's desk and watched her cross the road. She did not look back. He raised his view to include the window in the apartment where he had seen the woman with the dagger to her throat. The curtains were closed. He sat down and listened to the silence and then picked up the telephone and dialed seven numbers. Johnny Vodo himself answered. Adam said, "Do you know that photo of Honnie I lent you?"

For a moment Johnny forgot, he made hesitant noises, hums and uhs, and then remembered. "I passed it on to some guys I know," he said. "Some friends of a friend."

"What kind of guys?" asked Adam.

"Just guys."

"Why these guys?"

"Just because I thought they might have a lead."

"What, they are into tracking down lost women? Are you out of your mind? What are they, junkies? Junkies and pimps and pushers and murderers, right?"

"One of them plays a pretty good tenor sax, though," said Johnny Vodo. "Look, what's the matter with you, man, you out of your mind?"

"The photo, Johnny, that photo, that photo I gave you was found in an empty apartment. Honnie's face had been burnt out of it."

"What?"

Adam repeated the statement, he said, "I need to know who had the photo last, okay?"

Johnny said, "I'll do the best I can. I'll try, Adam, don't worry man, I'll try," though Adam knew nothing would come of it. The photo had passed through many hands, the world was a vast network of hands, grasping grabbing stabbing groping hands that never stopped, never rested.

He quietly replaced the receiver and idly pulled open the drawer in Gabor's desk once again and stared at the cover of the magazine. He thought of the woman in the sex shop, the nude woman who had seemed to recognize Honnie's name, who had instantly reminded Adam of his wife.

He picked up the revolver and placed the end of the barrel into his mouth. He closed his lips around the cold metal and found the taste rather bitter. He rested his finger on the trigger. The wind began to rise. He watched the leaves on the trees shudder. A pigeon strutted stupidly on the balcony, defining circles and bobbing its head. Adam felt the trigger beneath his finger. He thought of the Citadella Tool Works. In his mind's eye he saw his mother. He tasted metal. He remembered Honnie. He thought of a woman in a wall. The words *I am* no longer made any sense to him. A cloud passed over the sun, then another and still another until the sky was layered with grey. He began to walk around the office, the gun still in his mouth, a man chaperoning his own imminent demise. He looked at the building across the road. A child, a little girl, walked briskly before it, talking to herself and carrying a schoolbag decorated with a tartan pattern. The little girl stopped and unwrapped a sweet she had taken from her pocket. He probed the end of the gunbarrel with the tip of his tongue. It made a small sucking noise. An elderly woman walking a poodle stopped while the girl patted the creature. Adam thought of the cottage in Oberwil and the abandoned dog. He wondered if everything he would witness over the next few minutes would in some way, obscure or otherwise, reflect some past event in his and Honnie's lives. A man in a raincoat began to cross the road and then came to a sudden halt as a Fiat 124 raced by without stopping for him. The man crossed the road. He stood by the streetlamp and watched the woman and the dog and the little girl. The woman attempted to wave a bee away from the girl, she said something like *Oh, oh.* The man glanced momentarily up at Adam's window, put on a pair of sunglasses and disappeared around the corner. The clouds grew thicker, the air was dry. The possibility of thunder had been introduced. Adam considered how quickly and easily and efficiently he could make the scene he was watching disappear: the old lady; her poodle; the little girl with the tartan bag. There would be no future for any of them, they would have all disappeared, there would be a blackout and then eternal darkness, nothing, the essence of not being. He thought of pain, he speculated on how intense it would be, how long it would last. He felt the moist metal crescent under his finger. He traced the circle of steel with his tongue. He looked at the wall and the poster with the man in the doorway lighting a cigarette. He imagined it spattered with his blood and brains. He imagined LouLou coming to work on Monday and finding his decomposing body on the floor. He saw her put her hands to her mouth and heard her scream. He pictured Cuvillier rushing in and looking down at him and saying, This man's death is an admission of guilt.

Then he looked back at the street. He saw the little girl waving to the old woman. He saw the tartan schoolbag. But he was wrong: none of it would disappear. He would disappear and it would go on.

It would go on.

Even Honnie had not fully disappeared. Though dead she was still with him, strolling by his side, whispering under the breath of the wind, pressing her warmth against him at night, sitting across from him at table; inscrutable, invisible, riding the crest of his thoughts. She had not completely died. She had left something undone on earth and had not fully let go. She floated naked on a Swiss lake; sat motionless in a chair with an India print. Now he knew. She had died in solitude with her finger to her lips.

He removed the revolver from his mouth and put on his jacket. On his way to the place Pigalle he stopped at a florist. He asked that a dozen roses be sent to LouLou's apartment. The woman who worked there tried to explain to him the meaning of the various colors, white for purity, red for passion, and Adam could not concentrate on what she was saying, he just said "A dozen roses, you choose," and although that did not seem to please her one bit, this woman who took her job and everything connected to it quite seriously, she did not want to lose a customer. She said: "Monsieur, let us say four of each: red, pink and white, *ça va?*"

Adam nodded and kept nodding as he held the pen over the little white card. He wrote, *Please forgive me, I was an idiot, Your friend Adam,* then tore it up and on another jotted: *In hopes that we may be friends again,* then tore that one up as well. He thought of writing something witty about chicken paprikash. The woman in the flower shop waited and thought of her overheads and said, "Monsieur needs some ideas?" She took out a laminated page and wiped her sleeve across it. On it were printed various formulas for specific occasions:

—My darling, your lips are like
    rose-petals and my heart is smitten with thorns.
—With love from your secret admirer
—It was delicious, my darling ...
—To my favorite baby-sitter

—With all my love for ten glorious years of marriage
—With all my love for twenty glorious years of marriage
—With all my love for fifty glorious years of marriage
—Sincerest condolences on your recent loss

"You have nothing to commemorate a friendship?" Adam asked.

The woman took the laminated page from him. She said, "That depends, monsieur. That depends on what kind of friend you mean. Is it a woman friend, a man friend, a friend of a friend, a friend of the family, there are so many types of friends."

"Just a friend," he said, not wishing to elaborate, not wanting one jot to speak of a woman with freckled breasts who says *Hurt me, Adam, do what you like.* "A friend," he repeated. The woman suggested a few other salutations, A friend in need is a friend indeed; brother, Englishman and friend; forsake not an old friend; the friend of the bridegroom rejoiceth greatly; to my forever friend, and so forth. There were two or three other laminated pages full of such chestnuts and in the end Adam shook his head, signed the card simply *Love, Adam* and sealed the envelope. After he left the shop, indeed, when he was half-way to Pigalle, he regretted having sent her flowers and that idiotic card.

Love, Adam. His choice of words had been inappropriate. The Adam part of it was fine, he hadn't much scope for invention there. The problem centered on Love. He loved only Honnie. Surely LouLou would know that. Either she would interpret it to mean that he had actually fallen for her, or that he was lying and trying to be polite. No, he knew her only too well now, she would misconstrue the gesture. She would cook him another meal and take off her clothes, and so he had the bright idea to forestall this episode and invite her to have dinner with him in a restaurant.

Because it was daylight Adam did not want to be seen entering Sex à Gogo. Not that anyone in the place Pigalle would recognize him, there was little chance of some old chum suddenly spotting him and shouting, *There goes Adam Füst into the sex shop!*

Adam put on his sunglasses and ducked in sideways, colliding with a small man who was ducking out in a similar fashion. Standing around the magazine table were two North Africans and a Chinese man and a few German tourists. The fat proprietor of the shop sat behind his cash register reading *Le Monde*. Some American rock song, throb throb beat beat lalala, was playing on the stereo system, perhaps it was meant to get you in the mood for an afternoon of gasp and thrust. Adam stood by the table and leafed through a magazine. He eyed the doors to the booths. The magazine was called *Back Door*, he recognized it as the one Johnny Vodo had been reading. *I can sell you fire insurance, or house insurance or even insurance for your automobile, said Bill as he unleashed his throbbing member.* The photo, however, did not show an insurance salesman and his client; indeed, there was no correlation whatsoever between the photographs and text. Adam waited for the other customers either to leave or enter the booths. When he was alone he stepped up to the desk and then someone else walked in and he returned to the table. He looked at a few other magazines. One was devoted to large-breasted Englishwomen. Some of them were in boats. A few were having baths. One was eating a ripe banana and smiling. Adam wondered if she was smiling because she actually enjoyed posing naked for what she must know would be a vast audience of salacious men, or because she was being paid a great deal of money for taking off her clothes. There was a third possibility, one that depressed him greatly. The woman was smiling because she had been ordered to do so. Perhaps a penalty had been attached to the command. He thought of Honnie in a hotel room. He wondered how people could be so wicked. He wondered why women were held in such contempt. He touched his head with his hand, for a moment he felt dizzy. The shop was suddenly empty, the music continued throb throb lala and Adam stepped up to the desk, then retreated when an exhausted man charged out of a booth. He stood by the table again. He leafed through a magazine that showed photographs of a woman and a donkey in a sylvan setting, and Adam smiled because he thought there was something quaintly Shakespearean about it, and suddenly the shop was empty and he stepped up to the desk again and forgot what he had rehearsed saying.

The fat man looked at him and asked what he wanted, what the hell he wanted, he'd been in here for nearly an hour and he hadn't spent a centime, not a sou, did he think it was a library or something eh? Adam said, "I want to see a woman," and this caused the man much merriment, he laughed and showed Adam the interior of his mouth, teeth, a tongue. "The woman works for you," Adam explained. "She works in one of the booths. I must speak to her, it is most urgent."

The man stared at him while he tried to describe the woman, and it became rapidly clear to Adam that he was getting nowhere. He thought of returning in the nighttime and trying each booth in turn, and then felt quite empty and stepped outside, where Inspector Cuvillier was waiting for him.

"I was trying to speak to a woman who I think knows about Honnie."

"Sure, sure."

It dawned on Adam: "You've been following me."

"That's right."

Cuvillier took him by the arm and led him into a low café. He ordered two cognacs. They stood at the *zinc* among the prostitutes and pimps. Cuvillier said, "Any luck?"

"No."

"Of course not."

Adam said, "You think I killed Honnie."

Cuvillier bobbed his head this way and that, indicating *maybe yes maybe no*. He said, "For a while I did." He said, "That Borrel I told you about, the guy who lived in that apartment where I found the photograph. He's dead."

Adam was about to say *I know*, then thought better of implicating himself in yet another crime of which he was innocent.

"He died in a hotel near Orly. He was poisoned. His brother disappeared about two years ago. Probably went abroad. Six months later what was left of his body was found floating in the Seine."

Six months later.

Eighteen months ago. Adam recalled the moment in all its exquisite detail: Honnie in her black dress, the one with the thin straps; the enameled bracelet she had bought on that last trip to Budapest; the argument in the Vietnamese restaurant on the boulevard Montparnasse, the Woody Allen film, the blazing row in the apartment afterward; her return two days later, as if nothing had happened. Eighteen months ago. *Honnie; Borrel; Versailles; Fontainebleau; a warehouse in Nanterre.*

Eighteen months ago. Toto Roget: *Ask her why Borrel had to die, why she ran off so soon afterwards. Eighteen months ago.* The little spat in the restaurant, the way she held her chopsticks between her tanned fingers, her enameled bracelet sliding up and down her slim arm. *Eighteen months ago.*

Adam wondered if it would be going too far to imagine that Honnie had orchestrated the evening, from the argument to her stormy exit late that night. Indeed, the more he thought of it the harder it was to discover the origin of the misunderstanding. Yet why should she hide it, whatever it was: And Cuvillier watched him carefully as he wondered, as if the Inspector possessed the ability to read in the lines of Adam's face and the light in his eyes the truth about Honnie. He said, "We don't know very much about this Borrel, the first one who died, the one named Maurice. We knew his name, of course, and what he did, that sort of thing. His brother, though, this Jacques, he was another matter. Some of our people had been keeping an eye on him."

Adam looked at Cuvillier, he fingered the rim of his glass, he raised it to his lips, he sipped cheap cognac. He said, "What does this have to do with Honnie?"

Cuvillier lit a cigarette and smiled to himself. He looked at his disposable lighter and slipped it into his pocket. "And you needn't have wasted your time in that sex shop, you know. You could have gone in there and fallen to your knees and thrown money and that bastard wouldn't have told you the time of day. You haven't the clout, you see. You haven't the muscle, you don't speak the language, you live up there and they live down here, they do things differently." He turned to Adam. "I know the girl you're talking about, the girl you saw that night. I knew her immediately, the minute I laid eyes on her. I had a few words with her. A cute little thing, don't you think? I know most of the girls in this quarter. I gave her a few francs for her time. I bought her a drink at this very bar. I told her she was pretty. I told her she was wasted in a dump like that. I told her I'd have her up on a drugs charge if she didn't talk. She showed me her arms, she said she was clean. She said she was bored at the sex shop, she was sick and tired of sitting naked in a closet five nights a week. Her real money came from the specials. Private services. The more she's paid the more interesting the session. The sky's the limit with her. I asked her if she was into bondage. She said that was fine, as long as the money was good. She didn't mind a few straps and ropes as long as she was paid for her sufferings. Even a good beating wasn't out of the question. I told her I'd pull her in for something if she didn't come clean. I spoke to her like a wise guy, it's what these kids like to hear, a bit of the rough and tough. I asked her about Borrel. Sure she knew him. She worked for him for a while, this Jacques Borrel. A big shot. He was into whores, porn, the whole sex and women racket. And he was working for an even bigger man, the kingpin, the prince of the streets. Him we can't touch, much less find."

Adam remembered a man lying on the floor of a hotel lobby. He thought of a woman in an apartment with a dagger to her throat. He thought of private services. He thought of Honnie and his mouth went dry, he said, "Wh."

Cuvillier said, "I asked her about your wife. She said she didn't remember you, to her all men looked alike when they sat in that chair on the other side of the glass, they all looked like little boys. I had a good look at her and then I showed her the photo you gave us."

He reached into his inside pocket and took out the snapshot, a copy of the photograph she'd had to have taken when she applied for residency in France. It was a formal portrait, taken by a shopfront photographer on the rue de Rivoli. Honnie was unsmiling. She was wearing a grey cashmere sweater. She looked older than she was at the time, as old as she would be now. It was as if the past and present were coexistent in the photo, one image superimposed atop the other.

He remembered the night the gendarme came to take it away, how the stupid man looked at it, how he was about to say something, to comment on Honnie, and then touched the brim of his kepi and said *Bonsoir* monsieur and smiled faintly, as if all along he had known that Honnie was dead.

Now the photo was no longer in pristine condition. It had been touched by others, passed from hand to hand, perhaps even commented on and ogled over. On the night he gave it to the gendarme he had been certain Honnie was alive. Now he felt sure she was dead. That was the difference between then and now. Then there had been hope.

"Naturally, she reacted," Cuvillier went on. "I expected no less from her. I held the picture up alongside the woman's head. Your wife and she looked so much alike. Not like identical twins, of course. But there were striking similarities. Of course she said nothing. I don't know, perhaps it's only a coincidence, Monsieur Füst. What is it they say about the world?"

Adam looked at him. A reply was expected. He said, "World without end."

"No no, that's not it."

"Around the world in eighty days?"

"Really, monsieur."

"The world, the flesh and the devil?"

"It's a small world," said Cuvillier with a commanding smile. "This woman I was interviewing could have been your wife's sister. It's the sort of thing that throws a policeman off the trail, these little coincidences."

Adam again recalled the night he had spent in his office. The woman with the heavy breasts; the ornamental dagger with the curved blade; the man who looked at the gibbous moon, the man in the raincoat, the man with the Citroën, and now he recalled a man with a ring, a golden image of a bee set in onyx. He thought of these, he realized that viewed as such each element bore little significance; that even put together, as one begins to group together the pieces of a puzzle, they made little sense, they were like aspects of some obscure myth, a myth that would only begin to come clear when one had discerned the framework of it. He said, "Where can I find this woman you spoke to, Inspector? I'm sure I," and Cuvillier said: "She's gone."

"She's dead?"

"She quit the shop. She thought I was going to keep her under surveillance. She grew afraid, she ran. I don't even know her name. That's how it is down here, you see."

Cuvillier was on his third cognac; Adam had barely finished his first. It adhered to the top of his mouth and left a bitter taste on his tongue.

The Inspector said, "You know, I'm sure there's a perfectly rational explanation for the disappearance of your wife. There always is. Everything must have a rational explanation. Otherwise things get blown up out of proportion. Do I make myself clear? Your wife is dead. I'm certain of it. That's the way it usually ends up. I can quote you statistics. I have charts in my office. Eighty-nine per cent of all women who disappear are found dead. And there's a lot of it going around, you know. It comes in waves. It's almost as if people have gone out of their way to find death."

Adam thought of Gabor. He pictured him playing with his puzzle on the floor, *And the next thing I knew my father was in my room with all this blood pouring out of his throat, he blinked and then he was dead. I was the last thing in the world he. He blinked. He.*

His attention drifted to a woman standing at the end of the bar. She fanned herself with a magazine. She seemed tired, disgusted, half her face was swollen. Cuvillier looked at her with a mixture of contempt and desire, as if such a perspective afforded him the objectivity his job required. He slipped his right hand inside his jacket and fingered his wallet with his identification card. A portable radio behind the bar played inoffensive tunes from a bygone era, *"I read the news today oh boy,"* while Adam looked at the framed photographs that lined the wall above the bar, the soccer stars, television comedians, the strippers and showgirls. You live up there and they live down here, Cuvillier had said to him. Yet here he wasn't fifteen minutes from his flat in Montmartre. He imagined a line of chalk dividing the two cultures, an invisible frontier separating two alien peoples.

Adam stopped thinking about it and set down his glass. Two men stood in the corner, gesturing to each other, whispering, looking through the window into a breezy grey afternoon. Now the Inspector was beside the woman with the swollen face. He placed his hand over hers as it cupped the empty glass. The bartender filled it. Cuvillier indicated *More* with the lifting of a finger. He brushed his knuckles gently against her breast through the material of her cheap dress, he looked at his watch, he whispered into the pale curve of her ear. Adam thought of Honnie, naked, floating on the surface of a Swiss lake. At that moment she was untouchable.

Adam returned his look to the window. The wind had picked up. Traffic came to a standstill at the red light. Adam wished Cuvillier had not left his side. His voice was becoming a balm to him. Somehow all this rambling and indirection might lead to something, as if between the lines, the statistics, the crude implications of his jokes, might be found the key to Honnie's fate, a gleaming chink of truth amidst the gravel and silt. It was not enough to know she was dead. He had to know why, what it had to do with a woman floating in a Swiss lake, sitting in a chair with an India print, standing in a cold, disused chapel from which God had fled. He felt reduced, insignificant in the shadow of her terrible mystery.

Cuvillier was once again beside him. The bar was becoming crowded. Conversations erupted here and there, punctuated by loud bursts of laughter and the incessant chatter of the radio announcer, *"Et les autres!"* he seemed to be saying, *"Et les autres et les autres!"* The woman with the swollen face had disappeared. Adam imagined Cuvillier returning to the district later that night, meeting her in the bar and walking off to some cheap hotel room that stank of other men, prior encounters. He pictured Cuvillier amongst the pink frippery. There would be music on a radio, romantic tunes with strings and a male singer. He saw the Inspector passing money to the woman. He thought about Honnie. What if she weren't dead   if this were so, was she then thinking of him, Adam Füst? Perhaps it was he who had disappeared. Perhaps he had taken a fall and was suffering from amnesia. Perhaps the apartment was not his but one belonging to someone else, a place he had simply taken over. Thus everything he knew he would have had to learn since the time of the fall: the music of Ornette Coleman; how to work with Gabor; LouLou's freckled skin, her scent, her hair brushing his cheek. If that were the case, then who was Honnie? Was she a figment of his imagination, something devised by his heart, a repository of his dreams, his love, his past and future?

Or else he was dead, this was death, this grey Parisian universe of Gabor and LouLou and Coco and Cuvillier, inhabited by people with odd rings and waiters with stained teeth and men who salute the gibbous moon at three o'clock in the morning. He considered Honnie at home, ringing the police at odd hours, tearfully demanding to know where her husband was, viewing the corpse of a man in the morgue at Boucicaut, "Ah no," Adam said aloud and Cuvillier looked at him and smiled. Now Adam returned to reality. He felt his body relax. He caught his breath. It was time to go home.

Adam and the Inspector stepped outside. The wind had picked up. Subdued thunder played in the distance. The air smelled of rain. Cuvillier said, "Monsieur, I don't know. Perhaps we've been looking in the wrong place. All this... business with the sex shop and Borrel... Perhaps, monsieur," and he prodded Adam's chest with his blunted forefinger, "we should be looking more closely at Honnie, eh?" And he laughed and left Adam Füst standing alone, bereft.

10

WHEN HE REACHED THE DOOR TO HIS APARTMENT THE phone began ringing. He took out his key, tried to fit it in the lock, dropped it, picked it up, fit it in upside down, removed it, dropped it again, fit it in right side up, realized he had left the door unlocked anyway, and in the darkness grabbed for the receiver and toppled the apparatus onto the floor. He could hear LouLou's tiny voice, *Adam Adam*, it implored, *Adam Adam*.

He stood framed in the window, he held the receiver to his ear. Outside the sky was dark grey, almost night. In the distance tiny splinters of light branched down from the overcast. Rumble rumble went the sky as LouLou thanked him for the roses.

"I'm sorry about last night," he told her. "You must understand. I've not been myself lately."

An absurd line: *Not myself lately*. If he was not himself, then who was he? Errol Flynn? Herbert von Karajan? Louis Armstrong? Houdini? He thought about the other odd thought that had occurred to him a few nights earlier. He had eaten his dinner and had a shower, and then still in his underwear sat on the chair with the India print and listened to some music. And as he did so he realized that at least physically he was approaching the condition of Honnie, sitting in that chair, that pose, dressed as such … Perhaps if he had stayed there long enough he might, even for a moment, have somehow slipped into her identity, seen things through her eyes, come to comprehend the paradoxes of her life.

But of course that was impossible. She retained her mystery, just as he possessed his curiosity.

LouLou was continuing to be grateful, saying something again about thank you for the something or other, he could hear her voice but could not entirely grasp what she was saying, there was something distracting in the apartment. From where he stood he could not reach a lamp, and even had he stretched the telephone cord he still could not have switched on a light. LouLou was saying something about dinner, about having him over for dinner, and he saw it happening all over again, the tears, the imprecations, her freckled breasts, he said, "Have dinner with me, LouLou, we'll go to a restaurant," and she immediately jumped at the idea, it was a real treat for her, dining out, and then he hung up and turned and saw the man standing against the wall, the light from the streetlamps reflecting off his eyes, his high forehead, Toto Roget.

For half a moment they stared at each other, then Adam let out a little cry of fear and shock. He said, "*Ah, bonjour, ça va bien*, Toto?"

And because it was clear Toto had expected a reply out of Ian Fleming and not Anatole France he too gave a little cry. Toto said, "You bastard."

Adam said, "Yes."

"You owe me a door."

"How did you get in here?" Adam asked.

"The light."

"What?"

"A light."

Adam thought Toto was referring to some new electronic skeleton key, some sort of ray gun, whatever. "Put on a light,"

Toto finally said and Adam did as he was told, he switched on the lamp and the pale spider with the spindly legs retreated and cowered and watched the two men standing and staring at each other.

"Sorry about the door," said Adam.

"Bastard," Toto muttered without conviction. "Prick. Shit. Bastard."

"Yes," said Adam. "It hasn't been easy." He didn't know what else to say. He thought of a crab moving sideways on the floor of the sea. He indicated a chair. Toto put his hands in his pockets and looked at it. Adam said, "A drink?"

"Yes. All right."

He opened the cabinet in the kitchenette. The thought came to him of offering Toto a nice Bordeaux and giving him instead a glass of vinegar or shoe polish. He said, "Wine? Vodka?" He opened the fridge and poked about. "I've got some Evian." He removed an opened bottle of Stella Artois. "Beer. Milk." He shut the door. "Tea." He thought of what Cuvillier had said to him about the Borrel brothers and once more the notion of Honnie chained to a bed with grunting men standing about her came to mind, he felt his stomach turn, he said, "Ohh."

Toto said, "I was going to kill you. Then I decided to leave. Then I heard you coming to the door."

"My wife is dead," Adam said. "Honnie is gone."

"No no."

"I have coffee." He opened a cabinet: "Peanuts, if you like. Sardines." He shrugged. "Smoked oysters. Astro-Nuts." In bewilderment he again looked at the boy on the box. *Look, Mama, I can fly!*

Toto lit a cigarette. He looked around. He slid a record from the shelf, Cecil Taylor in concert. Adam said, "The one he made before that was better."

There was an explosion in the sky and then light rain began to fall. Toto said, "They say there won't be a spring this year. Just summer."

"I have coffee or tea or whatever."

Toto shrugged. "Your lock isn't very good. Anyone can get in here. I used a paper clip. I was going to kill you. I was going to kill you with my hands."

Adam edged closer to the door, he spouted inanities, "Long time no see, then."

Toto looked for an ashtray. He found the one Cuvillier had been examining a few nights earlier, filled with Honnie's stale, half-smoked Gitanes. He said, "So you found the letter. The one I'd written to Honnie."

Adam recalled the images. He saw the shirtless Peruvian sodomizing his wife. He saw her big breasts being oiled. He saw Honnie and Toto having a bite and a drink. He said, "That was a long time ago. I only mentioned it because."

"Don't mention it."

"I thought."

"I haven't seen her."

"But."

Toto shook his head. He had never seen the apartment, he began to take a little tour, he strolled around the living room, picked up Honnie's Aphrodite, examined its base, pulled out a few more records, some books, dragged his fingertips along the back of the furniture. He adjusted his cuffs, gazed at the Valloton print of the nude woman on the bed, he touched the knot of his tie and continued to make his rounds of the place, fitting the apartment to him as if it were a new shirt or a kid glove. Slowly Adam felt as if he were the intruder.

Toto said, "So this is where it all happened, hmm, Füst?"

"Where what all happened?" Adam shook his head slightly, as if trying to relieve his ears of water, or an unrecognizable accent. *This guy, he die strange death.*

"Just ... where it all happened. You and Honnie." He looked at Adam. "Sorry. Ah."

"You're in my house, Toto." The idea returned to him: Toto was the trespasser, not he. "This is my apartment, mine and Honnie's. You're in it. You broke into it. You've admitted it. You. You're in my place." He could phone the police, catch Cuvillier in a homicidal mood, watch the cop do in the Pimp of Lima.

"You broke my door," Toto said.

Adam remembered a name. "Borrel," he said. Toto looked at him. He lit another cigarette and opened a cabinet in the kitchenette. He took out the Astro-Nuts and examined the box, he said, "Borrel's the one that died, right?"

"Two years ago," Adam prompted.

"Something like that." He looked up at Adam as if just realizing where he was, who was addressing him, the circumstances of the meeting. He said, "What is this?"

"I bought it by mistake," Adam said. "Did you sleep with my wife, Toto?"

He said it so quietly that Toto squinted at him and tilted his head, he said, "What? What?"

"I said did you sleep with my wife. Did you make love to her."

Toto put the Astro-Nuts back on the shelf. He took out a crumpled paper bag, he reached inside it, he removed some empty peanut shells. "That's none of your business, Füst. I told you so in the restaurant."

"You said she was an actress."

Toto reversed the bag. Empty shells rained onto the floor. He made a disgusted face and threw the bag into the sink. In the flat above them the sound of laughter and glass breaking; the faint noise and rumble of rock music, bump-bump; bump-bump. That morning he had run into his neighbor from above on the stairs. He believed her name was Sabine. The lift had been out of order for a week. For two days a pair of workmen came and did something with the cables. Mostly they swore and listened to loud music on a transistor radio. Still the lift hadn't been repaired. He had met the woman on the stairs that morning. She had said *Bonjour* to him, he had returned the greeting, she had given him that disarming female look, two eyes meeting his, examining his features, summing up, boldly passing judgment, ingesting his essence in a matter of seconds. He didn't know her name. She knew nothing about him. Yet there was something intimate about their being strangers, it seemed to Adam as if in that short span of time she had understood what he was enduring, and her soft, enclosing smile comforted him.

He said again, "You said something about Honnie being an actress. Something about a second personality."

Toto Roget looked at him with disdain. He said, "Your wife was delicious." He said it as if Honnie had been nothing more than something you suck, a sweet, a jujube, or some culinary delight concocted at a posh restaurant, an hors d'oeuvre, a spoonful of pudding, a bit of puff pastry.

"My wife is dead," Adam reminded him, she was becoming dust. He parted the curtains and looked down at the street. The rain had stopped. The sky was a sickening shade of green. Crackles of lightning appeared in the distance, south of Paris, scratches on the horizon. The Café Picard seemed deserted. The tobacconist was darkened; no one stood in the doorway. There were no cars, no pedestrians. Paris seemed a ghost town. The sky turned bright yellow, there was a brief pause, then the building shook. He went to the fridge and took out the uncapped half bottle of Stella Artois. He sipped from it and spilled the remainder down the sink. Toto browsed through the records, he said, "I'm sorry, Füst."

"Who was Borrel?"

Toto looked at him. He looked down at the record jacket in his hands, a Beethoven piano concerto, and then back up at Adam, as if comparing the two images, Alfred Brendel and Adam Füst. He shrugged. "Some guy who died. They found his body in the Seine, I think."

Now Adam was almost too afraid to ask the question, the key question, the important question, the vital one, the one that might trigger off madness, despair, even death. His mind stuttered, he said, "What."

"What?"

"What did he have to do."

"With her? Borrel and her? I haven't the faintest idea, Füst. All I know is that on a few occasions she mentioned his name to me. She said something like, Borrel is a bastard. She'd seen his name in the newspaper, she just mentioned it in passing."

"Yet you said something about Borrel having to die and Honnie running away. And then there was something about Versailles and Fontainebleau and a warehouse."

"In Nanterre," Toto interrupted. He smiled. "That's right. The warehouse in Nanterre. She said something about a warehouse in Nanterre, something that happened there." His eyes glazed over for a moment, his memory was cast back, he thought of the delicious Honnie, the crystallized cherry, the bit of crumpet, Adam's deceased wife.

"Did you sleep with her, Toto?"

"Stop sniveling, Füst."

Adam realized that his eyes were welling with tears. Suddenly he felt helpless, it seemed as if the world was swallowing him, as if he were rapidly making his way down some pulsing canal. Toto stared at him, then sat heavily back into the chair with the India print on it. He touched his forehead with his fingers and winced, as if he were in pain.

Adam sat on the sofa. For what seemed a very long while he watched Toto. He said something, and as he said it he could hear his voice, small and tinny, in the hollowness of the silent room. He said, "It doesn't matter, Toto. I don't care whether you slept with my wife or not. I just want to know what has happened to her."

Toto looked at him. After a long pause he said, "I never slept with her. I wanted to, but she refused me, she said she wasn't interested. I hated her for it. You'll never know how much I wanted your wife, Füst. I would have paid anything for her."

Adam felt as if he were a priest hearing confession. He rested his head on his hand and averted his gaze. He wondered why Toto was afraid of referring to Honnie by her name. He wondered why at that moment he felt pity for the shirtless Peruvian, as if he were a cripple of some sort, someone with a handicap who excited one's sympathy. He looked at the shelves of records, he wondered if Toto required some background music, something that might ease the passage of words from him. He said, "Yes, go on."

"While you were at work with Gabor I sometimes took her out to lunch. Sometimes I met her for a drink. We never came here. She wouldn't allow it. She was a tease. She told me she loved sex, she loved doing it, she felt she was beautiful. She wasn't beautiful, Füst, she was gorgeous, she was delicious, she was beyond beauty. It's funny not seeing her here. It's funny. She said something to me about being in some sort of trouble." He lit a cigarette and rose from the chair. He turned acutely to look at the seat, as if something had fallen from his pocket. He puffed on his cigarette and walked to the window. He pulled aside the curtain and stepped back when he saw the rain, rain splashing against the tall windows, rain obscuring the view of the street, Paris, the sky. Adam now realized what he had been hearing in the background all this time. At first he had thought it was the woman above him taking a shower, or running a bath. Or it might have been the lift, come miraculously to life, sliding up and down between floors. Now he could also hear a Klaxon, and then he saw the lights, two smeared blurs reflected on his wet windows. He pictured a woman's mutilated body floating in the sewers of Paris. He thought of her murderer's short memory, how he would be laughing twelve hours later. Toto said, "It's an ambulance."

Adam joined him by the window. He could see the ambulance had pulled up to the front of the house. He knew instantly what had happened. He wondered if Madame Moreau's mother had died peacefully, in her sleep, or violently in a fit. Toto reeked of a strong cologne. There was a small oval discoloration on the shoulder of his jacket. Toto in himself was not perfect. He carried stains, like most people did. He splashed on scent to camouflage his own bodily odors. Adam felt sorry for him. He thought that Toto must hold himself in low esteem. He pictured Toto going home alone each night, putting on his carpet slippers and leafing through the newspaper and watching idiotic quiz shows on television, or the big film of the night, a worthy adaptation of a Balzac short story, and then afterward lying in bed, imagining himself dominating the women of the world.

He opened the door and stepped to the top of the stairway. Other tenants were already there, outside their doors, on the landings. Some were in dressing gowns. They stood silently and tried to catch a glimpse of what was happening. Adam saw the ambulance attendants. He saw a body with white hair on a stretcher. Her eyes were open. She seemed to be staring at him. She was dead. *Agn.*

Adam returned to the flat, he said, "Tell me, Toto."

Toto looked at him, as if at a stranger or a beggar or an employee of the métro. He said, "What?"

"Tell me about Honnie. It doesn't matter. I don't care what you did or didn't do. I don't care whether you had lunch with her or not. Honnie's dead, I'm the one who has to live with it." He felt anger rising inside himself, now he felt like murdering Toto Roget, because Toto would not mourn Honnie, only continue to fantasize about her, a nameless, long-legged whore. He said, "Tell me, Toto."

"Oh God."

"Who was Borrel?"

"Give me a drink." But he was already in the kitchenette, opening cabinets and cupboards, searching for a bottle. Adam gave him the cognac and a tiny glass, one of a set that he and Honnie had bought in Vienna. Toto returned to the chair with the India print and drank two cognacs in quick succession. Then he poured himself a third, set it down on the table with Honnie's Aphrodite, lit a cigarette and laid his head back on the chair. Adam was afraid he might fall asleep. Quietly he said, "Toto?"

"She once told me a story, some story, I don't know, something about a wall she was working on once. What was she in Hungary, a carpenter?"

Adam said, "She restored frescoes."

"Something about a body in the wall. She said it frightened her, finding the body." He looked at Adam. "Did she ever tell you this?"

"Honnie is my wife, Toto, of course she did."

Toto finished his drink and poured himself another. He said: "We used to meet at a café by Père-Lachaise, near Belleville."

"But."

"She said she liked the atmosphere of the place. The waiters there knew her, they called her Monique."

"What?"

"They called her Monique."

"I said why."

Toto poured himself another cognac. He had forgotten why he was in Adam's flat. He had forgotten about the door to his shop in the Marais. He lit another cigarette, he said, "She said she'd found a job, she didn't want you to know about it. She never told me what it was. She had to travel a bit, usually in the afternoons. Sometimes she said she went to Versailles, sometimes to Fontainbleau. Then there was something about a warehouse in Nanterre, I don't know." He looked at Adam through his slitty eyes. "I never much liked you, Füst. Do you know why? Because you never deserved her. You weren't worthy of her, you filthy little Magyar shit."

Adam remembered the letter, he laughed and held his stomach with his hands, he pictured Toto the frustrated Peruvian imagining Honnie being ravished by him, her husband. He stopped laughing and gave Toto a serene look. He remembered making love to Honnie. He remembered the feel of the skin high up on her thigh. He could smell her hair. He tasted the flesh on her neck, felt the curve of her breast, saw her mouth open in happiness. He said, "My wife loved me, Toto."

Toto rose from his chair and walked into the toilet. Adam listened to him urinate. He noted that Toto didn't wash his hands. He heard the Peruvian blow his nose. He heard the door open. He wondered if Toto had all along been taping their conversation, if it was being broadcast into the ladies' room in some posh Marais restaurant. It didn't matter. He had said little. He had heard much. He had learned nothing. Toto returned to the room.

Adam said, "Tell me everything, Toto. Tell me everything you know."

"Honnie isn't dead," said Toto, and Adam's heart leapt. "You've lied," he added. "You only said it to frighten me."

"The police think she's dead," Adam said. "There's an inspector on the case. He took me to a morgue." He remembered the basement. He thought of the pipes and the muck that ran through them. He saw the nude corpse on the table, he saw the look on Cuvillier's face, he shut his eyes and tried to think of something else. He saw an open space. He felt intense heat. He tasted fish oil.

He was twenty minutes late for his appointment with LouLou. He had completely forgotten about it. He had sat and listened to Toto and watched him drink cognac and forgot about LouLou as if she had never existed, Gabor as well. He hadn't wanted to go. He had allowed her to choose the restaurant. She was waiting outside the door of it on the rue de la Huchette, looking at her watch and gazing up and down the street. The rain had stopped. Dusk was approaching. People walked by her, avoiding puddles with little balletic twists and turns. The air was dense with moisture, it stank of the sea. Plunging through it were university students, most of them in pairs, making headlong progress and speaking knowingly about things of the mind, of the past, speculations on the state of the universe, on the nature of time, of space. She wore a crocheted shawl about her shoulders that made her look like an old woman. As he stood watching her he wondered if it had been her mother's shawl. He thought of her mother alive, and then dead, lying in the heat of a coffin, succumbing to rot and worm. He looked at his hands and stretched out his fingers. He thought of what Toto had told him and tried to unravel it. He considered the name Monique. He strained his memory to recall if she had ever mentioned it.

Monique.

Mmmmmonique. He sounded it out quietly as he stood at the corner of the rue de la Huchette. He placed a hand against a lamppost. He felt as if his sense of equilibrium might fail him. *Mmmm. Monique.* That was what the waiters had called her. Adam wondered who Honnie truly was. Monique: was she more herself living under this assumed identity? Or perhaps Honnie wasn't Honnie at all, but rather Monique, and was the woman to whom he was married, Agnes, Honnie, someone utterly unreal?

Toto said he met Honnie in a café near Belleville. Sometimes she would take little trips, to Fontainebleau, Versailles, a warehouse in Nanterre. She hated Borrel. Before Toto left he said that once a man stopped at their table. The man was in his forties, Toto guessed, but appeared much younger. He had short hair and was quite lean and tanned. He wore dark glasses and a gold bracelet. His shoes were expensive. He had stopped and kissed Honnie on the cheek, and then he excused himself to Toto and led Honnie a short distance away. There was some sort of argument, Toto said; Honnie was trying to pull away from him, the man kept holding onto her. Toto said that he thought he shouldn't get involved. He said that afterward Honnie had said something about Borrel. He assumed the man with the short hair was Borrel. He only heard the name again when Honnie read of his death in a newspaper and smiled.

Toto was standing by the door. It was still raining. He raised the collar of his jacket. The ambulance had driven off. Adam imagined Madame Moreau's mother lying in a morgue. He thought of Cuvillier surveying her wrinkled body.

"She'd said something about how glad she was that bastard Borrel was dead. She said he'd had to die. She said something about getting out of Paris for a while."

Adam stood on the pavement and recalled what Toto had said. He peered around the corner and looked at LouLou in her shawl. He wanted to tear the shawl from her shoulders and throw it to the ground. He wanted LouLou to become herself.

Toto took out a cigarette. Adam opened the door for him. Toto said, "I asked her if she wanted me to take her away. I suggested a weekend in Athens. I know people in Rome. I have friends in Monaco. She said she wouldn't leave you. She said she had to get away."

Eighteen months ago.

Adam again recalled the scene in the Vietnamese restaurant, the cinema, at the apartment. She had been away for two days. The dead man was Maurice Borrel. His brother Jacques died in a hotel lobby, *Thna-thna* he had said, then breathed his last. Jacques had dealt in pornography and prostitution. Maurice had been found floating in the Seine. Eighteen months ago. Private services. A woman with a curved dagger to her throat. A man salutes the gibbous moon. LouLou waved when she saw him approaching. His mind was not quite there, he smiled and wanted only to walk past her, to get back on the métro and return home, to hold his head in his hands and think. LouLou smiled and stretched her neck to kiss his cheek. He saw the skin of her forehead in the seedy blue neon of a shop sign. For a split second he caught a glimpse of the truth about Honnie, and then it escaped him, it slipped through his mind like a whispered syllable.

She had chosen a simple little restaurant that seated only twelve or thirteen people. It was run by a couple who were in some way related to her, second cousins, he thought she'd said, on her mother's side. Adam had never heard LouLou speak of her father. They sat down and the husband and wife came over and kissed her, shook his hand, looked at them in a congratulatory manner, as if he and LouLou were newlyweds, or about to become so; there was talk of a complimentary bottle of wine. LouLou said that her father had left her mother when she was still a baby. Her mother had never much spoken of him. The marriage hadn't been a happy one. She asked Adam about his parents. He said very little. He could see she was growing disappointed. He hated her shawl. He said, "What a pretty shawl, did you make it?"

"It was my mother's," she said, and he felt his stomach turn. He thought of LouLou in his bedroom. He imagined her on all fours on his bed. He heard her say *Do whatever you want to me.*

"I'm sorry about the other night," he said, and she smiled and shook her head and said it was all right, it didn't matter, it would be best if they just forgot about it. His emotions over Honnie's disappearance had now become adulterated. A new ingredient had been added. If Toto had been telling the truth, Honnie had been mixed up with other people, people who held onto her in the street, who kissed her cheek and were hated by her. Monique.

He thought of him and Honnie alone, in the flat. He saw her sitting in the chair with the India print, holding a cigarette to her lips, her knees up, thinking. It hadn't just been the two of them. All along there had been other people in the apartment, a great crowd of shady *messieurs*, Maurice Borrel and others, living memories who accompanied Honnie wherever she was. Perhaps at night she dreamed of them. He remembered that sometimes she would wake him with shouts and screams, exclamations and cries that emerged from the depths of her sleep. But when he turned to look at her she remained peacefully asleep, the only evidence of her distress being a slight frown on her lips; lips coolly defined in the pale light of the moon.

"The flowers were lovely," LouLou was saying, while the man who owned the restaurant ignored the other patrons and displayed a dusty bottle of champagne. Adam nodded his head and said *Bon, bon*, though at that moment he could have destroyed the restaurant and everyone within it. He could not understand precisely with whom he was angry. Honnie, for having led a separate life, for never having told him of it? Or was it with the people who had initiated her into it? But who were they? And what sort of life was it?

He looked at LouLou. She was smiling at him and holding onto his fingers. The man who owned the restaurant seemed unable to tear himself away from them, he kept bringing bread-sticks and breadrolls and bottles of mineral water and forks and napkins and flowers and pepper mills and salt shakers and news of Tante Delphine in Reims and Oncle Théo in Blois, and he kept asking Adam questions, *What do you do, monsieur? Who are your people? How do you like the weather? How do you prefer your veal?* and all Adam could say was *I work for Gabor, and my people are the Füsts of Budapest, and the weather has been very nice, and I prefer my veal cooked,* and the man said *Ha-ha,* he told LouLou that she was marrying a funny man, *Ha-ha.* And all he could think about was Honnie lifeless on satin sheets, a silk cord knotted around her throat.

He looked at LouLou. Except for the shawl she looked more attractive than usual. Her hair had grown longer. The shirt she was wearing, some sort of jersey with a low, curved neck, showed her cleavage. For the first time in his life he felt an unmitigated desire for her. For the first time in his life he had mixed feelings for Honnie. He grieved over her disappearance; he raged over her silence. He wanted to go home with LouLou, go to her flat and tear her clothes off. There would be no talk of making love. He would not make love to her. He would fuck her, and fuck her hard, he would push her up against the wall of her shower, he would turn on the hot water and plunge into her, he would dry her off and lay her on the bed and separate her thighs and fuck her. He would sodomize her until she screamed and then he would ejacu-late on her body, over her contorted face. He said, "You look nice tonight," then quickly apologized, he said he wasn't quite himself.

He realized he was being unfair to her. Here he was on a date with a pretty woman and all he could think about was Honnie. He was not giving LouLou the attention she deserved. When he was not thinking about Honnie he was imagining the humiliation of LouLou. He grasped her fingers and lifted his glass of champagne. He said, "*Salut*" and drained his glass in one swallow. He felt tears come to his eyes as the carbonation tingled painfully in his throat. He said, "I'm glad you liked the roses. I wasn't sure what to send you."

"You didn't have to send anything, Adam. It wasn't necessary."

"But I thought you were angry with me," he said. He remembered her silence in the office, the way she turned abruptly away from him when he apologized once, twice, a third time. He said, "And the other night, the dinner you cooked, the paprikash. Sorry."

She pressed her lips together into a smile and shook her head. Her smile told him it didn't matter but her eyes told a different story, they spoke of rejection and disappointment. Adam wondered how many men beside himself Honnie had slept with. Not counting the eighty-three before they'd met. Had she ever gone to bed with Maurice Borrel? Jacques Borrel? The waiter with the stained eyes and yellow teeth? The thought of it nauseated him, the notion of Honnie pressing herself against a man who stank of sweat and in whose universe people were transformed into pigs and slaves.

The man and woman who owned the restaurant brought them their meal. Adam had forgotten what he had ordered; then remembered that the *patron* had demanded to choose the meal himself. Adam looked down at the veal. He disliked veal. Honnie disliked veal, too, and that was why he disliked veal, because Honnie hated it, even the odor of it cooking gave her the urge to vomit. He thought it was unfair of the *patron* and his wife to presume to know the tastes of their customers. What if veal produced a violent reaction in Adam? What if he keeled over and died? That would be a big surprise to the couple, they would have to shut up shop and move to another town where their reputation was not yet known.

LouLou spoke of the film Gabor was making. That morning she had spoken to the German actress on the telephone. It seemed there was the question of the meals Gabor would be serving his actors and crew during the shooting. It appeared the German actress was on a strict diet. She required certain foods. "It seemed hardly worth the trouble of a phone call," LouLou said. "I mean, why couldn't she just wait and tell Gabor himself when shooting begins?"

"What did Gabor say?"

"Well he wasn't in, was he. I told her I would send the message on, that Gabor was out of the office. She didn't believe me. She said I was lying. She demanded to speak to him. I thought of passing the call onto you."

"But you didn't." He thought of the German actress in the film he and Honnie had seen in Zurich. He thought of Honnie sucking little circles onto the skin of his chest. He thought of a million bucks. He thought again of the circles and then thought of the ripples in a lake, ripples surrounding a floating woman.

"She became really rude, you know," LouLou went on. "She called me a lying bitch. I hung up on her. Gabor will be furious with me, he adores that monster."

"He won't be furious with you. You did the best you could. It was all you could. And then the. Fuck. Fuck fuck."

LouLou looked at him. She said: "What is it? What are you saying?"

Words had become nonsense. He remembered Madame Moreau's mother with her *agn agon agor agnes*. Words became nonsense in his mouth, they could no longer convey the content and power of his thoughts. He set down his champagne glass and thought it might be amusing to squeeze it tightly in the palm of his hand until the glass shattered. He thought of blood on the tablecloth, he thought of blood on LouLou, he took her hand and said, "Let's go, let's get out of here."

He thought, *I will never see Honnie again.*

11

BY THE TIME THEY ARRIVED AT THE APARTMENT ADAM'S lust had abated. Perhaps it was the ride on the métro that had caused it. The carriage was crowded. Only one seat was free. He had stood and gazed down at LouLou. He looked at her cleavage, at the top of her head, at her hands as they fidgeted endlessly on her lap. The light in the carriage made her seem pale and sickly, though when she looked up at him and smiled she appeared healthy and eager. She seemed to have two faces, two natures. Few men he had met in his life were so doubly graced. He looked at the freckles on her chest. Stepping into the carriage he had almost been pushed to the ground by a man in a raincoat. The man looked familiar, Adam had started to say *Hey, monsieur*, and then let it drop when LouLou took hold of his arm and helped him regain his balance.

His desire for her had subsided. Not disappeared: diminished. He knew himself well enough by now. One alien thought, an image flashing into his mind, even an abstract idea, goodbye to tumescence. He remembered the days of Oberwil. Sometimes as he and Honnie lay beside each other on warm evenings, as their hands explored their bodies, the notion of death would come to his mind, Honnie's death, and she would feel him and whisper "What is it, my darling?" And he would say nothing and try to think about Honnie alive, warm, and lying beside him. It occurred to him then that death was woven into life, it was an indestructible golden thread that glowed brightly against the dark backdrop of night, a bitter odor that lingered in the air, a quiet, continuous hissing like blood coursing through the veins.

He could not quite see what had caused it this time. He looked at another woman in the métro carriage. She was perhaps of Middle Eastern origin, Lebanese or Israeli, and then he realized that probably she was Persian. Her skin was dark, her features delicate. Her hair was black, like Honnie's; ornately clipped at the back of her head. He imagined her naked. He thought of the smooth, dusky skin on her belly. He thought of her breasts, thickly veined in blue. He looked at her legs emerging from the short skirt. He imagined the legs separating. He thought of her scent, the heat of her body. He looked at LouLou. She was looking at her fingers. She was pathetic, she reminded him of a puppy, simultaneously inviting both punishment and love. He thought of LouLou howling in pain. He stopped thinking about it when he looked at the beautiful dark-skinned woman. She invited only love, passion, speculation. Now he could feel it lying low, his lust, it had retreated and was preparing to rise up once again, it shifted his head. The Persian woman reminded him of Honnie. He pictured her lying unconscious on his bed, the Persian woman, he saw himself turning her over and exposing her dark cleft and ravishing the woman, and then he gasped and looked at his reflection in the window and realized that he had reduced the beautiful woman to a dead creature, a piece of meat.

A man lay in the lobby of a hotel. A waiter with stained eyes raped a delirious woman. Cuvillier returned to the bar in the place Pigalle. He fastened his trousers and paid the bruised woman a hundred francs. A young pink-haired woman with a sour apocalyptic expression stared sullenly through a restaurant window. Honnie in a warehouse, being beaten by Maurice Borrel.

LouLou had never seen his and Honnie's apartment. Like Toto before her she touched the walls, the objects: with a look of wonder on her face she felt textures, the India cloth, the fabric of the chairs; she stared at the Valloton print, the nude woman playing with a white cat, looking intensely at these things as if trying to read the intimate details of a life that had excluded her, that of Adam and Honnie Füst, as if attempting to absorb something of the mystique of this marriage that had always excited her curiosity, her envy, her desire.

Adam stood in the kitchenette and finished pouring out two cognacs. He looked at LouLou and thought of what she had said: *Do what you like with me.* No woman had ever said that before to him. It was a man's deepest, most shameful wish, yet also an expression of mutual contempt: *Abuse me, you prick.* Honnie would never have said such a thing. There were certain sexual acts that she refused to perform. In the beginning there were even more sexual acts she refused him, a repertoire of twists and turns and entrances and exits. And yet over the course of time she would make little forays into these dark forbidden regions, and these acts would be incorporated into their lives. Adam knew there was a line that Honnie would never allow him to cross. He wondered if she did that because it added the element of anticipation. And that one day she would surprise him and grant one further experiment, which in turn would become part of their routine.

And what would happen when there was nothing left to anticipate, when every orifice had been exploited, rubbed numb, become overfamiliar? Would sex lose its interest? Would death then become their obsession?

He could hear LouLou in the bedroom, he could hear her moving about, feeling things, sheets and curtains and clothing, trying to reconstruct in her mind the charmed life of Honnie and Adam Füst. He set down the drinks and looked through the living room window. It was the blue hour, that brief moment between day and night when Paris achieved its truest, most sensual coloring, a moment echoed by its counterpart that lay wedged in time precisely twelve hours later. He rested his forehead against the window and thought of a woman surrounded by ripples in a Swiss lake.

LouLou was waiting for him in his and Honnie's bed. As if she could possibly replace his wife. She was lying naked on the sheet. She had pushed the duvet down to the end of the bed. He saw her long legs. One of them was bent, it was as if she were posing for a magazine. She lifted her arms to him. He saw her freckled breasts, the gingery curls between her legs, the tufts beneath her arms, the pink curves of her body. She smiled, and her smile seemed pretty, it glowed with innocence. He unbuttoned his shirt and removed his trousers. He came over to her and raised her up in his arms. She shut her eyes and yielded her will to him. He maneuvered her onto her knees and held her tightly, squeezing her flesh with his hands. She let out a little whimper and then gasped with pleasure. He looked at the wall and thought of nothing.

The sound of the phone ringing woke him. He lifted his head from the pillow and looked at the window. A fine rain went pit-pit against the panes of glass. His arm tingled where it lay beneath LouLou's head. He felt her with his left hand, he felt her breast. It was damp with perspiration. He pulled his arm slowly away from her and ran into the living room to answer the phone. By the time he got there it stopped ringing. He wondered if it had been Honnie, he remembered that first call he had received from her, just before dawn, *I just wanted to ring to say that everything's all right*, she'd said. He recalled what Toto had said. *Monique at a café in Belleville. Maurice Borrel.* He wondered when the lies had first begun.

When he returned to the bedroom LouLou had rolled onto her stomach and was taking up most of the bed. He could barely hear her breathing, though he knew she was in a profound sleep. He stood over her in the darkness. He felt nothing inside him. He was dead, just as Honnie was dead and just as LouLou seemed to be. Only Gabor was alive, making films about people who leave red palm prints on the walls, who sign their deaths with indelible blood. *He blinked and then he died.* The phone rang again. He remained staring down at LouLou. He remembered Gabor's revolver, the taste of metal on his tongue.

It was Cuvillier. It was a few minutes past eleven. Adam had been sleeping for only a few hours. "Tell me, monsieur," Cuvillier said the moment Adam answered the phone. "When was it you said you met your wife?"

Adam could remember it almost to the day. He thought of Charlie Mingus. He thought of the café and Johnny Vodo. He recalled the newspaper Honnie had been reading. He tasted beer. He told Cuvillier the date.

The Inspector said, "And you say she claimed she'd been in France for only a month?"

Adam felt his throat go dry, he nodded, gasped for breath. Cuvillier said, "You're certain she said that, one month, she'd been in Paris only one month?"

"Yes," said Adam. "Yes." In the background, behind Cuvillier's voice, he could hear the sound of a typewriter. He could hear the muffled voice of a man, a door slamming, brief laughter.

"Can you meet me at the Café Achéron in ten minutes?"

"What?" Adam said. He had meant to say Where?

"The Café Achéron. On the Right Bank, across from the Préfecture de Police. Just outside the Châtelet métro. I may have some information for you."

Adam did not know what to say. He nodded his head. The Achéron. Across from the Préfecture. On the Right Bank. He pulled the phone away from his ear and looked at it. He pulled hard on it, as if it had been secured to a hard surface.

He stood, naked, holding onto the phone. He heard the dial tone return. The rain had come to an end. He saw a lighted window in a room above the Café Picard across the road. Waiters were moving to and fro while in the window two stories above them a man wiped his face with a towel. He was a large man with powerful arms. He draped the towel over a rail and then stared out the window. He pressed his hands to the glass and looked in Adam's direction. Adam sensed that the man was about to commit an act of violence upon himself, to throw himself out the window or put a bullet in his head. Adam turned and went back to the bedroom. Quietly he pulled on his jeans and sweater and sneakers, fetched his suede jacket, reached down to touch LouLou's head, left the flat.

The métro would be running until one. Two more hours. The idea of taking a taxi seemed absurd to him. The streets of Montmartre seemed less crowded than usual, the pedestrians subdued, as if collectively they had heard of the assassination of a world leader. He remembered the murder of Sadat in Egypt. It was before he had met Honnie. He had been in a bistro with Jeannot Debray and Suzy Rinaldi. Sitting at the next table were some Egyptian students. The radio over the bar was barely audible. Suddenly the students leapt to their feet and cheered. They overturned their table and loudly ululated and shrieked. It was impossible to tell whether the news had driven them into a frenzy of anger and revenge, or had filled them with joy. They ran out into the street, holding onto one another and performing a curious little dance. They had forgotten to pay their bill. In the west it was different. Sackcloth and ashes.

The road contained the façades of houses, shops, bars, restaurants. The images rippled in the puddles, in the shimmery membrane of water the rain had left behind. Whispering lovers huddled in darkened doorways, caressing, embracing. Adam walked slowly toward the métro station. He tried to picture the Right Bank across from the Préfecture on the Île de la Cité. He had never been in the Café Achéron. Perhaps it was a favorite watering spot for police inspectors. He wondered if they met their informers there, small men with shifty eyes and dirty fingernails, who reeked of stale urine and spoke too fast in a monotone, under their breath. He thought of Gabor setting up a shot. He saw the one-eyed man moving swiftly about, pointing, pushing people into position, shouting over his shoulder at his cameraman. He could imagine the finished scene in the Achéron, the closeups, the grainy texture of faces, the uncertain nightmarish quality of the backgrounds. He thought of the *pigeonnier* in Chantilly. He pictured how Gabor would shoot the scenes there, the lighting effects he could achieve, the splashy patches of sun on the German actress's slim body: like a million bucks.

He thought of Honnie in the Café Achéron, how the different aspects to her nature would be there with them, filmy guests of the night: Honnie, her Infidelity, her Lies and now her Death. That was why the Inspector had asked him to leave the flat in Montmartre. Honnie's body had been found.

Adam stopped by a streetlight and extended a hand to it and only then realized he had walked past his station. It didn't matter. He could go to another. A fine mist unfolded in the air as he thought this, and the feel of it refreshed him. There were no stars, no moon; only clouds, a bright grey blanket that occluded the great distances above his head.

He had grown accustomed to the notion of Honnie Dead. But he had become intimate only with the words, which in themselves broke down into abstraction. Honnie Dead. Honnie has been murdered. Honnie died in solitude, she had killed herself. The words had become detached from the images he had so terrifyingly conjured up. No longer did he see a woman in a pit, staring at a disc of sunshine. No more did he envision a woman with a bloodied bandage across her eyes. Neither was there a body bleached of its color being dredged from the river. Just words. Honnie Dead. Honnie was murdered. Honnie killed herself.

He tasted blood in his mouth. He had bitten the side of his tongue. He descended into the station at Pigalle and stood on the platform, his hands in his pockets. His eyes seemed to absorb all the light, his head throbbed with it. His body felt soiled, damp. He had forgotten to wash his face or brush his teeth or comb his hair. He thought of Cuvillier stepping outside the café to meet him, taking him by the arm and showing him a photograph inside his office across the Pont au Change. He would have to identify the woman in the photo as Honnie. That was why Cuvillier had asked to meet him at such an unholy hour: because this time there was proof. Honnie Dead would become reality, cold flesh on a gleaming chrome table; the attendant stands by, garbed in white, smoking a cigar; the world moves one quarter turn; a man with stained eyes laughs and slaps his knee.

He had just missed a train. At first deserted, the platform quickly came to life. There were perhaps seven people beside Adam. A young oriental man in a turtleneck sweater stood near him and sang quietly to himself in an unfamiliar language. A drunk man in a blue pinstriped suit staggered and fell into a plastic seat and then vomited onto his trousers. No one turned away. No one cared. The smell of shit and cheap drink filled the platform. A young woman with green hair and a leather jacket ran down the steps, followed by a boy similarly dressed. They looked at the drunk man and then came over and began speaking to him, they made small talk, *Bonjour, ça va, how do you like the weather, eh?* The platform stank of elemental things, shit and wine. The drunk man seemed unconscious.

Adam said nothing as the couple emptied the drunk man's pockets. A wallet, a passport, a cigarette lighter, a packet of Marlboros, loose change, a wristwatch. Adam turned and looked at a poster advertising a department store. A little girl smiled and sat on a swing. The photograph was meant to suggest Renoir. Summer. Innocence. Youth. Lost things, things irretrievable. When he turned he noticed that the green-haired woman and her boyfriend had disappeared. The drunk man was lying on the floor. His jacket was aflame. There was the odor of singed hair. The oriental man put out the fire by rolling the drunk man onto his back with his foot. Then the train pulled in. Adam stepped onto it and took a seat in a first-class carriage. He listened as the train surged ahead. A man in a raincoat sat across from him, reading a newspaper. A young man in a skullcap stood and read his prayer book. Adam stared at his sneakers, his filthy sneakers, and then his hands as they gripped his knees. The stench of shit and vomit remained in his nostrils. He thought of iron doors concealing flames. He felt like throwing himself to the ground, groveling in filth, lying in ashes.

When he stepped outside he saw the rain had stopped. The cool air refreshed him. There were breaks in the clouds, the reassuring grey face of the moon momentarily appeared and then withdrew. He looked at his watch and saw he was late for his appointment with Inspector Cuvillier. He breathed in the air and rocked on his heels, tried to catch his bearings. He saw the lights of the Hôtel Dieu glowing against the sky. Beside it was the Préfecture. The traffic on the *quais* was heavy. The people in the cars were smiling, some of them were dressed to the nines;

for them the night had just begun, there would be champagne and merriment until dawn. For others the night would never end.

He stood by the river and saw the lights from the bridges dancing upon the tips of the waves. A boat passed by. Through the windows he could see people sitting and dining. A disembodied female voice told them they were about to see the cathedral of Notre Dame. The boat carved a wake in the river that rolled twice over and eventually disappeared. Adam turned and saw the Café Achéron. He saw a figure sitting alone at a table, stirring something in a small cup. He saw the orange glow of a cigarette, he walked by it, quickening his pace until he stood opposite the Île Saint Louis. He looked at the houses on the tip of the island, he thought of the people within these enlightened structures, people with their feet in a past beyond his imagining, people who lived among ghosts. He pictured Cuvillier waiting inside the Café Achéron. He could continue walking until dawn. He could hitch rides until he came to the German border. He would proceed to Switzerland, to Oberwil, he would climb the stairs of the little cottage and seek out the shadow at the end of the corridor. He would never have to return to Paris, to hear the news of Honnie's death, to see her body in a coffin, to watch the earth fall in clumps onto the polished pine. It occurred to him: we live in order to conquer death. We die in order to conquer life. He laughed at the absurd pomposity of it, and then the rain grew harder, it dotted the river, and he was standing before the café window, watching a man stirring his coffee, Cuvillier.

It was as he suspected: the Achéron was a gathering place for the police, subdued baggy-eyed men with cynical smiles and the stink of murder about them. Cuvillier looked up as Adam stepped inside. A young man in a soft leather jacket played a video game. Adam caught a glimpse of a spaceship shattering into fragments, somewhere in the black depths of another galaxy, another time. Cuvillier shook his hand and indicated a chair. Cuvillier ordered him a coffee, he smiled, he placed calloused fingers on Adam's shoulder, he smiled and his eyes sparkled, "We are beginning to make progress, Monsieur Füst," he said. "But we have been very stupid. We never ran a check on your wife. At least not until now. You see, monsieur, and I'm not sure it makes much of a difference, but we've just put your wife's name through the computer at immigration and naturalization. Your wife first came to Paris nearly eighteen months earlier than you'd said she had. And before you and she met she left France on three occasions. Twice she traveled to London and once to Madrid. She only stayed a night or two on each occasion."

He listened as Cuvillier repeated what he had said. The Inspector referred to his pocket notebook, he gave the dates of Honnie's little trips to London and Madrid. He said that Honnie had been in France for a year and a half before she'd met Adam.

He thought of what Toto had said: *Versailles, Fontainebleau; a warehouse in Nanterre. She'd had to travel a bit, usually in the afternoons:* that's what Toto had said. These would never appear in the computer.

The Inspector said "What? What was that?"

"Monique," Adam repeated more clearly. "To Maurice Borrel my wife was known as Monique."

Cuvillier wrote it down. He asked Monique what? And Adam said Just Monique. Cuvillier looked at him and said, "Ah."

He said, "There's something else. The records at immigration and naturalization are very comprehensive. When she traveled abroad she was always accompanied by Maurice Borrel. Or at least he always traveled on the same flights. Some things are beyond coincidence."

He lit a cigarette and squinted at Adam as the smoke curled up to his eye. Adam watched the doorway as a man in a raincoat entered. A few of the people at the tables offered a few grunted syllables of greeting. The man seemed familiar to Adam; he said, "Who is that?"

Cuvillier smiled, he made a noise in the back of his throat, he said something about a big deal in the Sûreté, he asked the waiter to bring two more coffees.

Adam said, "My wife."

Cuvillier shrugged and shook his head. He said, "We don't want to jump to conclusions, monsieur. As I said, Jacques Borrel, the brother of Maurice and the man who recently had been murdered, was very deeply involved with prostitution. He wasn't exactly a pimp, a procurer. Most of his money came from the distribution of pornography, magazines, films, devices."

Devices. The word struck Adam as being profoundly evil. Devices. Such a neutral word, it could include anything, instruments of torture, surgical knives, things sexual, its meaning was manifold. "We knew he had women who worked for him," Cuvillier went on, "but he wasn't a pimp in the strict sense of the word, not the sort of man who works the streets and skims off the wages of his girls. Jacques Borrel was too big for that. He," and Cuvillier could not quite find the words, he shook his head slightly, his eyes shifted from west to east, "he, there was also the question of an unsolved murder a few years ago, just before his brother Maurice disappeared. A woman was found in an abandoned well on a farm outside Pithiviers. She'd been dead, oh, two or three weeks maybe. It was known she'd worked for Borrel. They found her floating on the scum of the well, in the water. Her name was Gina, a Corsican girl, on the streets she was known as Chita. Everyone knew she'd worked for him, she'd been working for him until the day she disappeared, but there wasn't enough evidence to convict him. He claimed he'd been in Australia at the time, visiting friends. Apparently it was true." He shrugged. "Perhaps Maurice was the culprit. But the man who owned the farm had a simpleminded son. They locked up the son instead of Borrel." He squinted at Adam Füst. "Easier that way."

Adam thought of Honnie in a well. He thought of her last moments alive. He saw an eclipse of the sun. The word *swagman* came to mind; he said, "You think Honnie was a whore."

"I never said that, Monsieur Füst. Never. I only said she'd traveled abroad on three occasions with Maurice Borrel. That could mean anything. Perhaps she was his mistress." He shrugged. "His secretary. She never spoke to you about any of this, her past?"

I have had eighty-three men, she once told him. He shook his head. "Never," he said.

"I've asked that the search for your wife's body be extended beyond the city limits. It's quite obvious that after Maurice Borrel's death she somehow got involved with his brother. Your wife disappeared shortly before Jacques Borrel's murder. Therefore, monsieur, we must conclude that," and then he was interrupted, he excused himself and walked away and took the telephone from the bartender.

Adam sat alone and looked at his coffee. Like meteors on an August night, questions passed brightly through his mind and then burned themselves out. He looked at the window of the café and saw the reflection of the bar, the other patrons, himself. He imagined what was beyond it all, the Hôtel Dieu, the Préfecture de Police, the Palais de Justice, the Seine. He thought of the night and the rain. Now he wanted to see proof of Honnie's death. Now he wanted a body produced. Now he wished the hauntings to end.

Cuvillier stood before him, he said, "I must return to work, something has come up, something unrelated to your wife's case."

The man in the raincoat passed by and patted the Inspector on the shoulder before leaving. "Big shot," Cuvillier wisecracked to Adam after the man had left.

When he returned to the apartment LouLou was sitting in the chair with the India print, in her underwear, a cigarette between her fingers, waiting for him. She looked lovely in the subdued light from the lamp, pink and lithe. She smiled at him, and this time her smile seemed less innocent. He felt something move within him and he held out his hand to her. She said nothing. She pressed her lips to his forehead and made him kneel on the floor beside the chair. He watched her thin thighs tighten as her knees dropped to the rug. Honnie had traveled abroad with Maurice Borrel. She had lived in France for eighteen months before meeting Adam. She had lied to him that first night, the night with Mingus and the bandage on her back and the delicate flesh at the top of her thighs, the earthy delicious taste of her sex, she had lied to him afterward. He remembered once thinking: *lovers for five years, a married couple for three, strangers for two weeks.* But he had been wrong. They had always been strangers.

12

THE FIRST DAY OF SHOOTING WAS FRAUGHT WITH CHAOS. It took place just outside and within the *pigeonnier* in Chantilly. Though chronologically late in the story, it was the key scene in the film, the opening scene, the point at which memory blossomed and fate was determined, the beginning, the end. Adam had caught a glimpse of the run-through staged earlier that morning. Through the door he saw the German actress in a torn dress. Her left breast was visible, the nipple highlighted with rouge. Wrapped around her head was a thick blindfold torn from an old sheet. Later she would be smeared with mud and fake blood. Her wrists were bound together with electrical cable. On her face was a distressing look of pain and resignation. Afterward she complained of a headache and Adam had to fetch two aspirins from the glove box in the Renault.

It had rained for the most of the night. Clipboard in hand, Adam stood in four inches of mud. When he tried to lift his right foot the earth clung to it, refused to let him go. It made a loud sucking noise as he freed it. Gabor's crew had laid down a plank floor for the director and his cameraman. Over it they had thrown two or three blankets to muffle the noise of the boards. In trailers hired for the location shots the actors and actresses were dressed and made up for their scenes. Adam looked at the sky. What had begun as a cloudless cool morning had rapidly become a hot, overcast day. The air was thick with the smells of manure and freshly cut grass, a trace of ozone. He inhaled the odors and felt his feet sink into the mud. His head cleared, for a moment he smiled, then the door to a trailer opened and the German actress, wrapped in a blue terrycloth robe, stepped hurriedly down onto a strip of plastic sheeting and proceeded toward the *pigeonnier*.

Though by now he knew it almost by heart, Adam referred to the script once again. His copy was heavily annotated. He knew which scenes were to be filmed on a closed set, which required authorization for location shots in Paris, which members of the crew were needed at various points. He watched Gabor as he raged about in his gumboots, waving his arms, screaming orders in three different languages. The owner of the farm kept his distance, standing beyond a fence, iron rake in hand, bemusedly watching the anarchy as he sipped coffee from a mug.

Five crows flew overhead, loudly cawing. Gabor looked up, pointed, waved his hand, spoke to himself. It was as if he wished to harness all of nature for his opening shot, from the weather to the birds of the sky, the weeds that grew in wiry abundance around the stone *pigeonnier*, the gnarled moribund trees skirting the perimeter of the property. Adam thought about LouLou back at the office, listening to the radio, answering the phone, reading a novel, waiting for him.

Since meeting Cuvillier that night three weeks earlier in the Achéron he had heard nothing more, nothing definite. He would never see Honnie again. It was what he had said to LouLou upon his return that night. *I will never see Honnie again.* LouLou had smiled and caressed his cheek with her fingertips. She no longer appeared pitiful to him. Now she seemed infused with power, with lust and triumph. She said that life would have to go on, with or without Honnie, it was what she had learned when her mother died. When they made love she spoke aloud, she spoke vulgarly, sometimes she shouted *Do this to me, do that, put it there, thrust thrust, push harder:* as if seeking the threshold of pain. Adam became lost in her sexuality, he sank into it as one without strength drowns in a river in flood.

The young English actress smiled at Adam as she watched Gabor shoot the bleak exterior shots. The film opened with a long static monochrome view of the round stone structure, followed by three black-and-white shots of it closer in, from other angles. Over it would be heard the sound of the ubiquitous crows, the lowing of a cow. Then, as the titles rolled, the audience would become aware of the quiet demented humming of a young woman.

Adam had come to like the young English actress. She was shyer and more intelligent than LouLou had made her out to be. She had studied at RADA in London. She had done some television work, stage plays as well. Her boyfriend in London was studying art at the Slade. They shared a flat in Battersea, south of the Thames. She smiled at Adam: in a childlike face a mature, sensual smile. That was what made her so attractive, so much the center of attention in a scene: that smile, it was alive, it sparked off hints, it moved your heart. In less than an hour she would become the licentious young English wife of a French security guard. LouLou came to hate her.

A week after meeting Cuvillier Adam had phoned him from a café near the Sacré-Coeur. He felt uncomfortable ringing from the apartment. *I will never see Honnie again*, he had told LouLou, and she had somehow interpreted this to mean that he would never speak of her, think of her again. It was as if she had, in one rough stroke, buried his past.

He wondered what images LouLou would create for him in the future. He could not imagine her sitting still, cigarette in hand, thinking. Neither could he see her floating on the surface of a lake. There seemed something unpoetic about LouLou. And this struck him as odd, he seemed to be entangled in a web of paradoxes, for Honnie, though sensuous, though a woman who made you constantly aware of her flesh, her body, conjured up emblematic, unworldly images that begged for interpretation; while LouLou, who at times seemed so airy, so lost in her thoughts, in her solitude elicited nothing but physical desire, domination. Even the notion seemed tangled, too many words, too many phrases, too much collision; no sense.

On the telephone Cuvillier sounded solemn, he said he was working on Adam's case day and night. "One of our informers had heard that Jacques Borrel was associated with a woman named Monique. He said he thought he'd even seen her once, about a year ago at a party on a yacht moored at Saint-Cloud. His description of her matches that of your wife. He hadn't seen her or heard about her for a few months. Then we're questioning someone who used to work for Borrel. And we've heard that human remains have been found in some woods near Fontainebleau." After a pause the Inspector said, "Borrel kept a house there, you see."

Adam asked if the Inspector had found the waiter at the hotel near the airport. Cuvillier claimed he'd questioned two or three of them, but none resembling the one Adam had met. Adam remembered the smell of perspiration, the stained eyes, the yellow teeth, the stink of corruption. He thought of a dark corridor, a room with lockers, the chill damp of chambers beneath the surface of the earth. He felt nothing, he said, "So you'll."

And Cuvillier interrupted, "I'll be in touch, Monsieur Füst."

He felt refreshed standing in the mud. He looked down and saw the worms gleefully twisting into the damp clumps of earth. He saw a bone, shorn of meat and bleached of its color, left perhaps by a dog. Ashes to ashes, he thought. He remembered what Cuvillier had said during the phone conversation. Human remains had been found in Fontainebleau. Adam looked at the earth. Above he saw layers of clouds, he heard the distant harmless rumble of thunder, he thought of the curvature of the earth. He looked at the *pigeonnier* and thought of a man wearing goggles, displaying a photograph of a naked woman. He felt intense heat. He smelled the richness of earth. He tasted fish oil. The English actress asked him for a light, she said, "You like working for Gabor?"

He smiled, he said, "Yes, of course."

She always giggled when Adam spoke, she said she loved his accent. He recalled the photos of her Gabor had shown him: sitting naked on a sofa, her small firm breasts bared. He wanted to say to her, *You have beautiful breasts, you have a beautiful body.* It was her first major film. Her complexion took his breath away. He said, "You look nice today."

She blushed, she said, "Thanks."

Honnie was dead. He was free to do what he liked: an idiotic expression. When Honnie was alive he had felt no sense of confinement, of suffocation. Within their marriage he was liberated, he was liberated with Honnie, together they enjoyed the easy living of a happy marriage. Now that she was dead he could ask the young English actress to come to his flat, to eat his food and drink his wine and listen to his music and giggle and make love. But that was impossible. Honnie absent had left him bound and gagged, unaware of direction, unable to take a definite step, vertiginous, sickened by his ignorance.

Gabor emerged from the *pigeonnier* and walked over to Adam. He looked at the woman, he looked at Adam, he smiled and touched the corner of his eyepatch, in Hungarian he said, "I'm sick and tired of this bullshit. Tomorrow we begin an hour earlier. Make sure it is posted, okay?" He turned away and announced something through his bullhorn. The young English actress said it was time to have her makeup applied, time to change into costume. She touched Adam's arm and he looked down at her short, slim fingers, at the lovely unpainted nails, at the pale hairs on her arm. Her costume for her first scene was a pair of tight shorts and a white blouse tied at the midriff, below her breasts. He smiled and wished her luck. She went up on her toes and gave him a friendly kiss on the cheek.

It was odd.

It was odd because as heretofore he had always had a rather complex view of Honnie as a woman of various faces, moods, images, reflections, he now saw her in a completely different way. He imagined her standing in a doorway, in some hellish back street of the demimonde, clicking her tongue at tired businessmen and ministers of state. He imagined her in a bedroom in some grim two-star hotel, asking what the gentleman would prefer this evening. He imagined her forgetting him, Adam Füst, her husband. He thought of private services. None of this could be reconciled with the Honnie who stood in a cold disused chapel and lost her faith, who floated naked on a still Swiss lake, who sat in the chair with the India print and remained immobile in thought, cigarette to her lips.

And what was most odd about it was that there seemed no earthly reason for him to reconcile the two Honnies. He knew one of them, he knew Honnie. Other men were unaware of her, they had known only Monique. He pictured some industrial magnate lying in bed, sweating and remembering that night with her. He wondered what she had done with the industrial magnate. Had she straddled him? Had she lighted his cigar? Had he offered her a hot tip on the stock market? Had the question of fellatio been introduced during the course of conversation? Had they drunk champagne? Or perhaps he was an aficionado of kink, perhaps he had asked her to bind him to the bed, to disguise herself in some peculiar way, as a nurse or Mrs. Thatcher or the Duchesse de Guermantes, to whip him until his body was wracked with orgasm. Adam shook his head violently to remove the image from it. He smelled the air. He felt the earth grasping at the soles of his sneakers. He thought of a lake in Switzerland. He listened as the German actress hummed quietly to herself within the *pigeonnier.*

Sometimes he would be walking with Honnie down a boulevard, or sitting at a café table having a drink with friends, and he would look at her as she discussed French socialism or the latest film by Resnais and remembered her from that morning, lying naked on their bed, grasping him between her thighs, moaning deliciously as they made love. Perhaps that was what made women so desirable: the contrast. Perhaps it was why men lusted and raped: to see a woman do what men thought was the unimaginable. It seemed absurd. Why unimaginable? Men were easy to picture in bed, grunting and gasping, the physical act of sex seeming to set a pattern for their lives: invade, conquer, thrust, plunge, dominate. With women it was different, they were like Chinese puzzles, they wore their secrets within. With them there was a contrast between propriety and sexuality; between lingerie and flesh; the nights and days of their moods.

He listened as Gabor shouted and raged and demanded a retake. The German actress stepped out of the *pigeonnier* and slapped her forehead. She had had enough. She had had enough, even though, as everyone very well knew, she had only been in front of the camera for all of three minutes. Gabor had intended to spend six weeks on the project. It would be a long spring; spring would extend into summer. The question of budget would be raised. Gabor went to her and put his arm around her petite shoulders. He whispered pleasantries and soothing homilies into her ear. Adam remembered her from the film he and Honnie had seen in Zurich. He remembered her naked body, how she had sucked circles into the Englishman's hairless chest. He thought of a woman's body, how it seemed to be divided precisely into two parts, cleft neatly down the middle, how much more complex and natural it seemed than a man's, as if it reflected the perfection of a seashell, the aesthetic certainty of an orchid. He wondered how much of Honnie he had ever really known. He considered it and the thought depressed him. He would return to the office, to LouLou, he would kiss her lips and he would think of this woman he had known as Honnie.

It was LouLou's idea to invite Johnny Vodo and Eva to dinner. Adam hadn't been at all keen on it. "Johnny is fine, I like Johnny, he is great fun," he said, though he wondered what LouLou would make of the cocaine, the opium, and hashish Adam hoped his friend would bring along with him, the tangy oblivions of the underworld. "It is Eva I find difficult, she is so silent, she gives me the creeps."

LouLou had never met Eva Vodo. She said, "It doesn't matter. We need to see more people."

We.

Adam had refused to move into LouLou's flat, despite her requests. The thought of spending the rest of his life in a pink apartment with his every movement overseen by the malign uncomical Coco appalled him. And he was still married to Honnie, the apartment was hers to return to, he would wait there in solitude until he knew definitely what had happened to her.

Yet four nights out of seven were spent together, usually at his place. LouLou had become a form of addiction for him; he wished to suck her dry of her narcotic properties, her gingery nature. She sat in the chair with the India print and smoked her Gitanes and looked at him.

Johnny was pleased with LouLou. He liked her looks, Adam could see that. Adam had rung him earlier from the Picard to beg him not to mention Honnie. There seemed little point extending the request to Eva. Johnny brought a chunk of Moroccan opium and some grass. He reached into his pocket and produced a ball of aluminum foil. He unwrapped it. Five pills of varying colors were revealed. He said, "I bought these from a man I met on the corner. A Senegalese."

Adam stared at them; he asked, "But what do they do? Make you sleep, keep you awake, give you visions?" He knew of Johnny's habit of trusting anyone who sold anything illicit. He thought of a man lying on the floor, blood and foam at the lips, dying of poison, *Thna-thna*. Johnny shrugged and popped one in his mouth. Adam pictured him becoming paralyzed. He thought of Johnny going insane and flinging himself out the apartment window, taking an unsuspecting LouLou with him. He wondered if Eva would remain silent. He shook his head and puffed happily on a joint and sipped strong red wine. LouLou took Eva by the arm and whispered under her breath.

Johnny said quietly, "Any news, man?"

Adam shook his head. "Nothing."

"I couldn't find out who'd had the photo last."

"It doesn't matter." He hadn't told Johnny about Monique or Maurice Borrel. He felt diminished in the shadow of Honnie's secret life.

Adam put on some music, Eric Dolphy at the Five Spot. Johnny tapped his feet and wiggled his head and slapped his hands on his knees and sang *Bop-bambam* when Ed Blackwell took a drum solo. Adam grew quickly disgusted. He grew disgusted with the musicians, Eric Dolphy and Booker Little and the rest of the band, Mal Waldron and Richard Davis, anything that deviated from stillness. Eva and LouLou sat on the sofa. LouLou was saying, "I'm interested in Sweden. Tell me about it.

I want to hear about the sun never setting." Adam thought of a vast tundra, of people going insane for want of night. Eva said nothing and looked intently at the floor, as if messages of import were to be found there, formed by ants perhaps, or microbes of some sort; Adam shook his head at the folly of it all.

Eva had lost weight, she looked less solid, more ethereal, curiously transparent. He could see the veins through her skin. He thought of her and Johnny together, he thought: like black and white. Adam conjured up an image of the Swedish woman defying gravity, gaining altitude, floating off into the clouds, her arms extended, circling the earth, touring the stratosphere, silently like a spy plane, passing before the eternal sun, he giggled and said "Pah!" and realized he was high as a kite, he hadn't felt so good in months. He heard himself say, "I once had a funny notion about Sonny Rollins," then realized he was about to relate the scene of Eva's death.

LouLou and Eva stood by the stove. LouLou could with some facility cook only soft foods. It was something she had had to learn during the last five years of her mother's life. Her mother had been unable to feed herself, she swallowed only with difficulty, and so LouLou had learned to reduce edibles to a soft vomitlike mush. Adam had taught her to prepare chicken so that it could be chewed. He revealed the secret of cooking sausages so that they remained within their skins. He took her to restaurants to show her how normal people dined. Over his shoulder Johnny looked at her, he said, "Sexy chick."

"Yes," said Adam. He had never thought of LouLou as a sexy chick. Sexy Chick. It conjured up images of Honnie in a tight skirt, tantalizing men of the street. It made him think of Toto Roget, with his grandiose fantasies, screaming sodomy and oiled bosoms and afterwards a bite and a drink. Sexy chick. Slick chick. Sick chick. He didn't want to give Johnny Vodo the impression that he had replaced Honnie with LouLou; he said,

"She's been a good friend through it all," and then Johnny and he laughed because it sounded like a line from an American television program.

Through it all. Honnie had rung him how many times? Once certainly; possibly twice. *Don't worry*, she'd said one morning just before dawn, *I'll be all right*. Adam puffed on the joint and passed it to Johnny as they stood by the window overlooking the Café Picard. Adam felt the delicious smoke fill his lungs, he tasted the bitter weed on his tongue, he looked forward to a bubbling bowl of opium: sleep; dreams: oblivion. It had been two months since that last morning, lying in her bath, *I'm fine*, Honnie was saying and then she was gone. Sexy chick.

Bitch. The word sprang instantly to his lips.

He thought of her during the long hours when he was working for Gabor, during the filming of *Reparations* and at other times, he wondered if she had been thinking of him while she fucked her clients, collected her fees. Cuvillier had never come out and said it: Honnie was a whore. He had wanted Adam to reach that conclusion on his own. The morals of society were the business of others. Death was what interested Inspector Cuvillier. He pronounced Honnie dead. He quoted statistics. He spoke deliciously of bodies found in walls. He lived from one corpse to the next. "What?" said Johnny Vodo, looking at him.

Adam shook his head. Bitch. Whore. Scum. He felt humiliated by Honnie. He felt his head reel. He looked out onto the street and watched the rain fall. He hated the people who darted across the road, huddled beneath their umbrellas. He hated humanity. He pressed his hand against the window until it shattered. The pain in his wound delighted him.

Now it happened that Adam Füst wished to kill his wife Honnie. He could not at first understand this homicidal impulse, especially as it had become quite clear that Honnie was already dead.

Already dead. Words without substance, meaning nothing. He felt cheated. Honnie's life had eluded him, as had her death. He wanted to track her down and push her against a wall and place his hands around her throat and squeeze the breath out of her lungs. He wanted to be present when her heart stopped, when her eyes went blank, when her last word was strangled into silence.

He thought of this as LouLou bandaged his hand and Johnny stared at him and Eva looked into her glass of wine and nodded her head, as if she had foreseen the terrible fall of Adam Füst.

"It was an accident," he said. Johnny was on the floor, on his knees, giggling and trying to pick up the pieces of glass. The smell of burning fowl filled the apartment. The music had come to an end.

Eva and LouLou went into the kitchenette. Adam could see that LouLou had fallen into the trap. Terrified of Eva's silences she was trying desperately to fill the void with sentences, recipes, memories, hopes, and delusions. Johnny said, "Oh man."

Adam smiled at him. He felt insane. Not like before, not as if things were out of control, but truly helplessly mad, beyond cure, a babbling idiot whose vision of the world was of the realms of dream and nightmare. Since the moment he had pictured himself murdering Honnie her name had lost something of its potency. And because of this his hatred had nothing in which to fix its claws, its teeth. Grief had given way to anger; anger to indifference, the indifference of one stranger for another. His disgust with Honnie now turned upon himself. He felt only waste.

He sat on the sofa and watched his bandage turn dark red. He wondered how much blood he would have to lose before he began to feel the effects of death. He imagined it as a gradual diminishing of strength, as after an arduous day one succumbs to a delicious exhaustion. Johnny bared his white teeth and giggled, "Oh man," he was saying. LouLou came to Adam and examined his wounded hand, letting it rest on her ten fingers. She shook her head, she said, "Dinner will be ready in a few minutes." Adam wondered if she were of peasant stock, if her ancestors accidentally hacked off their arms or legs and happily stumped back to work, because the harvest demanded it. She raised her eyes to his. Honnie would have kissed his hand, called him *silly boy* and worried about it for an hour or two. LouLou gazed at him with contempt, as if she possessed the ability to read his thoughts, to see the images that played upon the screen of his mind. He wondered if when her mother died she had dismissed her memory with such insouciant ease. He looked at LouLou and thought her sick. She was mad, insane, delirious with the morbidity of her life. He thought of Coco the Clown. He pictured a pubescent LouLou carefully sketching the monster, her body blossoming into womanhood, her imagination feeding her images of a happy fulfilled life. Now what had she? An empty apartment that stank of her dead mother. A thankless job working as secretary for a famous one-eyed film director who vomits on the rug. A wounded lover who mourned a wife he had never truly known.

He thought of her in bed, thrusting her body at him, demanding pain, shouting in the misery of her pleasure. Perhaps she believed she had found in Adam Füst a kindred soul, a disappointed man who wished only to die in the naïve heights of ecstasy. He saw her now as a small animal wracked by terrible disfiguring disease. The idea of putting her out of her misery came to him. He saw his hands snapping her frail neck. He looked at her and felt only pity. He pitied her because he could do nothing for her. He could not carry her away into a better life. He could not love her. Paradise did not reside within Adam Füst.

13

NOW CAME THE HEAT WAVE.
Now it came back to him.

It began the following Monday, when Gabor was expected to complete location shots in Chantilly. He was already behind schedule. The German actress had twice walked off the set, on each occasion disappearing for twenty-four hours, only to be discovered staying with an old boyfriend in Montparnasse, pouting when Gabor came to the door, saying No no and bursting into tears. It was a personal matter, Gabor explained to Adam, though it was obvious Gabor was at sea, he was losing his lover, his best actress. That morning at the office Gabor had said to Adam, "Tomorrow we shoot at Printemps. You phoned the people there to remind them, yes?"

Adam nodded, he said all the arrangements had been confirmed, Gabor and his crew were expected at the department store at half past eight the next morning.

Gabor smiled and scratched his head. He was wearing faded black jeans, black T-shirt, a jacket he had bought in a New York boutique, a strange satiny garment advertising a bowling club in Kansas City. His hair had grown long, it fell almost to his shoulders. He hadn't shaved in a week; a small handsome beard, tinged with red, lent definition to his tanned face. Adam wiped his brow with his sleeve. The air was thick with moisture, it smelled of decay. Guy Lanson and Gabor had spent the weekend working on rewrites. LouLou was expected to finish typing and photocopying them later that day.

Today Gabor was due to reshoot the opening scenes of the film: the *pigeonnier* alone, viewed from a distance and then closer up; afterward the action that was taking place within the round stone structure. He would have the sound of crows. He would try to calm the rages of the German actress. He would attempt to capture the ineluctable horror of the scene, the contrast between the beauty of the day, the cows lowing, the blades of grass, the wildflowers, and the tortures Solange was enduring at the hands of her fellow human beings. That was how Gabor had put it in his latest draft for a press release: Cannes, its festival and starlets, was very much in his future. There would be controversy: the scenes of sadism, of sexual terror, were to be intermittently graphic, shocking, always suggestive. Adam leafed through his copy of the script. In one of the *pigeonnier* scenes Solange would be tormented by the young Englishwoman while her husband, the store detective, looked on through a hole in the door. He would glimpse the bare flesh of the two women. He would listen to his wife's whispered taunts. He would break into a sweat as the imagination of the audience twisted and delighted in its wickedness. Gabor would once again be accused of exploitation. Adam remembered the red palm prints, the way the director's mother was led backward toward her bedroom. He pictured the father collapsing onto the floor, the blood spurting from his throat onto Gabor's uncompleted puzzle. *He blinked and then he.*

Gabor felt the less people who were there that day, the easier it would be for the German actress to finish her scenes. Adam was asked to remain at the office with LouLou. There were phone calls to be made on the director's behalf. There were script rewrites to proofread and collate, documents to prepare. There were things to do, small, mindless things.

He stood by the window and watched as Gabor climbed into a van driven by the sound technician, a Corsican named Tony. Gabor lifted his face toward Adam's. Adam thought of the young English actress. He imagined her stripping off her clothes in the hot, damp *pigeonnier*. He felt nothing but the heat. Now it was coming back to him.

It was the first day of summer. Even at half past eight in the morning the sun was blazing behind a thin haze, a disc yellow and aflame, low on the horizon. An old woman walked a poodle along the pavement, before the shops and houses. The creature moved its wet black nose along the surface of the ground, it sniffed out the scents of Paris. Adam tasted metal on his tongue. He felt something go chill inside him, in his heart, his memory. He thought of a door holding back the winter. Now it came back to him.

LouLou stopped typing a few minutes after Gabor left. She appeared in the doorway as Adam turned from the window. For the past two nights they had slept apart, in their own flats, a result of the argument they had had the night Johnny and Eva Vodo came to visit. After Johnny and Eva left she had said, "You are like a child, you only want pity."

He was sitting on the chair with the India print, he looked at his hand. The bandage had grown stiff with dried blood. It gave off a peculiar odor, like wine on the verge of becoming vinegar. He looked at the plates on the table, the incinerated, uneaten chicken, the pale slops of puréed vegetables, the vile yellow pudding LouLou had prepared for dessert. Eva had eaten nothing, she had sat and stared at the edge of the table. Johnny only picked at the crisp black skin of the chicken and occasionally burst into uncontrollable laughter as it turned to cinders between his fingers. Adam kept saying, "Mm, this is delicious,

LouLou, a little dry perhaps, but very tasty. Very nice," and he, too, could not keep from laughing, the universe had outdone itself, turned inward, become absurd.

"You are a child," she was saying. He remembered the Citadella Tool Works. He remembered being a little boy. He wondered if maturity meant outgrowing mysteries. She said, "Come to bed. Come to bed now, we'll take care of the dishes in the morning." He looked at her without desire. He wondered why it was impossible to make love to a pitiful woman. He looked at his hand, at the Eric Dolphy record revolving silently on the turntable, the tone arm immobile on its little post. He reached forward and switched it off. He watched the little blue light on the amplifier fade to black. Everything seemed to shimmer with mystery, to radiate with question. LouLou unbuttoned her blouse. He said, "Go."

That Monday morning, the first day of the heat wave, she had greeted him with a nod and a cool *Bonjour* when she arrived at eight. Adam had been there since seven, expecting to drive Gabor to Chantilly.

The image of the van turning the corner, disappearing from view, lingered in his memory as he watched the old woman with her poodle. He thought of a woman interred behind a fresco. The smell of corrupt flesh passed elusively through his mind. He saw himself on his knees in the cottage in Oberwil, carefully removing a floorboard with a screwdriver he kept in the Fiat, trying to locate the source of the odor.

From the office doorway LouLou said, "Your hand."

He looked at it. He no longer needed a large bandage. He had not bothered going to a hospital, the idea of it revolted him, it brought to mind a female corpse on a chrome table, scribbled writing on the wall, the dampness of a basement, he said his hand was much better, fine.

LouLou smiled coldly. He looked at her eyes, he turned away and looked at the sun. She said, "We've got the place to ourselves. Do you remember that morning I came in and found you sleeping on the floor?"

He looked across the road toward the window of the apartment. The windows were open. Flowers grew in a window box. A middle-aged woman fed them water from a china pitcher. He recalled the night, the dagger and the gibbous moon and the woman with her knees raised, her legs parted. Now everything seemed part of a vast mystery. The world seemed strewn with waste. He had wasted his pity on LouLou, she had stolen it from him. He had spent it on her instead of the woman who needed it most. He thought of Honnie after the incident in the chapel. He felt that whatever had happened there was somehow connected with her life as Monique, her past, her disappearance, her death.

She had lived in Paris for a year and a half before meeting Adam. Eighteen months. Had she been Monique before that evening at the café, the Mingus, the smiles and the looks? He remembered the bandage on her back. She said she had fallen down the steps of the métro near the Jeu de Paume. She took his hand and placed it on her breast. He pictured some man hurting her, breaking the skin, making her suffer, throwing money at her naked body and disappearing from sight.

The pity had been wasted on LouLou, because this pity had been reserved for Honnie. Perhaps life had somehow disappointed Honnie. Not disappointed: repelled, disgusted, he could not find the word to express what she must have felt. Bereft. Now it came to him. Honnie felt bereft, just as he felt bereft, it was a kind of algebraic equation with scattered unknowns appearing throughout.

Now his life with Honnie seemed somehow different, as if the knowledge of her career as Monique added other colors, provided new perspectives. He thought of her in the chapel; floating on the lake near Oberwil; sitting on the chair with the

India print; and it seemed to him that perhaps all this stillness had been deceptive, that beneath it was raging a battle between Honnie and Monique. It was beyond him now.

LouLou said, "You'll never see Honnie again." She sat on his desk and looked at him. Her eyes were filled with contempt. Honnie had become a kind of dreaded disease, a great contagion that threatened the future of human life. Adam looked at her bare knees, the muscular ascent of her thighs. He smelled her scent, Honnie's scent, L'Heure Bleue. Her mouth was twisted. He looked across the room at her desk. He could hear the hum of her typewriter. Momentarily he thought of going into Gabor's office, taking out the revolver and murdering LouLou. Afterward he would shoot himself in the mouth, he would scatter his sodden grey memories across the walls, the posters, the windows. He tasted metal. He thought of a great door. He felt simultaneously hot and cold, he said, "Does it matter that much to you?"

"I want to marry you, Adam," she said.

Honnie was dead, he would never see her face, he would never speak to her again. That was it, that was the curse: he would never speak to her again. He would never be able to ask her why this had happened. The mystery seized his brain. The telephone rang.

It was Cuvillier. His voice startled him. The Inspector said, "I tried to reach you at your apartment." He said, "Don't try to ring me at the office today, I won't be in, I think I may be on to something."

Adam's vision became acute, things on his desk leaped out at him in terrible detail, he said, "Have you," and Cuvillier said, "Nothing like that, nothing definite, there's no body, not yet, no. The remains we found in Fontainebleau had nothing to do with your wife." His voice fluttered with agitation, excitement, the thrill of a corpse to be found beneath six inches of soil, fished from the rapacious vegetation of a river. He said, "But I think we're finally getting someplace. Look," he said, "all I can say right now is that the investigation may be nearly over."

Adam strained to grasp his meaning. LouLou had disappeared. Gabor's office had disappeared. The block of flats across the road had disappeared, as had the sun, the sky, the present and future, the universe was full of eclipse and anticipation. Cuvillier spoke in a raspy, sober whisper, from the background noises it was clear he was in a café or bistro; he said, "Just don't try to contact me at my office or speak to anyone else here, you understand? Don't tell anyone that I rang, not even another cop. I'll try to get back to you later, monsieur. Just stay where you are, I may have some news for you then," and then there was a click and the dial tone, and Adam looked up at LouLou, his face tingling, burning. He said, "There may be news about my wife today."

LouLou returned to her desk. Before resuming typing she looked at Adam. She tried to find the words to express herself. She said, "Bastard," and then pressed her fingers to the keys.

Adam walked into Gabor's office. He pulled open the windows and stepped onto the narrow balcony. He gripped the railing and looked down and felt afraid, as if something within him, some incomprehensible corner of his heart, might compel him to throw himself onto the pavement below. He stepped back into the room and watched life resume. The old woman with the poodle reversed direction. He listened to LouLou's typing. He felt his heart beating. He sat behind Gabor's desk and stared at the telephone. He thought of how quickly LouLou's adoration of him had turned to hatred. She was filled with violence, in bed she directed it against herself; beyond the walls of his flat she victimized him. Now it was as if something had clicked inside her, as if an already weakened fault line had begun to give way, her equilibrium about to be shattered forever. He thought of what she had told him about her mother, how when she first became ill her father became a philanderer, how he picked up women and gave them money and had a son by some other woman he knew. Her mother detested men, she spoke of them in generalities, with distrust, her contempt was of complex design, fraught with degrees like ripples surrounding a violent fall. She had bequeathed it to her daughter. Adam wondered if people who so easily fell to hatred at heart only loathed themselves. LouLou had become like a loaded pistol in the hands of a lunatic, it was impossible to say who would suffer next. He thought of Honnie walking through the door, smiling, raising her arms to him, being shot dead by the insane secretary.

He put his hands to his face and laughed. He remembered Cuvillier's voice, the excitement punctuating his phrases, and as he thought of this he looked through the window and saw the world in a different light. Now Adam Füst filled with hope; now he began to think of the future.

He sat at Gabor's desk and began to sort out some papers that would have to be sent to Gabor's lawyer, Maître Blanchet, before Wednesday. For a moment the silence of the office startled him into stillness. He listened to it and held his breath, it frightened him, it was the stillness of death, it brought to mind the mute mother of Madame Moreau. The day after her body had been taken away he had gone down to the concierge to pay his respects. A great weight had been lifted, Madame Moreau said, her old mother had suffered so. Adam said he was sorry, and Madame Moreau put her handkerchief to her eye and smiled and said *Merci*, how kind you are, Monsieur Füst, though it was clear to him she was the second happiest person in the world, the first being Monsieur Moreau, who was staggering boozily about the kitchen in his bedroom slippers.

Adam heard a click and then the sound of rock music on the radio, the ticking and tocking and shifting of LouLou's typewriter. It took him thirty-five minutes to go through the papers. He copied six of them on the office machine and placed them in a folder. The envelope was already addressed. In a song on LouLou's radio a sinister American man sang *This is the end my only friend the end.* He checked through the documents one last time and prepared them for posting.

The activity soothed him, it calmed his excitement. He thought of Cuvillier tracking Honnie down. He remembered the Inspector sniffing her camisole, inhaling the scent of her breasts, trying to reconstruct her face, the texture and curves of her body. He rose from the chair and moved quietly to the doorway. He watched LouLou's back as she continued typing. He wondered which scene she was working on. He wondered if it was stimulating her imagination. He thought of the tune "Lonely Woman," Ornette's grieving alto sax, the itchy rhythm of bass and drums. She seemed so small, LouLou, sitting at her desk, and yet that was an illusion, she was a tall woman, per-haps even an inch taller than Honnie.

It was funny. Now that he seemed on the verge of finding Honnie, of being reunited with her, he felt suddenly aroused by the presence of LouLou. She was wearing a pale yellow dress with thin straps over her shoulders. He looked at her freckles. He looked at the back of her neck. If Honnie was alive, came back to him, he would never make love to LouLou again. In his mind her voice said, *Do whatever you want to me, hurt me.* He thought of the things Honnie had never let him do. He walked to her and pressed his lips against her skin, suddenly he felt as if all control had left him. She turned and raised her arms and at that moment, as they rose as one and went into Gabor's office, he saw that the two of them, Adam and LouLou, were wrapped in a blanket of deception and loss. She lay back on Gabor's desk and lifted and parted her legs as she unbuttoned her dress and exposed her breasts to him. In the hot sunlight he looked at her smooth thighs, the gingery hair between them, the darkness; he felt the sweat on his face.

Afterward she smoked a cigarette and said, "You'll marry me, then," and he stared out the window and said nothing, the sun beat down upon merciless Paris. Her hair was tousled, her eyes red from lack of sleep. Her dress still unbuttoned, she idly browsed through Gabor's desk drawers. Adam wondered whether she had ever done this before, especially as she spent so much time there alone. She looked at the magazine with the Swedish women and their Filipino beaux. She laughed and said the women were beautiful, she wished she were a blonde. She found Gabor's revolver and lifted it for a moment, her finger falling naturally to the curve of the trigger before replacing it.

Adam looked at his watch. It was almost eleven. The sun was nearly overhead, the obscene white dome of Sacré-Coeur blinding him with its brilliant indifference. He felt LouLou standing behind him. He hoped she would say nothing. He equated her marriage proposal with the idiotic false nose of Coco; her motives with the clown's vindictive, incisive stare. He looked away from Sacré-Coeur. He thought of the people buried beneath the soil of Paris. He considered Madame Moreau's mother in her coffin, in the heat wave, he thought of parched flesh and discolored bone and the warm, exhaled soul of a woman who said *Agn*.

From behind him LouLou pressed her hands to his chest and rested her head against his shoulder. He looked down at her slender fingers. She whispered, "Come home with me tonight."

He lied, he said, "Perhaps," and she was overjoyed, she smiled and hugged him and then the phone rang and Adam forgot she had ever existed, it was Gabor. "I thought," said Adam.

Gabor was interrupting in his native tongue, he said, "Listen."

Adam turned to LouLou. She was standing in the doorway, she looked horrified, the color had left her face. Gabor said,
"Something terrible has happened."

Adam stared at LouLou as he listened to Gabor. He swiveled
to look at Paris, the lowlands by the river. He saw nothing but
the words of Gabor. The director said, "Listen. I want you and
LouLou to stay in the office until I ring back, okay? There were
people who heard about it, witnesses, the fucking press will get
hold of it and they won't leave me alone. Listen to me. Stay in
the office. The newspapers will probably start calling at any
minute. Tell them she's all right. Tell them everything's under
control, the film is proceeding on schedule, everyone is confi-
dent, tell them to go fuck themselves, tell them whatever you
like, just don't repeat what I've told you, okay?"

Adam nodded, he said Yes. He replaced the receiver on the
hook, then thought twice and removed it and left it lying on the
desk. The dial tone hummed like an angry bee. Adam looked at
LouLou, he said, "There's been an accident."

He could almost see LouLou's imagination beginning
to work, like a child's kaleidoscope turning circles, changing
images, suggesting people dancing, people flying, people lying
down, animals gorging, she said, "Oh my Christ."

The face of Coco flashed into his mind. Adam said, "It wasn't
Gabor who was hurt." He stood by the window and related what
Gabor had told him. During a break in the filming the young
English actress had gone for a ride with one of the crew in his
hired jeep. They had raced off up a road and then cut across the
upper reaches of the farm on which the *pigeonnier* was located.
Gabor had thought nothing of it, he was sure sex was involved,
sex and a chat and a cigarette, that was all. The owner of the
property had been putting up some fencing.

Adam pictured the remainder of the scene. He saw the jeep
veering uncontrollably off the road, into the ditch, he saw the

pretty young woman being flung from the open vehicle, he saw her throat striking the wire, he saw her head rolling away in the dust, he said, "Ahh," and then ran off and vomited into the toilet.

When he returned to the office LouLou was in tears, even though he hadn't finished the story. He said, "Shut up," and when she didn't shut up, even after he repeated himself twice more, he slapped her across the face. He laughed as she stared at him. He saw her eyes shift an inch away from his face, toward Gabor's desk. He said, "I'm sorry." He held her. "It's horrible. She was so pretty."

"Yes," said LouLou. Her voice was suddenly distant, literally distant, as if she were speaking through several thicknesses of gauze, or a thin wall, or from the far end of another room. The scene of the young woman's death remained branded to his mind. He recalled what Gabor had said, that the guy with the jeep had returned screaming and in shock and Gabor had driven out with Tony the sound technician and found the actress, both parts of her, lying in a vast pool of blood. He remembered how Gabor described the scene. He though of Gabor's mother being pushed backward into her room, his father bleeding from the throat, blinking and dying. He thought of a head detached from its body. He remembered the actress vividly, the way she giggled whenever he spoke: now he is wishing her good luck, she stands on her toes and kisses his cheek and for a moment has sprung into life before dying, her head lies on the ground, a crow's meager supper.

For a moment the landscape went flat, he thought of nothing. LouLou stood gazing out the window. Adam sat in Gabor's chair. A little girl on the street sang to herself, tentatively, as if she weren't quite sure of the words. A man laughed, some woman said a bright *Au revoir*, silence returned.

Adam wondered what might have happened between him and the English actress. He had been quite taken by her, she had obviously fancied him. He wondered if things might have gone one step further. He pictured himself mourning Honnie. He saw himself at the funeral, as whatever remained of her descended into the ground. He saw himself marrying the English actress. He saw Gabor's smile at the wedding. He saw himself in London, in the rain. Honnie had once gone to London, Cuvillier told him. He imagined himself making love to the young English actress. He listened as LouLou stirred. She said, "Well."

He watched as she returned to her desk and resumed typing. She didn't only hate men. She despised women as well, she reserved her contempt for members of the human race, regardless of sex, race, or religious persuasion. Adam looked at the telephone receiver, he heard the incessant buzzing, he replaced it on the hook and a moment later picked it up when it rang. LouLou appeared in the doorway, he said, "Gabor Productions, good afternoon."

It was a reporter from *France-Soir*. He had heard that the German actress had been murdered by Gabor on location in Chantilly. Adam listened to the urgency in the man's voice. He could not keep himself from smiling. He said, "I am happy to report that the story is completely untrue. Thank you for ringing." He hung up and stared at the phone and then picked it up again when it rang a moment later.

It was a someone from *Libération*, indeed, the same woman Adam had met at the hotel near Orly, Dominique something. He recalled the dark roots of her blond hair. She had called him a prick. Together they had watched Jacques Borrel die on the carpet. She said, "Can you confirm the rumor that an accident has occurred on the set of Gabor's latest film?"

Adam considered the question. A novice when he'd first met her, she had quickly learned how to probe for answers. He said: "I can't say either way."

"You have no comment, then?"

"Not at the moment."

"Which means that an accident has taken place," she said drily.

He said, "I have nothing more to say."

There was a pause. He was about to hang up when she said, "You're of course aware that this could bring Gabor's career to an end."

He wondered what Gabor would do were he deprived of his medium. He pictured the director becoming nocturnal, roaming the streets, murmuring to himself, living rough in disused métro tunnels, cooking rats over an open fire near the Canal Saint-Martin. Adam said, "Look. I know nothing about this. Gabor isn't here to speak for himself and."

"You're a cocksucker," she said, slamming down the phone.

Adam sat for a moment and then stood and crossed the room. He realized his shirt was adhering to his skin. He felt as though he had just emerged from a body of rancid water. He went to the bathroom and washed his face. There was a faint putrid odor of vomit. He thought of the English actress. He felt his head spin. He listened as LouLou answered the phone. He prayed she would not betray too much. Clearly Gabor would have to tell everything the next day. There would be a press conference to organize; reporters, cameras, questions, a written statement. The woman's death had been an accident, something Gabor could never have prevented. LouLou was standing before him. She indicated the desk with a nod of her head, she said, "It's Gabor, he wants to speak to you again."

Now Gabor sounded more calm. He told Adam that the police were on the scene, the actress's body had been taken away. He kept returning to the decapitation, the detail that would haunt him for the rest of his life. Adam told him about the two calls. Gabor said that Adam was to say nothing more but that a statement would be released next morning. He asked if Adam wouldn't mind remaining at the office until he returned in the evening from Chantilly. They could work together on the press release for the morning. Gabor also wanted to speak personally to the actress's relatives in Britain, he wanted to extend his condolences. Adam imagined them cursing the one-eyed Hungarian. He imagined Gabor telling them about his father bleeding all over his puzzle. *He blinked and.*

Adam said: "So you've canceled shooting for the day?"

"Are you crazy? We have an agreement with this guy, we've got to complete the *pigeonnier* scenes by the day after tomorrow. Everyone here is willing to do it, why shouldn't we go on, for Christ's sake."

In a more subdued voice he asked Adam to ring an agency based in London. It was too late for rewrites, they would have to find another English actress willing to step in at a moment's notice. Adam made a note of this. He rang the agency and in heavily accented English said nothing more than that Monsieur Gabor needed to hire an actress in her midtwenties who would be willing to fly to Paris that same evening. The woman at the agency asked if that was all, if there were no further requirements. He checked his notes, he read off exactly what Gabor had said, he told the woman he wanted a dark-haired woman who was willing to shoot most of her scenes either partially dressed or completely nude. There were to be a few explicit scenes of intimate contact between women and several others of a heterosexual nature. Adam was surprised Gabor hadn't for good measure thrown in coprophilia and cannibalism. The woman laughed to herself, she said, "You'd be surprised what our clients will do for their wages," and Adam felt sick to his stomach. He thanked the woman and left his number and hung up.

LouLou said, "Lunch?"

Lunch.

All Adam could think about was the English actress, youth and giggles and beauty lying bloodied and headless in the dust of the hottest day of the year.

14

T WAS FOUR O'CLOCK WHEN INSPECTOR CUVILLIER RANG back.

Adam had been on the phone for most of the afternoon, parrying reporters' speculations, putting them off with increasingly professional ease. He had forgotten about Honnie, Cuvillier, the investigation. LouLou continued typing. A hot breeze blew through the offices and then withdrew. The afternoon grew still, as if the air were on the point of boiling.

Adam looked through the file Gabor had compiled on the English actress. He looked at the photographs of her face, how different she appeared in each one: now a snot-nosed punk, now a debutante. He looked at the glossy view of her on the leather sofa, her breasts bared. Now he would never kiss her lips, caress her skin, see that smile. Now he would never hear her voice again. He shut the folder and returned it to its place in Gabor's drawer. He looked at the revolver. The sun disappeared behind a cloud as the phone rang. Cuvillier said, "I've located your wife, Monsieur Füst."

Adam felt his heart move, he said, "Uh."

"She's alive."

Cuvillier did not sound relieved. For a moment Adam thought that perhaps something horrible had happened to

Honnie, disfigurement, torture, amputation, he thought of a head in the dust, he said, "What?"

"I won't explain now. It's," and he paused for a few seconds, "it's too complicated to go into, monsieur. I'll meet you at six. At the Achéron. No later than six. You remember where it is? Wait there for me, you understand? Don't speak to anyone there, just wait for me."

"But."

"Oh yes, Monsieur Füst. She's all right."

Adam held the humming receiver tightly in his hand. His palm felt moist. He thought of six o'clock. Quite loudly he said, "Honnie is alive," his voice reverberated and the sound of typing ceased.

He stood behind LouLou. Without turning her face she said, "I'm glad for you, Adam."

He said, "Gabor wants someone to stay here until he comes back. Someone has to answer the phone."

She said nothing. He returned to Gabor's office and sat behind the desk. He held his head in his hands and felt the pressure grow within it, the pain of a potential storm. He wondered if he should go home first, shower and change and try to look his best for the reunion with his wife.

His wife. To whom was he married, Honnie or Monique? Did it matter? For a passing second he felt intense joy, then the funny thought came to him that perhaps on some days she could be Honnie and on others Monique. He thought of Monique in bed with her repertoire of tricks, novel positions and strange pressure points she had perfected with her industrial magnates and cabinet ministers. In the morning she could wake up as Honnie, stretch like a cat and stroke his head with her fingers, lie in the curve of his arm and speak about Budapest, Oberwil, Zurich and Paris, *Do you remember this?* she would say, *Do you remember that?*

But when she was Monique would she still be Honnie?

The phone rang. It was the woman from *Libération* again. She had just heard that the English actress had been strangled by Gabor. Adam gripped the phone as if it were the reporter's throat, he said, "That is incorrect. A full statement will be released tomorrow morning."

"A full statement," she said dubiously. "Fucking excuses."

"Look," said Adam.

"Sexist bullshit."

"Look."

"Prick."

He wondered if the reporter would have been so angered had a male actor died instead. He felt suddenly calm, he said, "In the light of what has actually happened I find your words irrelevant," it was how Gabor paid him to behave, and then he took the phone and in one inelegant movement smashed it to bits on the edge of Gabor's desk, "Shit," he said afterward when LouLou came in to see what had happened.

"That was an expensive desk," she said, and he must have given her a murderous look, for she backed away and returned to her work.

The haze thickened over Paris. The city looked like stale wedding cake. He thought of maggots gnawing through the center of it. A red Citroën passed rapidly beneath his window, its powerful engine roaring as it accelerated. A woman walked her toy poodle, a child stopped to play with it. The phone continued intermittently to ring, though Adam was unable to answer it. He looked at the apparatus, at the wires that dangled uselessly out of the earpiece like ruptured nerves from a severed head. He would leave LouLou to speak to the press.

At five he went into the outer office, took her phone off the hook, gripped her by the shoulders and made her look him in the eye. He said, "Listen. You must understand. Honnie has been in terrible trouble. She is my wife. I have lived with her for five years. You are my friend, I have enjoyed being with you. But tonight I am going to have Honnie back. You must try to understand what this means to me." His head throbbed, he felt his strength drain away, he thought of the English actress, the dust, the blood. He was surprised LouLou remained so calm. She took his hand and held it, she said, "I see."

"Things haven't been easy lately."

"No."

"And now Gabor."

"Yes," she said.

"You'll manage all right this evening?"

"Of course."

He wondered what Honnie would look like after two months' separation. He stood by the window with his hands in his pockets as LouLou spoke to a man from *Le Monde*. The pressure in his head seemed to lessen. Now there was only numbness: in his mind, his memory. He thought about asking Gabor to allow him a week off. He would take Honnie away from Paris, to Italy perhaps, or Greece, possibly Spain. He thought of bulls. He thought of blood. LouLou said, "Well."

He turned. "Yes."

"So you'll be off soon."

His laughter was edgy, he said, "I'll be back."

"Tonight?"

"I don't know when. Tomorrow. Tonight. Gabor asked," he began.

"Of course," she said. She seemed distant again, there was a disturbing, dreamy quality about the appearance and movement of her eyes. He took hold of her arms and pressed her to him, he said nothing. When he left to meet Cuvillier she was standing in the doorway of Gabor's office, her back toward him.

Cuvillier arrived a few minutes before six. Adam was waiting for him in the entrance of the Achéron. He had not bothered to go in for a drink. The terrace was deserted. The threat of rain was in the air. Paris felt like the inside of a large drum. The Inspector unlatched the door of his Renault and gave Adam a grim look, he said nothing, he pulled the car away from the curb and merged with the evening traffic on the quays. The sky had grown dark with an oncoming storm. Adam felt pain as if it were a small stone rolling freely about his head, shifting and swaying with the caprices of the weather.

Adam said, "Where are we going?"

He noticed Cuvillier was wearing a blue blazer. On the pocket was a patch of some sort, an elaborate wreath encircling two crossed oars. He wondered if the Inspector was a keen sailor, if he knew port from starboard and how to jibe and drop anchor. He thought of a bottle of rum and a man with an eye-patch and peg leg. The image of a death's-head came to mind. Cuvillier said, "We have to cross the river," then retreated into silence as they turned onto the Pont au Change. To the left was the Préfecture de Police. The street lamps of the Latin Quarter glittered in the premature nightfall.

Adam watched the thickening darkness of the impending storm. It was as if the seam between day and night had been erased, as if the brief period of transition had for this one occasion been obliterated. The blue hour: a whispered name; the elusive image of a shadow in a hallway. He concentrated on Honnie. There was nothing else to think about, not now, not ever.

For fifteen minutes Cuvillier said nothing. They were moving southward. For a while the traffic was heavy, it started and stopped, it progressed in slow spurts along the boulevard Saint-Michel and then on the A6. Adam recalled driving Gabor to the hotel near the airport. He scrutinized the faces of the people in the neighboring cars, the tired men, the resolute women, their knuckles white against the steering wheels. He imagined they were listening to the radio. He imagined they were hearing the news about the death of the English actress.

Adam said, "Where are we going?"

And Cuvillier replied, "I can't tell you that, monsieur." For the first time since they had left the Achéron the Inspector turned his face to him, he said, "Besides, it doesn't matter."

Adam watched his profile. At irregular intervals lightning struck the horizon. The clouds resembled thick grey billows of smoke. Cuvillier blinked and lit a cigarette. A large American car came abreast with them. A man with dark glasses smoked a cigar and listened to loud rock music. He seemed unmoved that he was disturbing the peace of the evening. Adam watched the man sip whiskey from a bottle. He laid his head back on his seat. The Renault was quiet, it hummed reassuringly. In Adam's mind the events of the day took on a diffuse glow of unreality. It seemed ironic to him that only now could he begin to put things into perspective. He thought of the death of the young English actress. Now it was nighttime. She would never know this night, this hour, the look of the sky, the lightning. Perhaps she had been invited to a party somewhere in Paris. Or her boyfriend the art student was expecting her to ring him in London. Perhaps the great pity of death is that we live on to savor the night, and the ones we have lost do not. And thus the night appears to us all the more delicious, terribly bitter.

Suddenly Cuvillier broke the silence; Adam opened his eyes, the Inspector said, "It seems she first began working for Maurice Borrel about three months after arriving in France. That would make it just over a year before the two of you met."

What? Adam must have fallen asleep, suddenly there were words, words without meaning, noises tumbling from the cop Cuvillier's lips, filling the night. Adam rubbed his eyes and watched the clouds throw great forks of light toward the ground.

The Inspector said, "Apparently she wasn't working at the time, what was it you said she was? An artist?"

Adam said, "She," and Cuvillier interrupted: "She met Maurice Borrel quite casually, by chance, at a café on the Champs-Élysées, Borrel was no fool, he knew where he could find the tourists, the naïve women who come to Paris looking for a lucky break, a rich man. So he took a fancy to her, your future wife. He probably bought her dinner, probably kept his hands off of her. He was a smooth man, our Maurice Borrel, professional, slick."

Cuvillier rolled down his window and tossed out his cigarette. Adam could hear a deep rumbling of thunder. A drop of rain splashed against the windshield, then another, they threw out appendages, shattered in the wind. Cuvillier switched on the wipers. At first they squealed against the dry glass, then moved swiftly, smoothly in two wide, damp arcs. He said, "Somehow he got her to work for him. He told her he had an associate, a businessman who needed to be impressed, softened for the big deal. The businessman took her out to dinner, back to his hotel room, into bed. The next day Borrel paid her and probably paid her well." He turned to Adam. "You can imagine how she felt, eh? Cheap, like trash. But she needed the money, the cash came at the right time. Borrel waited a few weeks. Then he looked her up and told her about another businessman. This time there would be more money coming her way."

Adam felt as if the Inspector were speaking about a character in a novel, a film, he could not for the life of him recognize this woman named Honnie.

"There's no proof, but he might even have gotten her hooked on dope. So she needed him: for drugs, for money. On a few occasions she traveled abroad to see special clients, highfliers, men who demanded something extra, something spicy, out of the ordinary. In those days Maurice was working mostly on his own, trying to make a reputation for himself. His brother Jacques was already deep into narcotics, porn, women. That girl in the sex shop, you remember her? She worked for him. He liked her type, those looks. He liked your wife, he liked that girl, he had others like them." He turned to Adam. "About a year ago someone else became involved, someone big, a guy we'd never been able to find." He looked at Adam again. "We didn't even know his name. He began taking over one business after another. You connected your wife to Monique, Monique to Maurice, Maurice was of course working with Jacques. In tracing your wife we found the first hints of the identity of the big man, the big shot behind Jacques, the guy we've been looking for."

He said, "Then Honnie met you, Monsieur Füst."

In the headlights from an oncoming truck Adam could see a smile forming on Cuvillier's face. The Inspector said, "You were different from Maurice's clients, you were someone from her own country, a person her own age, you knew nothing about her work with Borrel. You wanted her for herself, you see. You respected her."

Adam saw Cuvillier reach into his pocket. He took out a tube of pills, placed two in his mouth. He continued, "Now, of course, she can't very well walk out on Borrel's little game, can she? Things aren't that easy, Borrel would have killed her if she'd refused. So she sees her clients when you're at work with Monsieur Gabor. Perhaps she even found a way of slipping out at night and not disturbing you, eh?"

Adam tried to recall his life with Honnie. He thought of the incident in the chapel. The lake. Stillness and solitude. His head filled with pity for her.

"She had no way of getting away from Maurice Borrel. Two years ago he disappeared. Six months later his body was found in the Seine. He'd been murdered, stabbed to death with a knife. We never knew who was responsible, we never cared, the man was worthless scum. If we hadn't put two and two together we wouldn't be here tonight. The story would have ended there, your wife would still be listed as missing.

"You said that eighteen months ago your wife disappeared for two days. That was when Borrel, Maurice Borrel, was murdered. He had been dead only a week when his body was discovered. Until then he'd been traveling: in France, Tahiti, Australia, other places."

Cuvillier pulled off into a parking area by a roadside restaurant. He left the engine running. The rain had stopped. He stood by the side of the car and urinated on the ground. Adam opened the window and listened to the thunder, now almost continuous. A plane blinked its lights as it defined a circle before approaching the runway. They were near the airport, near Orly. Cuvillier returned to the car, he took out his revolver and checked it in the dim light from the dashboard, replaced it in his holster. Now Adam saw what had happened, he felt as if he were made of ice, he said, "Honnie killed Borrel."

Cuvillier smiled, he coughed and put the car in gear and moved slowly off into the night.

He switched on the radio. A man read off sporting results, he said, *"Zero-zero,"* there was a splash of static, then Cuvillier pressed the button and listened to the silence.

Cuvillier said, "Of course we have no direct proof she'd done it. But we're certain she did and we now know why, she wanted to be free of Borrel, she wanted to live a normal life, that's why she'd disappeared for those few days, you see, monsieur. She'd heard Maurice was back in Paris. She did the dirty job and wanted to lie low. Then she came back to you when she realized she'd never be connected to Maurice Borrel's death."

Now they were circling the airport, bypassing exits. Adam stared dumbly at the signs, Air Canada Air France British Airways TWA Air India. His head felt swollen, inflated, pain

competing with words, memories. After a time Cuvillier opened
his window. The rumbling continued, the sky became momentary
day, a drop of water hit the windshield, the Inspector said,
"Your wife was a whore, Monsieur Füst. It wasn't her fault,
Borrel was using her. She killed him. She did us all a big favor.
But she'd forgotten about Jacques Borrel. After a while he got
in touch with her. He knew she'd murdered his brother, he said
that if she didn't work for him he'd kill her."

Adam felt thick, stupid. He had known nothing about this.
The sound of a grieving saxophone passed slowly through his
memory, he felt the agitation of time. He felt tears in his eyes,
he felt small in the light of Honnie's life, unworthy of her.

Cuvillier said, "I suppose it doesn't matter if I tell you. We're
meeting them at a hotel. I left it up to them. It doesn't matter.
Nothing matters."

Adam said, "Who? What?"

Cuvillier said, "Jacques Borrel died only recently. He'd been
poisoned." Adam remembered the man on the floor of the lobby,
Thna-thna-thna. This guy he die strange death.

"Your wife didn't kill Jacques Borrel. She'd left you two
months ago because Jacques demanded she return. She owed
him, that's probably what he said, she owed him, everybody's
in debt in this world, Monsieur Füst, everyone's in thrall. She
probably thought she'd be able to clear things up with Jacques
and then come back home. That's why she phoned you, you see,
she thought it would be over in a day or two." He shrugged just
as lightning struck, he said, "But the new man, the big guy
behind Jacques, had some clients lined up for her. Sometimes
she worked out of a room in that hotel near the airport, she
serviced visiting businessmen, high-roller friends of Jacques
Borrel. The woman you saw in the apartment across from your
office that night was probably the girl from the sex shop. Private
services." He looked at Adam. "On the other hand it may have

been your wife." He shrugged, he said, "There are always a few mysteries left behind, monsieur."

The Renault entered the hotel area. Valets unlatched doors, helped with luggage, parcels, pointed this way and that. Adam felt pain in his stomach.

A small blue light indicated the entrance to a subterranean parking garage located directly beneath the hotel. Cuvillier said quietly, "There's where we're meeting them. That's where Jacques Borrel died." He drove the car around to the rear of the hotel and switched off the engine. It seemed a wasteland. The ground was littered with paper, some foamy substance oozed from a pipe, something small and alive was momentarily caught in the blaze of the headlights. "They're probably there now." He turned and faced Adam. He lit a cigarette, he said, "The man who had Borrel killed was the man we'd been looking for, the guy who was behind the whole business. We've spoken to him. He told us Borrel had become dangerous, a threat. Now your wife is working for him." He placed a finger on Adam's arm and tapped twice. "Listen to me, monsieur, you must try to understand what I am saying. This man is a cop, someone with the Sûreté, an important man. That's why we'd never been able to catch him. All along he was a cop, a crooked cop, of course, but a cop; now a rich cop, a very rich cop. And tomorrow he won't be a cop at all, just a wealthy exile. This is who we're supposed to meet tonight. This man, and your wife. Now listen to me, monsieur, I must tell you," and then his voice trailed off.

The Inspector stared blankly through the windshield at the dark sky, the rage. He placed his fingers around the key, the car defined a half circle in the deserted road, they approached the mouth of the parking garage. Cuvillier said, "Let's go underground, shall we?" and then the Renault dipped and descended.

There were three levels. The ramp was like a corkscrew, twisting and boring into the earth. There were few cars parked there. Adam thought of nothing. He felt his body go cold. He tasted blood, he had bitten the side of his cheek. Cuvillier came to a stop when they reached the bottom level. In the dim light from the few ceiling lamps still intact the Inspector looked into the corners of the space. There were areas of broken glass; a shoe lay on the ground, a few empty wine bottles. Adam saw a red Citroën parked in a corner. Its lights were off. The smell of dampness, of rot, was everywhere. Cuvillier said quietly, "That's them." He took hold of Adam's arm, he said, "Don't get out of the car, not until he says it's all right. Remember who he is, Monsieur Füst. Try to understand what is involved here."

Cuvillier backed the car slowly into the space beside the Citroën. Adam saw something of Honnie's face through the tinted window glass, her long hair, her unreadable expression in shadow, he said, "H—" and then Cuvillier raised a finger, he lowered the window, he said, "So," and his voice echoed briefly, the sound flattening into something indefinable between the concrete walls of the garage.

The window on Honnie's side slid down. Beside her, behind the wheel, was a middle-aged man with tired eyes and a moustache. He smiled at Cuvillier, he said, "I suppose you've explained to Monsieur Füst precisely what has taken place?"

"Most of it," said Cuvillier. "Let him see his wife, let him touch her."

"He understands, though?"

Honnie stared at Adam. There was no smile. She looked fatigued, thinner than before. Briefly Adam recalled that first night at the café, the Mingus, her smile, her touch.

Cuvillier said, "No. Let them meet, just for a moment. That's all. That was our agreement."

The man in the Citroën considered it for a moment, he said they were to stand together in front of his car, and he took out his revolver and pointed it at the Inspector. He said, "If it goes one step beyond that I kill the woman, does everyone understand this?"

Cuvillier turned to Adam, he said, "Don't be stupid, don't try to run. Just talk to her for a few minutes. You must understand what is happening here, things could get very dangerous back in Paris," and suddenly Adam lost all comprehension of the scene, Cuvillier was pushing him out of the car and in the glare of the headlights they were together again. Adam pulled her unresponsive body against his. He pressed his lips to her mouth and smelled her hair. Her arms lay limp against her body, she said, "I'm sorry, I'm," and he went Shh and held her some more. In his ear she whispered, "You know. Now you know."

"It doesn't matter."

"He won't let me go back to you."

Adam held her with his hands. He listened to the sound of the engines idling. He thought of flight. The air grew thick with fumes. He saw Cuvillier drawing on a cigarette, the end of it glowed bright orange. She said, "The guy is a cop. That's why he won't let me go with you. He's leaving the country tonight, in an hour, he's taking me with him." Again she said "I'm sorry," and Adam waved her apology away with his fingers, he said, "It could have been worse, it doesn't matter, you're still," and he stopped because words seemed superfluous.

Adam looked at Honnie, at her face, her mouth. There were swollen pouches beneath her eyes. He noticed a small bruise on her forehead. She seemed older, ravaged, strands of grey were visible in her hair. Her expression spoke of pain, loss. For no reason he said, "One of Gabor's actresses was killed today." Honnie didn't seem to hear him. She felt his lips with the ball of her thumb, gently, as if trying to read his words, their inner meaning, his secret. He could not keep his hands from her, he touched her face, her shoulders, her arms, he wanted to devour her, to make her a part of him. For the first time he seemed to know her completely, to understand her.

She said, "I'm sorry," and when he tried to quiet her again she said into his ear: "Forgive me, my darling. I gave you the best part of me. Just remember that." The headlights on the Citroën flickered from bright to dim and then back again. Honnie looked lost, she said to Adam, "Just don't turn around," and then she was no longer with him, he could hear someone running, the shot rang out and then there was another, and the sound echoed and filled his ears, he could taste the pain of it. The air was smoke, exhaust and burning oil. The windshield on the Citroën was splashed with red. Cuvillier said, "I'm sorry." Adam turned. Honnie was lying on the ground, on her back, her arms and legs spread wide, as if she were attempting to float on water. He knelt beside her and watched the blood ooze from her wound, he felt it with his finger and touched it to his lips. He pressed his hands to her chest, he felt the warmth rising from her body, evaporating in the night. He touched her face, her cheek. She was no longer there. Cuvillier put his gun away and pulled open the door to the Citroën. The man from the Sûreté fell sideways toward him, the revolver still in his fist, the hole in his head leaking blood and brains, his eyes expressing mute surprise.

Adam was kneeling beside Honnie. Cuvillier lit a cigarette and held it out. Adam ignored him. Cuvillier went off to find a telephone. Adam thought of Honnie lying on the lake near Oberwil. He thought it astonishing, miraculous that she could remain floating on the surface. He wondered what was passing through her mind. He considered the terrible mystery of her life. Honnie was dead, she had died twice, perhaps even more than that: at a café on the Champs-Elysées, in a disused chapel in Switzerland, in a damp cavern in the bowels of the earth. There was nothing to forgive, nothing could diminish his love for her. Cuvillier was saying, "You'd have lost her anyway, Monsieur Füst. He would never have let her come back to France." After a moment he said, "Shall I take you home, to your apartment, monsieur?"

Adam thought of what was left to return to. He thought of LouLou, alone, waiting for him in Gabor's office. He would go back to her and weep for Honnie, he would speak endlessly about his wife, their life together. The car pressed forward in the downpour as the ambulances moved slowly past them. Sheets of water poured from the sky, as if some great vessel were overflowing. There seemed no end to it. He'd had the best part of her, she had said. He watched the lights of the airport recede in a blur. He thought of deep still water. He thought of intense heat. He thought of descending into the earth. Honnie, he thought.

Honnie.

About the Author

J. P. SMITH IS THE AUTHOR OF THE novels *The Man from Marseille*, *Body and Soul*, *The Discovery of Light*, *Breathless*, and *Airtight*. His screenplay *Chasing Daylight* was a quarterfinalist for the Nicholl Fellowships. Smith was born in New York City and currently lives in Beverly Cove, Massachusetts, with his wife.

14930990R10143

Made in the USA
Charleston, SC
09 October 2012